WASHOE COUNTY
3 1235 02872 4966
P9-DWF-655

A Fine Line

Also by William G. Tapply

THE BRADY COYNE NOVELS

Past Tense
Scar Tissue
Muscle Memory
Cutter's Run
Close to the Bone
The Seventh Enemy
The Snake Eater
Tight Lines
The Spotted Cats
Client Privilege
Dead Winter
A Void in Hearts
The Vulgar Boatman
Dead Meat
The Marine Corpse
Follow the Sharks
The Dutch Blue Error
Death at Charity's Point

NONFICTION

Pocket Water
Upland Days
Bass Bug Fishing
A Fly-Fishing Life
The Elements of Mystery Fiction
Sportsman's Legacy
Home Water
Opening Day and Other Neuroses
Those Hours Spent Outdoors

OTHER FICTION

Thicker Than Water (with Linda Barlow)
First Light (with Philip R. Craig)

A Fine Line

William G. Tapply

St. Martin's Minotaur
New York

www.minotaurbooks.com

Library of Congress Cataloging-in-Publication Data

Tapply, William G.
A fine line : a Brady Coyne novel / William G. Tapply.—1st ed.
p. cm.
ISBN 0-312-30352-1
1. Coyne, Brady (Fictitious character)—Fiction. 2. Missing persons—Fiction. 3. Boston (Mass.)—Fiction. 4. Ecoterrorism—Fiction. 5. Teenage boys—Fiction. 6. Naturalists—Fiction. I. Title

PS3570.A568 F56 2002
813'.54—dc21

2002068131

First Edition: November 2002

10 9 8 7 6 5 4 3 2 1

For Mum

Acknowledgments

Writing a novel is a solitary—even lonely—occupation. But whipping the thing into shape cannot be done alone. I am lucky to have so many supporters and consultants and critics who want my books to succeed and know how to help:

My wife, Vicki Stiefel, who manages to give me tough editorial criticism and loving support all at the same time;

My father, H. G. "Tap" Tapply, who nurtured my love of words by reading Winnie the Pooh stories to me when I was too young to read them for myself, whose interest and pride in my work sustained me while he was alive, and whose editorial voice ("short is good," "mind your verbs") will forever echo in my head;

My mother, Muriel Tapply, who promotes me wherever she goes and urges her friends to buy my books rather than borrow them from the library;

My kids—Mike, Melissa, and Sarah—who think it's pretty cool that their old man writes novels and who keep me going when the going gets difficult;

My agent, Jed Mattes, who has steered and nurtured my writing career for lo these many years;

My lawyer, Ken Quat, who makes sure I don't mess up the legal stuff;

And my editor, Keith Kahla, who is simply the best.

The only obligation which I have a right to assume is to do at any time what I think right.

—HENRY DAVID THOREAU

About half the practice of a decent lawyer consists in telling would-be clients that they are damned fools and should stop.

—ELIHU ROOT

What was the best thing before sliced bread?

—GEORGE CARLIN

One

A pair of ruby-throated hummingbirds—a male and a female—were darting and hovering and dipping their beaks into the pink hollyhocks that grew against the brick wall. Up there inside Walt Duffy's patio garden on Mt. Vernon Street at the crown of Beacon Hill, the June sun had sunk behind the walls and the late-afternoon city noises were far away and muffled, and I could actually hear the soft buzz of the hummingbirds' wings.

Walt was sitting on his chaise with his useless legs sprawled in front of him, watching the birds through the long telephoto lens of his Nikon. He snapped a couple of pictures, then put the camera on the patio table and picked up his gin-and-tonic. "Beautiful, aren't they?" he said.

I nodded. "They are beautiful."

"Old habit," he said, "taking their pictures. I like to frame them, bring them close, catch that iridescence when the sun hits their breasts." He took a sip, held it in his mouth for a moment, then swallowed. Then he laughed. "Pretending I'm still the great globe-trotting bird photographer. Hummingbirds in my garden. Jesus."

It had been a little more than a year since the drizzly May morning when Walt Duffy climbed a granite outcropping near the Quabbin Reservoir to photograph a nesting pair of bald eagles. He'd somehow slipped and crashed onto the rocks thirty feet below. It took him half a day to crawl out of the woods to the cell phone he'd left in his car, dragging his lifeless legs behind him.

And that, abruptly and irreversibly, ended Walt Duffy's career as the country's—maybe the world's—best-known photographer of wild birds.

I'd handled his divorce nine years before his fall. I'd helped him organize his various business ventures. I'd vetted his publishing contracts, counseled him on tax law, and helped arrange syndication in forty-two city newspapers nationwide for his weekly "The Urban Birder" columns, which combined natural history, practical advice for city-dwelling bird lovers, and environmental polemic.

After his accident I helped him negotiate the medical insurance maze and did all the other things a jack-of-all-trades lawyer does for a client—including drop in for gin-and-tonics with him most Tuesdays on my way home from the office.

He, in turn, paid me a pretty nice retainer.

Walt Duffy, who had photographed birds on every continent on the globe and in every state in the Union, who had climbed mountains and traversed deserts and floated jungle rivers, was now stuck in his Mt. Vernon Street townhouse, and as far as I knew, aside from weekly visits from me and biweekly sessions with his physical therapist, his only companions were his son, Ethan, a freshman at Emerson College who'd come to live with Walt when he got out of the hospital, and Henry, his fat Brittany spaniel.

Well, he did have his birds. When Walt bought the townhouse after his divorce, the first thing he did was build what he called his "bird garden" in the little twenty-by-thirty-foot walled-in patio area that backed up to the alley. "If you build it, they will come," he liked to say. He cleaned out the junk, dug the whole place up, trucked in yards of topsoil, laid the bricks, planted the bird-attracting flowers and vines and berry bushes, installed the water fountain and bird-bath pool, and hung the feeders. When he wasn't on the road, he liked to sit quietly among his birds, photographing them and admiring them and writing about them on his laptop computer.

When it came to birds, Walt Duffy was a democrat. He liked the English sparrows and blue jays that came to his Beacon Hill backyard as much as the rare and exotic species he'd tracked down in Belize and Madagascar and Hudson Bay before his accident.

Now a robin was splashing in the pool and a downy woodpecker was jackhammering the suet. Three goldfinches pecked thistle seed from the feeder. The hummingbirds continued to buzz among the hollyhocks, and squadrons of chickadees and titmice were swiping sunflower seeds.

Walt drained his gin-and-tonic, put his glass on the table, then lay back on his chaise and closed his eyes. He was, I happened to know, forty-eight years old, just a few years older than me. He had once been a tall sinewy man with a ruddy sun-creased face, a quick smile, and boundless energy and enthusiasm. But in the year or so since his accident, his hair had grown thin and gray, his belly had thickened, and the skin on his face and neck had begun to sag.

Suddenly, the door in the back wall to the alley pushed

open. All the birds whirred away, and Henry, the pudgy spaniel, came bounding into the patio. He headed straight for Walt and leaped onto his chest.

"Jesus," muttered Walt. "You're all wet." He pushed Henry off his lap, and the dog came waddling over to me. I held my hand down to him, and he licked it a couple of times. Then he sat beside me and gazed into my eyes.

"I like dogs," I said. "Dogs make eye contact."

"They think if they look at you lovingly, you'll give them something to eat," said Walt. He snapped his fingers. "C'mere, you."

Henry stood up, sauntered over to where Walt was sprawled on his chaise, and lay on the bricks beside him.

A moment later Ethan came in through the door in the wall and shut it behind him. "Hi, Brady," he said. He came over and held out his hand.

I shook it. Ethan was a small kid, skinny and quick like Walt used to be and with the same lopsided smile. Even with his shaved head and the gold stud in his left nostril, he looked about twelve. He was studying screenwriting at Emerson.

"The damn dog got mud all over me," said Walt.

"We went down to the duck pond," said Ethan. "I told him to wipe his feet."

"Get a towel or something. I don't want him tracking mud all over the house."

Ethan gave Walt a quick salute. "Aye, aye, sir." He looked at me and rolled his eyes, then went into the house.

Henry had rolled onto his side beside Walt's chaise. Walt's arm dangled down so he could scratch the dog's belly. "You see that fucking earring in his nose?" he said. "What's with that?"

"One of my sons got an earring when he was in college,"

I said. "Wore it for about a year, then let the hole heal up."

Walt rolled his eyes. "You should see the kids he hangs out with. Purple hair, pierced tongues, girls dressed like boys, boys dressed like girls. You can't tell one from the other. They all think they're artists."

At that moment, Ethan came back with a towel. "We *are* artists," he said. "We're just not very good at it yet." He knelt down on the bricks, wiped Henry's feet, then stood up and looked at Walt. "What do you want for dinner?"

"I don't care," said Walt.

"Pasta okay? I can make some pesto sauce."

"Don't overcook it," said Walt. "Last time you overcooked the damn linguine."

Ethan looked at Walt for a moment, then turned to me. "Brady? Join us?"

I shook my head. "No, thanks."

"Stay," said Walt.

"Nope. Thanks. Gotta go."

He waved the back of his hand at Ethan. "Go cook," he said. "I got something I want to talk to Brady about. And bring the damn dog with you. He scares the birds."

"What do you expect," said Ethan. "He's a bird dog." Then he whistled to Henry, and the two of them went inside.

"I don't know how he puts up with you," I said.

"Me, neither," said Walt. "What kind of kid moves in with his crippled-up father, cooks and cleans the house and runs errands and takes all his bullshit?"

"A boy who loves his father, I'd say."

"It's not natural."

I shrugged. "Count your blessings." I glanced at my watch, then stood up. "I've got to get going."

"Wait a minute," said Walt. "I need you to do me a favor."

I sat down again. "What?"

He pointed at a manila envelope that had been lying on the patio table. "I want you to deliver that for me."

"What is it?"

"Take a look."

I picked up the envelope and opened it. Inside was another envelope made of stiff transparent plastic.

"Be careful," said Walt. "Don't touch the paper. Keep 'em in the plastic. Your fingers will wreck them."

Showing through the plastic was an unlined sheet of paper with a small pen-and-ink sketch of a bird's head surrounded by handwriting. It was a letter. The ink had faded to a sepia color. The date was June 12, 1807. The salutation read: "My dear Mr. Wilson."

I looked at Walt and arched my eyebrows.

"Meriwether Lewis to Alexander Wilson," he said. "There are seven letters in that envelope. I picked them up at a little out-of-the-way antique shop in the Poconos about ten years ago. The old lady who ran the shop didn't have the foggiest idea of their significance. She wanted to charge me a hundred dollars for them. I gave her five hundred and made her promise to contact me if she came up with any others. I suspect they're worth a hundred times that."

I whistled. "Meriwether Lewis. Wow."

Walt smiled.

"Who's Alexander Wilson?"

"He was the most eminent ornithologist of his time. An excellent watercolorist, a very precise writer, and probably the greatest authority on birds who had ever lived up to then. He was hoping to do a book about the birds of the American West based on the observations of the Lewis and Clark expedition."

I looked at the sketch. It appeared to be some kind of shore bird. It had a very long, curved beak. "What's this bird?"

"Long-billed curlew," he said. "The long-bills were unknown to science before Lewis discovered them near the Missouri River. He covered two sheets of paper, both sides, describing their appearance, their behavior, their habitat, and so forth. The other letters are also about birds. It's great stuff. I want you to take these letters to Ben Frye. I've never had them appraised. You know Ben, right?"

I nodded. "Ben's an old friend."

Walt Duffy had been collecting bird-related artifacts—old documents, manuscripts, books, paintings, decoys and carvings—all of his adult life. His will stipulated that his entire collection would be donated to various museums and archives. His lawyer—me—had been urging him to get the whole business reappraised and adequately insured.

"I told Ben you'd be bringing them over," said Walt. "It's on your way home."

"You just assumed I'd do this for you, huh?"

"You're my lawyer," said Walt.

I shrugged and looked at my watch. It was a little before seven. "Is he still at the shop?"

"I'll give him a call, tell him to expect you. He's very hot to see those letters."

I slid the plastic envelope back into the manila one, put it into my briefcase, and stood up. "I better get going, then."

"Ethan!" Walt yelled.

A moment later Ethan opened the door and poked his head out. "You screamed?"

"Brady's leaving. Show him out."

Ethan rolled his eyes, then jerked his chin at me. "Follow me. We don't want you to get lost."

I shook hands with Walt and left him slouched on his chaise pecking at his cell phone.

At the front door I turned to Ethan. "What're you doing now that school's over?"

"Oh, I've got a part-time job at a record store in Central Square. It gets me out of the house."

"Well, that's good. Getting out of the house, I mean."

"Sometimes it's necessary." He smiled. "Sorry you're not staying for dinner. I wouldn't mind the company. Might steer the conversation to something other than my shortcomings."

"Another time," I said. "I promise."

Two

It was about a ten-minute walk from Walt Duffy's townhouse on Mt. Vernon Street, down Joy Street, and across the Common to Ben Frye's bookshop on Temple Place on the other side of Tremont. As I walked, I was acutely aware of the value of the letters I was carrying in my briefcase. I felt faintly furtive, as if I were some kind of spy disguised as a lawyer and carrying top-secret documents. It would be a lousy time to get mugged.

We were approaching June 21, the summer solstice, the longest day of the year, and even at seven in the evening, the Common swarmed with after-work secretaries in short skirts, college girls sprawled on blankets wearing halter tops and shorts, men in business suits walking their dogs, college boys with their T-shirts hanging from their hip pockets playing Frisbee, and homeless men parked on benches feeding the squirrels.

Well, there were some homeless women, too. For some reason, I'd never seen the women feeding the squirrels.

Temple Place, where Benjamin Frye's bookshop was located, was one of those narrow, dark, one-way alley-like Boston streets that connected Tremont to Washington. You had to know it was there to find it.

I crossed Tremont, turned down Temple Place, and stopped at the unpretentious sign beside the door: "Benjamin Frye Books—Second Floor."

I climbed the narrow stairway to the second floor landing. The hand-lettered sign on Ben's door read: "Benjamin Frye. Rare Books and Manuscripts. Appraisals. Hours by appointment," followed by a phone number.

I knocked on the door. It was ajar, and when I got no reply, I pushed it open and stepped into a small, square, windowless room lined with bookshelves. A long table dominated the middle of the room. It was covered with stacks of books. Against the walls were cartons that, I assumed, contained more books.

All of the books in Ben's shop, I knew, were old, rare, and valuable. There were no three-for-a-dollar used-paperback specials here.

"Ben?" I said. "You here?"

When there was no reply, I called louder. "Hey. Ben."

"Who's that?" came a voice from another room.

"It's me. Brady Coyne."

"Who?"

"Brady Coyne. I've got something from Walter Duffy."

"Oh, right," came his voice. "I'm out back."

The door to Ben's office on the other side of the book room was open. I sidestepped the table and went in.

This was a smaller version of the front room—two walls of bookshelves, one wall of file cabinets, a single dirty window that opened onto a fire escape in the back alley, and a big oak desk with a telephone and a computer and piles of papers. Ben was sitting behind the desk peering at a computer monitor. He was sipping from a coffee mug. I doubted it was coffee.

Ben Frye was a gangly, stooped, heronlike man with a long beak and big sad eyes. He had a half-bald head and a long gray-blond ponytail and a scraggly beard. He wore a hoop in his left ear, an Indian bead necklace around his neck, and a red bandanna around his head. He'd occupied the admissions office at B.U., he'd marched with Dr. King, he'd gotten arrested in Chicago, he'd danced in the rain at Woodstock, and he'd been stoned at a hundred rock concerts all over the nation.

Later he'd earned his Ph.D. in cultural anthropology at Duke. Typical old hippie.

I cleared my throat, and he turned, pushed his glasses on top of his head and grinned at me. "Well?" he said. "Where are they? You got those Lewis letters with you, right?"

I nodded.

He pointed at my briefcase and snapped his fingers. "Lemme see 'em, man."

A straight-backed wooden chair was pushed against the wall. I dragged it to Ben's desk and sat down with my briefcase on my lap.

"So how have you been?" I said.

"Come on, dammit," he said. "Gimme the letters. I've been peeing my pants since Duffy told me about them. Meriwether Lewis to Alexander Wilson? You realize what you got there?"

"Walt seemed to think they were worth something."

"Listen," he said. "If these letters are . . ." He shrugged. "I'm getting ahead of myself. I've got to look at them. Hand 'em over."

I opened my briefcase, took out the manila envelope, and held it against my chest. "Could they be forgeries or something?"

He nodded. "It's possible, sure. There's a lot of interest in documents from the Voyage of Discovery nowadays. Ever since that Ambrose book and the PBS series. Ambrose pointed out that there seems to be a lot of missing stuff. Big chunks of time, no journals, for one thing. Some of it's probably lost forever, but once in a while something turns up. And, yeah, there have been some forgeries." He reached across the desk. "So I gotta see that stuff."

I handed him the envelope.

He took it, adjusted his glasses onto the bridge of his nose, opened the manila envelope, and slipped the plastic envelope out. He bent close to it. "Oh, my," he muttered. "Holy shit." He groped around on his desk, found a magnifying glass, and peered through it. "Long-billed curlew," he mumbled.

"Is it genuine?" I said. "The letter?"

He looked up at me and blinked. "I wish it was that easy," he said. "I'll have to test the paper and the ink, study the handwriting, the spelling and syntax, all that. Meriwether Lewis was a poor speller but a knowledgeable naturalist."

"Suppose they're genuine?"

"Then I do my research and come up with a value for them."

"How do you do that?"

Ben shrugged. "Check the auctions. Talk to the curators. It's not a science. I gather as much information as I can, then try to estimate what Duffy could sell them for. It's supply and demand, like anything else. This is a good time for Lewis and Clark stuff, but I might advise Walter to keep them off the market for a couple years. We're coming up on the two-hundredth anniversary of the beginning of the expedition. They departed in the summer of 1804, you know."

I smiled. "Yes, I knew that."

"Well, we shouldn't get ahead of ourselves." He smiled. "I really get off on this stuff. This is better than free love in Harvard Square. Remember the night LBJ announced he wasn't going to run?"

I smiled. "I was in seventh grade in sixty-eight, Ben." I stood up. "I assume you'll be in touch with Walt?"

He nodded.

I reached across his desk. "I'm outta here, then."

He gripped my hand quickly, then said, "You can find your way out?"

I nodded and turned for the door. When I looked back, Ben Frye was hunched over the plastic envelope of letters, peering through his magnifying glass.

On the way home I stopped at Skeeter's for a burger, and I ended up watching the ball game on the TV behind the bar, so I didn't get to my rented sixth-floor condo unit on Lewis Wharf until after eleven. I dropped my briefcase inside the doorway and headed straight for the bedroom.

The red light on my answering machine was blinking. Two blinks, pause, two blinks. I hit the "play" button, then began to strip off my office pinstripes.

The recorded voice said, "First message, today, eight-forty-seven P.M." Then came the voice of Billy, my older son: "Hey, Pop. Whatcha doin'? Just wanted to say Happy Father's Day. Knowing me, I'll forget to send a card. Fishing's been great. When you comin' out?"

Billy had dropped out of UMass in the middle of his sophomore year to pursue his dream of becoming a trout-fishing guide and ski instructor in Idaho. Now, at twenty-two, he seemed to have realized his dream. I kept wondering what he'd do next. Most people go through their whole lives without ever fulfilling their dreams.

Father's Day. I had no idea it was approaching. Joey, Billy's younger brother, was a junior at Stanford. Joey would remember to send me a card. He was that kind of boy, just as Billy was the kind who'd forget. I loved them both equally.

The annoying recording on my answering machine was saying, "Second message, today, ten-thirty-two P.M.," and then came Evie Banyon's soft, seductive voice: "Hi, sexy man. Where are you? If you get in before midnight, call me. I need you to tuck me in."

I hung my suit in the closet, pulled on a pair of sweatpants, and lay back on my bed. I had known Evie for nearly two years. We had both spent the first year fighting ourselves—and each other—against growing too close. Then she disappeared. I could have let her go. I almost did. But I didn't. I tracked her down to the other side of the continent where she was holing up in her father's houseboat in Sausalito. She and I spent two weeks driving back to Massachusetts, more or less retracing the route Lewis and Clark had taken. We listened to local radio stations on the car radio, we made love in motel rooms, we ate in diners.

We'd been lovers for a year, but after that cross-country road trip, we became friends, too. It was our own voyage of discovery.

Evie and I were both independent people. We'd had lots of relationships. None had endured. Even my eleven-year marriage to Gloria seemed, in retrospect, transitory. Evie and

I figured that in all cases, it was our own fault. We decided that the best way to keep our own relationship going was to enjoy the present and not think too much about the past or the future.

But we also agreed to keep our options open. One day one of us might want to change the deal. Live together. Get married, even.

Or call it off.

We promised each other that if that happened, we would say so—openly, freely, immediately. Neither of us was very good at talking about our feelings. It had made that first year rocky. That was the main insight we got from two weeks together in her Volkswagen Jetta. That and the fact that we did love each other.

I picked up the phone, and Evie answered on the third ring.

"It's me," I said.

"Hello, you."

"You in bed?"

"Mmm."

"I woke you up," I said. "Sorry."

"What time is it?"

"Amost eleven-thirty."

She sighed.

"Hard day?"

"Oh, like usual." Evie was the assistant administrator at Emerson Hospital in Concord. She was responsible for patient services and public relations, which meant she handled everyone's complaints and problems. She was very good at her job. "I fell asleep in my bubble bath," she said. "I might have drowned. No strong man to rescue me."

"Or to wash your back."

"Or any other achy, tingly body part," she said.

"You're a cruel woman," I said. "I'll let you get back to sleep. Just wanted to kiss you goodnight."

"Mmm," she murmured. "That's sweet."

"Well . . ."

"I had an idea," she said.

"What?"

"Tomorrow after work? Let's have a picnic."

"Sure. Sounds good."

"Meet me at Walden? I'll pick up some sandwiches, bottle of wine. You bring the blanket."

"I can be there by seven," I said.

"I'll meet you down by Thoreau's cairn. I'll be the girl watching the swallows chase fireflies over the water. After it gets dark and the owls start hooting maybe we can make out on your blanket."

I smiled at the thought.

"Brady?" she said after a moment. "You there?"

"Yes. I'm smiling."

"Good. I'm going to sleep now. See you tomorrow." She hesitated. "Love you."

"Me, too," I said.

After I hung up, I lay there staring up at the ceiling wondering why Evie always said, "Love you," and not, "I love you." There seemed to be a difference.

Of course, it was I who said, "Me, too." Not: "I love you, too."

Evie and I still had a few things to work out.

Three

I'd already put in six boring hours of lawyer work, and now Herm Alberts, my last appointment of the day, was hemming and hawing, trying to decide whether he wanted me to draw up a prenuptial agreement for him. I was trying to help him understand the pros and cons, and trying not to reveal my personal feelings about the whole distasteful subject, when Julie buzzed me.

The only time Julie ever interrupted a client conference was if one of my sons was trying to reach me, and my sons virtually never called me at the office. So naturally I assumed something bad had happened.

I asked Herm to excuse me and picked up the phone. "What's wrong?" I said.

"Nothing's wrong," said Julie. "It's Mr. Duffy. Can you talk to him?"

"Why don't I call him back?"

"He's rather insistent, Brady. It's probably important."

I smiled to myself. What Julie wasn't saying, but what I knew she meant, was that prenuptial agreements were not only unimportant, but positively distasteful. Any discussion of prenups could and should be preempted. "Okay," I said. "Put him on." I covered the receiver with my hand and said to Herm, "This'll just take a second."

He shrugged. "No problem."

I uncovered the receiver. "Walt? What's wrong?"

"Nothing's wrong," he said. "I need to consult with you."

"You okay?"

"Sure. I'm fine."

I glanced at my watch. It was ten after four. I figured I could get rid of Herm by four-thirty or so. "I'll call you back in three-quarters of an hour."

"I'd rather it was face to face, Brady."

I sighed. I'd rather it was on the telephone, but Walt was the one paying me the retainer. "I can be there around five, five-thirty," I told him. "Okay?"

"Sure. Great."

"I can't stay long. I've got a date."

"That's okay. Time for a drink?"

"Just about. You want to tell me what's up? Something about those letters?"

"Sort of, yes." He hesitated. "I've gotta go."

And he hung up, just like that.

I went back to my conference table and sat beside Herm.

"Look," he said, "if you've got something important, this can wait."

"It's not that important," I said.

Not that Herm Alberts's prenuptial agreement ranked as a crisis, either.

Professionally speaking, I believe in prenups. It's always better to have things spelled out, to be prepared for the unanticipated, to acknowledge the well-documented fact that bad things happen to good people. That's why they invented life insurance and wills. Nearly half of American marriages end in divorce. Divorces are messy. Legal, binding contracts minimize the mess. Besides, Massachusetts law tilts to the wife in divorce settlements.

But personally I hate the idea of covering your bases before you get married. It makes divorce too easy. Prenups seem to me to put a price tag on love. They're calculated, cold, squinty-eyed. Getting married is about romance, about infinitely wondrous possibilities, about forever and ever, for richer or poorer, in sickness and in health. Not money.

So my strategy with my clients is always to lay out the options and refuse to advise them. I tell them to discuss it with their prospective spouses, I insist on meeting with both of them, and I require the spouse-to-be to have her lawyer with her when anything is signed. If it becomes emotional, as it often does, I urge the couple to get counseling—which I don't provide.

Better before they get married than afterward.

Herm Alberts had not yet discussed the subject with the woman he loved, a forty-something divorcée named Lauren Metcalf who would lose her alimony—and therefore virtually all her income—when she married Herm. Herm owned a chain of hardware stores and had a lot to lose, too.

It was a tough call, and I was glad I didn't have to make it.

I shooed Herm out of my office around quarter of five and changed into my faded jeans and my old Adidas and my Yale sweatshirt—my picnic outfit, which I'd brought to the office in anticipation of my rendezvous with Evie at Walden Pond.

I had driven my car to work that morning and parked it in the garage across the street for a quick getaway. I kept my old Army blanket in the trunk, as I had done since I was a teenager, where it was always handy for spontaneous fun in the woods.

But first I had to go see Walt Duffy. The question was whether I should drive or walk.

Walk, I decided. I'd get there twice as fast at rush hour on a Wednesday afternoon, and I wouldn't have to worry about parking illegally under a "Residents Only" sign on Beacon Hill—or not finding a space at all.

Julie was shutting down the office machines when I went out to the reception area. She looked at me and arched her eyebrows. "Going fishing? That your worm-digging outfit?"

"You know I fish with flies," I said. "Evie and I are having a picnic. I'm supposed to meet her at Walden in—" I glanced at my watch "—in a little less than two hours. First I've got to go see Walt Duffy."

"Why?"

"Why what?"

"Why are you seeing Mr. Duffy if you've got a date?" The only thing that Julie considered more important than accruing billable hours was getting me married and settled down. She had high hopes for Evie and me.

"It's your fault," I said. "You're the one who insisted I take his call."

"Sure," she said. "Blame me if you're late."

"That's why I pay you all that money," I said. "To take the blame whenever there's blame to be taken."

"Well, don't stand around here talking to me. Go take care of Mr. Duffy, and make it snappy. We women don't like to be kept waiting."

"Don't I know it," I said.

It was another spectacular June afternoon—cloudless skies and warm sun, with a soft salty easterly breeze puffing in off the ocean. As I strolled down Boylston Street, I was acutely aware of what Julie called my "worm-digging" attire as I passed women in high heels and short skirts and men in their summer-weight suits and ties.

I cut through the Public Garden and across the footbridge over the duck pond, crossed Beacon onto Charles, climbed Mt. Vernon Street, and banged the brass knocker on the door to Walt Duffy's townhouse around five-thirty.

I'd give Walt a half hour, max. Time for just one drink. Then I'd walk back to Copley Square and rescue my car, and with any luck I'd only be a few minutes late for my picnic with Evie.

I waited, hit the knocker again, and when there was no response, I headed around to the back alley. Ethan was probably out walking Henry, and Walt couldn't answer the door even if he heard me knock.

The alley behind Walt's townhouse was barely the width of an average driveway. It was lined on both sides by ten-foot brick walls with wooden doorways cut into them. Walt's was the fifth door on the left. I called his name, and when he didn't answer, I checked the door. He'd left it open a crack for me.

When I stepped inside, a gang of sparrows flew off in a panicky whir of wings.

Walt was not sitting on his chaise, and it took me a moment to see that he was sprawled on the brick patio on the other side of the table from where I stood.

"Hey, Walt," I said. "You okay?"

He didn't answer.

I went over and knelt beside him.

He was sprawled on his back. His crutches lay on either side of him, as if he'd been using them and somehow lost his balance, fallen backward, and hit his head on the bricks.

A dribble of wet blood ran from one nostril halfway down his cheek. His eyes were half-closed and he was gasping in rapid, shallow breaths that barely moved his chest. A little puddle of blood was pooling under his head.

"Oh, Jesus," I muttered.

I hurried inside, found the telephone, and dialed 911. I gave Walt's address and my name and told the woman that Walt had apparently fallen and hit his head on the brick patio.

"Is he conscious?"

"No."

"Is he breathing?"

"Yes. Rapid, shallow breaths."

"When did this happen?"

"I don't know. I just got here. Recently, I think. The blood is wet."

"They're on their way, sir. Please wait there. Cover him with a blanket, but don't try to move him."

"Right," I said.

I found a blanket folded up on Walt's sofa, took it out to the patio, and spread it over him.

"Hey," I said. "Hey, Walt."

His eyelids fluttered.

"What happened, man? Talk to me."

His lips moved.

I bent closer to him, put my ear near his mouth, and said, "Say it again."

But he closed his eyes and said nothing.

About then I heard sirens in the distance. I went back through the house, opened the front door, and stepped out to the sidewalk.

The emergency wagon pulled up a minute later and two paramedics, an Asian man and a blond woman, jumped out.

I waved at them and pointed to the open front door. "This is the place," I said. "He's out back."

The woman was carrying a black satchel. Both of them jogged into the house without acknowledging me.

I followed them out to the patio. They'd already clamped an oxygen mask over Walt's mouth, and the woman appeared to be taking his vital signs.

The other paramedic was kneeling beside her speaking into a cell phone. When he snapped it shut, he looked up at me. "What happened here?"

"I don't know. He was like that when I got here."

"He doesn't have use of his legs, right?"

"That's right," I said. "They're paralyzed from an accident."

"Fell on his crutches here, you think?"

"I guess so. Is he going to be all right?"

"Hard to say."

"What about—?"

"Sir," said the paramedic, "the police will be here. They'll want to talk to you." He turned to his partner. "We should bring the wagon around to the alley."

She nodded.

I stood back and watched them get Walt's head immobilized, strap him on a board, and load him onto a collapsible gurney. Then the Asian guy jogged back through the house, and I held the door while the blond woman wheeled Walt out to the alley.

Just about the time their siren started up, I heard a voice calling "Hello?" from the front of the house.

I went to the front door. Two uniformed Boston police officers were standing there. One looked about forty. He was beefy and pink-skinned. The other one was a little younger and trimmer and darker.

"This the place?" said the older one. His nameplate read: Sergeant A. Currier. "The accident?"

"Yes. The paramedics just took him away."

"The victim's name is—" Currier checked his notebook "—Walter Duffy?"

"That's right."

"And you are?"

I gave him my name, told him I was Walt's lawyer. He asked for my address and both my home and business phone numbers, too. He wrote everything into a notebook.

"We gotta ask you some questions, Mr. Coyne," he said, "and take a look around."

"Sure," I said. "It happened in the garden out back."

I led them to the patio and showed them where I'd found Walt lying. There was a patch of half-dried blood about the diameter of a grapefruit on the bricks. Walt's crutches still lay where I'd found them.

"He was expecting me," I said. "When nobody came to the door, I went around back and came in through that doorway." I pointed. "I found him lying here."

"Was he conscious?"

"Sort of, at first. I think he recognized me. Then he seemed to lose consciousness."

"Did he say anything?"

"He tried to. He whispered something, but I couldn't understand what he said. I asked him to repeat it, but that's when he closed his eyes."

Currier was writing in his notebook. "When you got here, the door, it was unlocked?"

I pointed. "The back door. He knew I was coming. I guess he left it open for me."

"Nobody else lives here?"

"His son lives here with him. Ethan. Ethan Duffy. Oh, and he has a dog. They're not here. Ethan's probably walking the dog. Henry. That's the dog."

Sergeant Currier was writing it all down in his notebook. I wondered if he included Henry's name. He looked up at me. "You figure, um, the son, Ethan, and the dog, they were gone when this happened?"

"Right. Otherwise Ethan would've called for help."

"When did they go?"

"I don't know," I said. "I've been here about twenty minutes, and they weren't here when I got here."

"They go for long walks?"

I shrugged. "I wouldn't know. Yesterday when I was here they went to the duck pond on the Common."

"You were here yesterday?"

"I'm Mr. Duffy's lawyer."

"Here on business, then? Yesterday?"

"Mainly a social visit. I've been dropping in on him just about every Tuesday evening since his accident."

"Accident?"

"He's paralyzed from the waist down. It happened a little over a year ago."

The cop jerked his chin at the crutches. "Those are his, then?"

I nodded.

"You said 'mainly.' About your visit yesterday. It wasn't entirely social?"

"Like I said. I'm his lawyer."

"Meaning you can't tell me his business?"

"No, I can tell you. He wanted me to have some old documents appraised for him." I told Currier about the Meriwether Lewis letters and how I'd delivered them to Ben Frye.

He asked me for Ben's address, wrote it into his notebook, then said, "And today? Why were you here today?"

"He called me, asked me to come over."

"What'd he want?"

"I don't know."

"Something about those letters?"

"He didn't tell me. Maybe he just wanted company. Look," I said, "he fell and banged his head. I didn't see it happen. That's about all I know. Where did they take him?"

"Mass General," he said. "What time did you say you got here?"

"Five-thirty or so."

"And you found him lying there."

"Yes."

And it was about then that it finally dawned on me that the cop suspected I might've had something to do with Walt's accident—and that it might not have been an accident at all.

Currier proceeded to ask me the same questions over again in a different sequence, and I proceeded to answer them truthfully, and finally he snapped his notebook shut. He handed me one of his cards. "If you think of anything," he said, "cell phone number's there. Call any time. Now I'm going to ask you to leave, Mr. Coyne."

"Leave?"

He nodded.

"Somebody's got to tell Ethan what's happened when he gets back," I said. "Let him know his father's in the hospital. Will you be here?"

"For a while. We've got to, um, secure the area, talk with neighbors. You know how it works."

"Crime scene," I said.

He shrugged. "For now."

"You think there was a crime committed?"

"I have no idea," he said. "We'll know better when we can talk with Mr. Duffy. And we'll want to talk to the son, of course."

"Ask Ethan to call me, would you?"

"We don't run a messenger service here, Mr. Coyne."

"Sure," I said. "You don't mind if I leave him a note, do you?"

"He won't be allowed inside."

"I'll put it on the door."

Currier shrugged. "Go ahead. I'll be in touch with you if I need you."

"Okay if I wait out front for him?"

"It's a free country, Mr. Coyne," he said. "Just stay out of the house."

So I took out two of my business cards, and on each of them I wrote: "Ethan. Call me ASAP. Brady." I wedged one under the knocker on the front door, then went around back and stuck the other one under the latch on the garden door in the alley.

As I left the alley, Currier's partner came out and began draping crime-scene tape across the door to Walt Duffy's bird garden.

FOUR

I sat on the front steps of Walt's townhouse to wait for Ethan. The sun had sunk behind the rooftops, and overhead the sky was turning purple.

I was torn. I wanted to go see how Walt was doing. But I didn't like the idea of Ethan coming home to a house wrapped in crime-scene tape.

I smoked a couple of cigarettes, and finally I decided that Ethan had taken Henry with him somewhere. He could be gone for the evening. When he got home, he'd see my card on the door, and he'd call me, if the police didn't get to him first.

Right about then I remembered my picnic with Evie.

I glanced at my watch. It was a little before seven-thirty. She'd already been waiting for half an hour. By the time I walked to the parking garage where I'd left my car and drove to Walden Pond, it would be nine o'clock and Evie would be gone.

Anyway, I couldn't just leave Walt in the hospital.

So I walked down Mt. Vernon Street to Charles Street,

went into the first restaurant I came upon, and found a pay phone inside the doorway. I dialed the number for Evie's cell phone, knowing it was a futile hope. She'd never bring a cell phone on a picnic at Walden Pond. She liked the quiet of the place the way Thoreau did. He would've considered an electronic gadget to be a profound violation of everything the pond and the woods represented, and I knew that Evie shared his transcendental sensibilities.

Her voice mail clicked in immediately, meaning she'd turned the phone off, and invited me to leave a message.

"I guess you noticed I didn't make it," I said. "Sorry about that. I had a meeting with Walt Duffy this afternoon. You met Walt, remember? The man with the bird garden? He's paralyzed, writes that column you like? Anyway, when I got here, he'd fallen and banged his head, and he was unconscious and nobody else was here, so I called 911 and the paramedics came and took him to the hospital. Then the cops came and asked me a lot of questions, and now it's about seven-thirty and I'm supposed to be at Walden with you, but I'm not. I'm still here in the city, and I'm about to head over to Mass General to see how Walt's doing, so—"

At that moment the time for my message expired with a rude click.

I redialed the number and told Evie's voice mail, "Just to clarify, I can't make it tonight. I hope you're having a nice picnic without me. I'll call you later."

Massachusetts General Hospital was about a fifteen-minute walk down Charles Street on the other side of Cambridge Street. It's a massive series of structures, and it took me some time to locate the emergency room. People of all descriptions and speaking myriad languages huddled in the waiting room, and various interns and residents and nurses and orderlies were bustling around ignoring them.

When I finally got the attention of one of the women behind the glass-fronted counter, I told her I wanted to see Walter Duffy.

"Spell it, please," she said. She had black close-cropped hair and pink lipstick and dark skin and a faintly Bahamian accent. She sounded neither rude nor friendly. Mainly stressed.

I spelled "Duffy" for her.

She poked at the keyboard of her computer, frowned, then checked a clipboard. "Walter Duffy?" she said.

"Yes. That's right."

"Upstairs. Surgery." She jerked her thumb over her shoulder.

"How do I find him?"

She shrugged. "I can't help you. He's not here." She looked past my shoulder dismissively.

I turned. A young man holding a baby in his arms was standing behind me. Both of them were crying.

I went outside, walked around to the front of the building, and went in the main entrance. It was less chaotic there. A white-haired woman behind the information desk told me that visitors were not admitted to the surgical floor.

I asked her if she could give me any information on Walt Duffy.

She said she was sorry, but she couldn't.

I asked her what she'd do if a friend of hers had been brought to the hospital for emergency surgery.

She pointed to a bank of telephones. "House phone," she said. She gave me the extension number for the surgical unit.

I went over and dialed it. A woman answered.

"I'm calling about Walter Duffy," I said.

"Who is this?"

"A friend of his. I'm in the lobby."

"Mr. Duffy is being prepared for surgery," she said. "That's all I can tell you."

"Is he going to be okay?"

"I have no more information for you, sir."

"How can I get more information?"

"Call when he's out of surgery. Ask for Acute Care."

"When will he be out of surgery?"

She sighed. "I have no idea. I'm sorry."

I hung up the phone. Now what?

Well, Walt was alive and being treated in one of the best hospitals in the world, and there was nothing I could do for him.

I went outside and lit a cigarette. I realized my stomach was grumbling. So I walked over to Skeeter's and had a burger and a glass of ale from a microbrewery in Vermont that Skeeter recommended.

While I ate, I watched the Red Sox game on one of the big TV's over the bar, but my mind kept wandering. I was thinking of Walt, how he looked lying on the bricks with blood dribbling out of his nostril and pooling under his head, how his eyelids had fluttered and he'd tried to tell me something before he lost consciousness.

I assumed he'd fallen and hit his head. Standard police procedure required them to proceed on the assumption that a crime had been committed.

The crime, if there was one, would be shoving a man on crutches, causing him to fall backward hard enough to make him bleed from the nose.

Who'd do that?

The only name I could come up with was Ethan.

That struck me as far-fetched and unlikely. On the other hand, a lot of unlikely things happened in this world.

"Another beer, Mr. Coyne?"

I blinked. Skeeter was leaning his elbows on the other side of the bar frowning at me.

"No," I said. "Thanks, Skeets. I'm heading home."

"You okay? Nomar hits a home run, you don't even smile?"

"A friend of mine's in the hospital," I said. "He got hurt pretty bad. I'm worried about him."

Skeeter nodded. He'd played a little second base for the Red Sox back in the seventies. When he blew out his knee, he bought this seedy little bar down the alley off State Street, named it Skeeter's Infield, paneled the walls, installed several big television sets, and turned it into the first sports bar in Boston. Skeeter still wore his faded and stained old Red Sox cap when he was behind his bar.

"You been to see him?" said Skeeter. "Your friend?"

I shook my head. "He's in surgery."

He took a swipe at the bar in front of me with his rag. "They do magic with surgery nowadays, Mr. Coyne. If they'd had arthroscopic surgery when I was playing, I might've had another four or five years."

"My friend banged his head," I said. "He was bleeding out of his nose."

Somebody down at the other end of the bar called to Skeeter for a refill. He reached over and touched my arm. "Your friend, he'll be okay," he said.

I left in the middle of the eighth inning. I didn't even notice what the score was.

When I got home, I checked my answering machine. No messages, from Ethan or from Evie or from anybody else.

I found my portable phone, took it out to the little iron balcony outside my apartment, and tried Evie's home number.

She didn't answer, and I didn't leave a message. It was a little after eleven o'clock. She had to be home from her solitary picnic at Walden Pond by now. Probably in the tub. Or maybe she was already in bed. She always turned off the ringer on her phone when she went to bed.

The point was, she hadn't tried to call me back.

I lit a cigarette and gazed across the harbor at the lights of East Boston and Logan Airport. Overhead, the moon was an orange wedge that reflected off the water.

When I finished my cigarette, I called Mass General and asked for surgery. They wouldn't tell me anything.

I went inside and poured two fingers of Rebel Yell over three ice cubes. Took it out to the balcony. Smoked another cigarette while I sipped.

Then I fished out the card Sergeant Andrew Currier had given me. He'd invited me to call any time. So I did.

"I was wondering if you had any news on Walt Duffy," I said when he answered.

"No news," he said.

"Did you talk to him?"

"By the time I got there, they were prepping him for surgery."

"The doctors say anything?"

"Nothing I'm at liberty to share with citizens," he said.

"Is he going to be okay?"

Currier sighed. "Look, Mr. Coyne. I understand your concern, okay? But when I gave you this number, the idea was you'd call me if you thought of something. So have you thought of anything?"

"You think this wasn't an accident, right?" I said. "You think somebody knocked him down, meant to hurt him."

"Supposing they did," he said. "Who could've done it?"

"I can't think of anybody."

"Call me when you can," he said.

I slept poorly and woke up early thinking about Ethan Duffy. The entire night had passed, and he hadn't called me.

I turned on the coffee machine, took a shower, shaved, and by the time I was dressed, the coffee had finished perking.

I took a mugful out to the balcony to wait for the sun to rise, which it did, right on schedule, an event that never ceased to fill me with wonder.

When my mug was empty, I went inside and refilled it. Then I did what I'd been dreading. I called the hospital and asked for Acute Care.

"I'm calling to see how Walter Duffy is doing," I said when the woman answered.

"Hold on, please," she said.

I held on.

Several minutes later, she came back on and said, "May I ask who's calling?"

"My name is Brady Coyne. I'm Mr. Duffy's lawyer."

"You're not a relative, then."

"No. I'm his lawyer. And his friend."

"Well, I'm sorry, sir, but we've been told not to speak with anybody except a relative about Mr. Duffy's condition."

"Told by whom?"

"I can't tell you that."

"Can you at least tell me if his surgery was successful?"

"I'm sorry, sir, but—"

"I just want to know if he's okay."

"Sir, please."

"That's okay. Forget it."

I was willing to bet it was the police who gave the Acute Care people those instructions. That did not comfort me.

Ethan was a relative. I wondered if he'd talked to the folks at Acute Care, or if the police had talked to him.

I left earlier than usual for work and headed for Walt's townhouse. I was hoping that the crime-scene tape would be gone and Ethan would be there, and he'd offer me some coffee and we'd sit in the bird garden and he'd tell me that he'd spent the night at the hospital, that Walt was fine, and that he was sorry he hadn't called me.

But when I got there, the front door was still crisscrossed with yellow crime-scene tape and my business card was still stuck under the knocker where I'd left it.

I went around to the alley. When I approached the door to the bird garden, I saw Henry.

He was lying against the door, curled in a ball. His white-and-orange fur was smudged with mud. For a moment I thought he was dead.

"Hey," I said. "Henry."

He lifted his head, blinked at me, and yawned. Then he stood up, stretched, and came over.

I squatted down and held out my hand, and he sniffed it. Then he gave it a cursory lick, just to be sure he hadn't missed a morsel of something edible.

"Where have you been?" I said. "Where the hell is Ethan?"

Henry sat beside me and watched my face.

I scratched his ears. "Did you spend the night outside? I bet you're hungry."

"Hungry" seemed to be a key word in Henry's vocabulary. He stood up and pressed his nose against the door. His stumpy little tail was wagging hard.

"You can't go in there," I told him. I blew out a breath. "What the hell am I going to do with you?"

He turned to look at me. His ears were cocked, and he seemed to arch his eyebrows.

I sighed. "Okay, okay. You better come with me. I hope you know how to heel."

We headed down Mt. Vernon Street and turned left on Charles. Henry heeled nicely all the way. I picked up a large black coffee and a cinnamon bun at the Starbucks on the corner. They didn't object to Henry, who sat quietly just inside the doorway while I waited at the counter. Out on the sidewalk, I gave Henry half of the bun. It went down in one massive gulp. I nibbled my half.

Then we strolled to my office in Copley Square. It was slow going, as Henry insisted on snuffling every shrub and bench and trash barrel in the Public Garden. He lifted his leg on most of them. That dog must've had a bladder the size of a dirigible.

I got to the office a little after eight. Julie wouldn't be in for almost an hour. I made the coffee, went into my office, and found an old sweatshirt hanging in the closet. I dropped the sweatshirt on the floor beside my desk and pointed to it. "That's for you," I told Henry.

He sniffed it, scratched at it with his front paws to get it properly arranged, then lay down on it.

I sat at my desk, snapped the cap off the Starbucks coffee, lit a cigarette, and tried to think.

If Henry had spent the night in the alley, it meant he hadn't spent it with Ethan. Ethan—and Walt, too, for that matter—doted on Henry. That conjured up several scenarios.

One: Ethan had left Henry in Walt's care and spent the night with a friend, and he didn't know what had happened to Walt. That was the least ominous scenario I could think of.

Two: If Ethan was gone all day and night, then Henry had somehow slipped away when Walt wasn't looking. Maybe Walt fell when he got up to go after Henry.

Three: If somebody had pushed Walt down, then Henry ran out into the alley when whoever did it escaped through the garden door.

Four: Ethan had been taking care of Henry, and Henry ran off because something had happened to Ethan.

Or, five: Ethan had, for some reason, been compelled to abandon Henry.

Scenarios three, four, and five frightened me.

I figured there were other scenarios that I hadn't thought of. They'd probably occur to me eventually.

On the floor beside me, Henry twitched and growled in his sleep. He seemed quite content to be snoozing on my sweatshirt.

Just what I needed. A dog.

Back when I lived with Gloria in our house in the Boston suburbs, we rescued a little black six-month-old mutt from a shelter. Gloria thought the boys, who were then in elementary school, should have a pet to care for. She thought it would teach them responsibility. The shelter people had named the pup Muffin, and I was unable to convince Gloria that he deserved a more dignified dog name.

Muffin?

Billy and Joey loved Muffin, and if we reminded them, they took turns feeding him. Naturally, most of the responsibility for the dog fell to me. It was I who housebroke Muffin, who taught him to sit and lie down and stay and come, who built the doghouse and erected the fence around the backyard, and who took him for his walks before bed every night and at the crack of dawn every morning.

Last I heard, Muffin was arthritic and deaf and still sleeping on the foot of the bed with Gloria.

In the decade or so since she and I had split, I'd forgotten how much attention dogs demanded.

At a little before nine, about the time Julie always gets to the office, I heard voices out in the reception area. I got up, opened the door, and peeked out.

Julie was standing beside her desk talking with two people, a uniformed man and a woman wearing tan pants and a matching jacket and a burnt-orange blouse. The man was Sergeant Andrew Currier.

I didn't recognize the woman. She was short and stocky, with straight black hair cut shoulder length, olive skin, and dark eyes.

I went out into the reception room. "Good morning," I said.

Currier looked at me. "Mr. Coyne," he said, "I'd like you to meet Detective Mendoza."

Detective Mendoza took a step toward me and held out her hand. "Saundra Mendoza," she said. "Boston PD. I'm with homicide."

FIVE

Walt Duffy?" I said to Detective Mendoza.

"That's right."

"Shit," I said. "When?"

"A little after midnight. He died on the operating table."

"The fact that you're here . . . You don't think it was an accident."

She nodded. She wore a thin gold chain around her neck and a man-sized gold watch on her left wrist. Otherwise, no jewelry. No makeup, either, that I could detect.

Under her jacket behind her right hip I detected the small bulge of a holster.

"Who did it?" I said.

She jerked her head toward my office door. "Can we talk?"

"I'll get some coffee," I said. I turned to Julie. "Would you mind showing the officers into my office?"

"Sure," she said, and she ushered Mendoza and Currier into my office.

I was pouring coffee into a carafe at the machine in the

corner of our reception area when Julie came back. "What, pray tell, is *this*?" she said.

I turned. She was standing in the middle of the room. Henry was standing beside her wagging his tail.

"That's our newest client," I said.

"It's a dog."

"A Brittany, to be precise. They used to call them Brittany spaniels. Now they just call them Brittanies. They're bird dogs, originally from the province of Brittany. That's in France."

"What happened to his tail?"

"All spaniels have little stubby tails like that. They're born that way."

"He's a bit chubby."

"He's struggled with it all his life. He was never very good at sports. Always had a complex. His name is Henry."

"Henry?"

"He was named after Henry David Thoreau."

Julie smiled, then scooched down beside Henry, who obliged by licking her cheek. "He's quite friendly," she said.

"He's all yours," I said.

She looked up at me. "What's the story?"

"He's very good with children," I said. "Megan will love him. Having a pet will teach her responsibility."

Julie stood up. "Megan is quite responsible already. She's also allergic to animals."

"You're making that up."

She shrugged. "We already have a goldfish. Seriously, where'd the dog come from?"

"He belonged to Walt Duffy."

She nodded. "Let me take care of the coffee. You go ahead and talk to those officers."

"Thank you." I started for my office, then stopped and turned back to Julie. "Henry needs a loving home for a few days. What do you say?"

"Fuggedaboudit."

Mendoza and Currier were sitting side by side at my conference table. Henry followed me in and went over and lay down on my sweatshirt. I sat across from the two cops. "Tell me what happened to Walt."

"The back of his skull was crushed," said Mendoza. "Splinters of bone in the brain. Massive hemorrhaging. He was in surgery for about four hours. The doctor said he never really had a chance."

"He fell on the brick patio," I said. "You think he was pushed or something?"

Mendoza shrugged. "Unattended death, Mr. Coyne. You know how it works. Why don't you just tell us about what happened yesterday."

"I already told Sergeant Currier."

"Tell me," she said.

So I repeated my story about how Walt had called with something he wanted to discuss, how when I got there I found him lying supine on the brick patio, how I'd called 911, how the paramedics had come, and then the two police officers, and how I'd told them everything I knew.

About halfway through my recitation, Julie tapped on the door. I called for her to enter, and she came in with a tray bearing a carafe of coffee, three mugs, a pitcher of milk, and a bowl of sugar. We fell silent until she went out of the room and closed the door behind her.

I resumed my recitation, and when I finished, Saundra Mendoza said, "So the dog was in the alley this morning and the son—Ethan—you haven't been in touch with him?"

I shook my head.

"We haven't, either." Mendoza glanced at Currier. Then she turned to me. "So what do you make out of that?"

"I don't know."

She pointed her chin at Henry. "That's Mr. Duffy's dog?"

I nodded. "His name's Henry. I stopped by Walt's place this morning and Henry was in the alley. Want him? He's all yours."

"Ha." She glanced at the notebook she was writing into. "Let's go back to when Mr. Duffy called you in the afternoon. He didn't say what he wanted?"

"No. He just said he wanted to talk with me. Consult with me, I think he said. I had the impression it was . . . important. Not urgent, but important."

"So what do you think was so important?"

I shrugged. "I've been thinking about it. I haven't got a clue."

"Something about those letters?"

"He didn't say," I said.

Mendoza nodded. "Let's go over it again, okay?"

This time the two of them kept interrupting my story for clarification and elaboration, and they kept asking me to estimate the times when things happened. In a couple of places I confused the sequence, and they picked up on them instantly.

When we finished, Mendoza said, "You're Mr. Duffy's lawyer. Does he have a will?"

"Certainly. What kind of a lawyer would I be if I didn't insist my clients had wills?"

"I don't know what kind of lawyer you are," she said. "What's the will say?"

"I'd have to check the details," I said, "but basically,

everything except Walt's bird stuff goes to his son, Ethan."

"Bird stuff?"

"He collected artwork and books and old manuscripts about birds. Some of it's quite valuable. His will stipulates that it's all to be donated to various libraries and museums. Walt Duffy was an expert on birds, you know."

"I know who he was," Mendoza said. "And the rest of his estate goes to his son?"

"Basically, there's just the townhouse. Walt didn't have a lot of money stashed away. No stocks or bonds. He invested everything in those old books and manuscripts and artwork."

"What about insurance?"

"Walt didn't believe in life insurance."

She nodded as if she'd expected me to say that. "Tell me about those letters. The ones you delivered for him."

So I told her about Walt's Meriwether Lewis letters and how I'd given them to Ben Frye to be appraised.

"This was day before yesterday? The day before he died?"

"Yes."

"The letters are valuable?"

"Both Walt and Ben seemed to think so. Assuming they're genuine."

She took a sip of her coffee, then set the mug down. She stared into it for a moment, and peered up at me. "Who might want to kill Walter Duffy, Mr. Coyne? Any idea?"

I shook my head. "No. No idea."

"Somebody did, you know."

"I figured that's why you're here."

"Ethan Duffy? Benjamin Frye?"

I flapped my hands. "I'm sorry. I don't know. I don't even have a theory."

She blew out a breath. "I need you to give us a hand."

"Sure," I said. "What can I do?"

"You've been in Mr. Duffy's townhouse a few times, right?"

"Many times."

"If something were missing or out of place, you'd notice it?"

I shrugged. "I might. It's harder to notice something that's not where it should be than something that is there that doesn't belong."

She shrugged. "Sergeant Currier and I are going over there now. We'd like you to come with us."

"I'm happy to help," I said. "Just let me check with Julie, see what I've got this morning."

I went out to the reception area. Julie told me I had only three clients scheduled for the day, one at eleven and the other two in the middle of the afternoon. I told her to reschedule them all.

"Evie called," she said.

"What'd she say?"

"She wanted to talk to you."

"You always chat with Evie."

"She told me about a new sushi restaurant in Harvard Square. Mentioned a book she was reading."

"And?"

"And I told her about Megan's soccer team."

"That's it?"

Julie smiled.

"Did she sound . . . upset?"

"With you, you mean?"

"Yes."

"We didn't talk about you," she said. "Sorry. She wants you to call her."

I went back into the office where Mendoza and Currier were waiting and told them I'd freed up my morning and just had to make one phone call. They nodded, got up, and went out to the reception area.

I sat at my desk and dialed Evie's office number at Emerson Hospital. When she answered, I said, "Hi, honey. It's me."

"Oh, Brady. Hi. Is everything all right?"

"Not entirely. Walt Duffy—one of my clients—died last night."

"I got your message," she said. "You said he'd been hurt. I'm so sorry. I met him once, remember?"

"That's right," I said. "You talked about decoys. I'm sorry I crapped out on our picnic."

"Under the circumstances . . ."

"I was worried you might be upset."

"Well, of course, I was upset. It was lovely at the pond, and I brought some great food. Couldn't eat it all myself. I missed you."

"I meant . . . like, angry."

"Why should I be angry?"

"Well . . ."

"We're supposed to be past that, you and I," she said. "I knew when you didn't show up that something must have happened. I was a little concerned that you might've had an accident. But angry? Nope. Not me."

"I'm relieved," I said.

"Dammit, Brady," she said, "we've talked about this. You seem to have these expectations of women. Negative expectations, I mean. We're not all selfish angry bitches whose main purpose in life is to lay guilt trips on men, you know."

I found myself smiling. "I know. I apologize for the fact

that it even crossed my mind. What about tonight?"

"A picnic?"

"Let's play it by ear. They're forecasting thunderstorms. I'll meet you at your place after work. Okay?"

"Okay," she said softly. "I look forward to it."

We drove from my office in Copley Square to Walt's townhouse on Beacon Hill in Sergeant Currier's cruiser. Mendoza rode shotgun, and I rode in back.

Currier pulled into the back alley. Saundra Mendoza pulled away the yellow tape and we went in through the door in the brick wall. They didn't bother slipping on rubber gloves, nor did they warn me not to touch anything, which meant, I assumed, that their forensics people had already been there.

The cops glanced around the patio, and then we went into the house. "Just tell us if you notice anything," said Mendoza. "Anything out of place or missing."

I led them to Walt's library where he kept his treasures. It was a large, dimly-lit inside room with no windows. It had air conditioning and a humidifier, which Walt kept fine-tuned to preserve his collections. Framed oil paintings, etchings, pen-and-ink drawings, pastels, and watercolors—all of birds—hung on the walls.

Three walls contained shoulder-high bookcases. On top of the bookcases Walt had lined up his collection of antique decoys and bird carvings. None of them seemed to be missing. The glass doors of the bookcases were all locked. Inside were hundreds of volumes of first editions and rare old books. There seemed to be nothing missing there, either.

The fourth wall—the one that included the doorway—was lined with steel file cabinets. These, I knew, held Walt's collection of letters, manuscripts, and bird-related documents. They were locked, too. There was no evidence that any of the locks had been tampered with.

We went through the rest of the three-story townhouse, floor by floor, room by room, and we ended up back in the garden.

"Nothing, huh?" said Mendoza to me.

I shrugged. "Not that I could detect."

"Think about the last time you were here. Before yesterday, I mean. Picture it. Tell me what you see in the picture."

I shut my eyes. "It was two nights ago," I said slowly. "Walt was sitting right there, on his chaise. He had those Meriwether Lewis letters in a manila envelope on the table. And . . ." I opened my eyes and looked at her.

"And?" she said.

"His computer," I said. "Walt had one of those new Apple laptops. He always kept it handy. And a camera and a cell phone, too, come to think of it. He always had them within arm's reach."

"There's no laptop computer here now," she said. She turned to Currier. "No cell phone or camera, either. You didn't notice them?"

He shook his head.

She turned to me. "Think, now. Were they here when you came yesterday and found Duffy's body?"

I tried to visualize it. "I don't think so," I said. "My attention was on Walt, of course. I mean, he was lying on the ground right there. But . . . no. His computer and his cell phone and his camera were not here. I remember thinking

I'd call 911 with his cell phone, but it wasn't there."

"They're not inside the house," said Currier. "And they're not out here."

"Well, then," said Mendoza.

"You think somebody killed Walt for his high-tech gadgets?" I said.

She smiled. It was the first time I'd seen her smile since I'd met her in my office. It transformed her face. "People have been killed for a loaf of bread," she said. "Let's talk about the son."

"Right," I said. "Ethan killed his father so he could steal his computer."

She shrugged. "Tell me about Ethan."

So I told her how Walt had separated from his wife about twelve years ago, when Ethan was six or seven. I'd handled Walt's end of the divorce. His wife couldn't tolerate the fact that he traveled the world photographing birds and was never home, and, from what I'd inferred, even when he was home he wasn't a very attentive husband or father. Walt told me that his wife believed he had women friends scattered across the globe and never lacked for company when he was on the road. He hadn't denied it.

In any case, after the divorce Ethan was raised by his mother. Walt went through the motions as a father—attended the school plays and concerts Ethan was in and met him for dinner now and then—but he didn't have much of a relationship with his son.

Then came Walt's fall at the Quabbin. It left him paralyzed, and Ethan, who was a senior in high school when it happened, enrolled at Emerson College in downtown Boston to study screenwriting and moved in to help take care of his father.

"You suggested that Duffy was cruel and ungrateful to his son," said Mendoza.

"He was worse at the beginning," I said. "He was all wrapped up in his condition. He was used to going everywhere. Climbing and hiking. Walt Duffy was a bundle of energy and enthusiasm. Suddenly, his legs didn't work anymore. He was angry and depressed, and he took it out on anyone who happened to be there, including me when I was with him. Ethan especially, of course. Ethan was handy. But it seemed to me that lately he was mellowing a bit. Accepting his situation, maybe, appreciating what Ethan was doing."

"But still . . ."

I nodded. "He could be nasty and sarcastic to Ethan, yes. But Ethan had a pretty good attitude about it. He shrugged it off, made jokes about it. He loved Walt. You think . . . ?"

"We're trying to find the boy, Mr. Coyne."

"The fact that he didn't come home last night."

"Yes. It raises questions."

"He told me he has a summer job in some record store in Central Square."

"Yes, you mentioned that to Sergeant Currier yesterday. We found the store. Place called Vintage Vinyl on Mass. Ave. Ethan Duffy didn't work there last night. He was scheduled to, but he never showed up."

I blew out a breath. "That doesn't sound good."

Mendoza shrugged.

"You never told me what happened to Walt," I said.

"No," she said. "I didn't."

"He was my friend and my client," I said. "It was I who found his body, for Christ's sake. I've got a right to know."

"I told you he died."

"From banging his head on the bricks, yes. But how did—?"

"Okay," said Mendoza. She narrowed her dark eyes at me. "We're keeping this under our hats for awhile, understood?"

I nodded. "Understood."

"Mr. Duffy didn't take a spill," said Mendoza. "And he wasn't pushed. According to the doctor who operated on him, the only way he could've sustained that injury was if somebody hit him with great force on the back of his head with something hard and heavy. Probably a brick."

"Jesus," I said.

She shrugged. "We'll know more when the ME gets a look at him."

"And you're thinking Ethan did this?"

"There was a lot of passion in that blow," she said. "Whoever hit Walter Duffy intended to hurt him. Probably meant to kill him. You figure it out."

I shook my head. "I can't."

Six

Sergeant Currier and Detective Mendoza dropped me off at my office a little after noontime. When I walked in, Henry scurried out from under Julie's desk and wagged his tail at me. I told him I was glad to see him, too.

Julie didn't seem all that glad to see me. She said she wanted to check out a shop on Newbury Street and would pick up lunch for us on the way back. I told her to take her time. She said she intended to.

That's how she always behaved when I canceled appointments.

Henry and I went into my office, and he waddled directly over to my sweatshirt, curled up, and went to sleep.

I poked through my Rolodex and found the number for Barbara Cooper, who had been Walt Duffy's wife's attorney for their divorce. Among those of us who generally represented the husbands in divorce proceedings, Barbara Cooper's name was pronounced "Barracuda." She defended her clients' interests relentlessly—which, of course, was how it was supposed to work.

Her secretary put me through to her right away.

"Mr. Coyne," she said when she picked up the phone. "To what do I owe this pleasure?"

"Not much of a pleasure, I'm afraid," I said. "The name Walter Duffy ring a bell?"

She hesitated, then said, "You and I did their divorce—what, ten, twelve years ago? They had a son?"

"That's the one," I said. "Walt died last night. I wanted to speak to his ex-wife. With your permission."

"You don't need my permission," she said.

"Actually, I wondered if you had her phone number. She's remarried, as I recall. I don't know her new name."

"I have the number right here. Hang on." She paused for a minute, then recited a number to me. "Her name is now Bramhall. Ellen Bramhall. She's living in Sudbury. What happened to Mr. Duffy?"

"He fell and fractured his skull. Didn't make it through surgery."

"I'm very sorry to hear it," she said. "How's the boy taking it? What was his name?"

"Ethan. He's a college freshman now. He seems to be bearing up okay."

"I don't recall if Ellen was a beneficiary in Mr. Duffy's will," she said.

"He didn't carry life insurance," I said. "I haven't even had a chance to check the will. It only happened yesterday."

"And the alimony?"

"It terminated when Mrs. Bramhall remarried, of course."

"Of course," she said. "Well, I know you'll be in touch with me."

"Sure," I said.

Barracuda.

I lit a cigarette and dialed the number Barbara Cooper had given me. It rang a couple of times, then a woman's soft voice answered.

"Mrs. Bramhall?" I said.

"Yes?"

"This is Brady Coyne," I said. "I'm Walter Duffy's attorney."

"Oh," she said. "I remember you. What's wrong?"

"I have some bad news, I'm afraid." I hesitated. "Walt died last night."

She didn't speak for a minute. Then she said, "What happened?"

"Evidently he fell and hit his head on the bricks in his patio." I felt uncomfortable lying about the manner of Walt's death to her, but Detective Mendoza had been very clear on the subject. I had not felt at all uncomfortable lying to Barbara Cooper.

Ellen Bramhall laughed quickly. "That man climbed mountains and prowled around jungles, and he ends up falling down in his own home." She hesitated. "I don't mean to make light of it. I'm terribly sorry. I never wished any harm to him. He wasn't a bad man. It's just that . . ."

"I understand, Mrs. Bramhall. It is kind of ironic."

"How's Ethan taking it?"

"That's one of the reasons I'm calling," I said. "I was wondering if you've talked to Ethan in the past twenty-four hours or so."

"Me?" She blew out a breath. "I don't hear much from my son anymore. Since he went off to college and began living with Walter." She paused. "Wait a minute. Why are you asking me about Ethan? Where is he? Is he all right?"

"Oh, I'm sure he's fine," I said. "It's just that he wasn't

there when Walt had his accident, and I'm trying to get ahold of him to tell him what happened."

"But he lives there," she said.

"He apparently stayed somewhere else last night. I thought maybe he was with you."

"Now you're upsetting me, Mr. Coyne. Where is my boy?"

"I don't know," I said. "If you should talk with him before I do, please ask him to call me."

"I will," she said. "You do the same."

"Of course."

"The police might come around looking for Ethan," I said.

"The police," she said. "Why?"

"Nobody saw it happen, that's all," I said. "It was what they call an unattended death. They're obliged to investigate."

"And they think Ethan . . . ?"

"It's just their routine," I said.

"Routine," she said. "Of course." She paused for a moment, then said, "Mr. Coyne?"

"Yes?"

"Do you think something has happened to Ethan?"

"No," I said. "I think he's a college kid who was at a party or something and ended up spending the night with friends, the way college kids do. I just wanted to tell him what happened to his father before he read about it in the papers."

"Sure," she said. "I'm sure you're right." She cleared her throat. "I am sad about Walter. He wasn't much of a husband. Or a father, for that matter. But he was a good man."

"I agree with you on all counts," I said.

After I hung up with Ellen Bramhall, I reached down and gave Henry a pat. He opened his eyes and looked at me for a moment, and when he decided I didn't have something for him to eat, he sighed and went back to sleep.

Julie returned around one-thirty. She brought a large plastic bag into my office and put it on my desk.

"What's this?" I said.

"It's not for you."

I peeked inside. The bag held a small green sack of Iams dry dog food, four cans of Alpo, two aluminum bowls, and a leash.

I took out the leash. It was one of those retractable gizmos with a square handle. "Thank you," I said to Julie. "We'll have a lot of fun with this."

"Maybe he's hungry," she said.

Henry was sitting there watching us. His ears perked up at the word "hungry."

"I bet he is," I said.

So I spread an old newspaper on the floor in my office and put half a can of Alpo and a handful of Iams and a splash of water into a bowl. I filled the other bowl with water.

Henry sat there looking at the bowls. "For you," I told him.

He cocked his head.

"Okay," I said.

He leaped up and went at it.

Julie had also stopped at the deli for tuna sandwiches with lettuce, tomatoes, and onions on wheat bread, bags of chips, dill pickles, and cans of Coke. Regular for me, Diet for her.

We ate at my conference table while Henry, having burped a couple of times, lay down beside me. His chin rested on his paws and his eyes followed my hands as I moved food into my mouth.

I tried to convince Julie that the house in the suburbs she

shared with Megan and Edward, her husband, would be a perfect place for an orphaned Brittany spaniel.

She still wasn't buying it.

"So what am I supposed to do with him?" I said.

"You rescued him," she said. "That makes his life your responsibility. Old Chinese saying. Confucius, I think."

"Confucius say," I said, "woman who fly upside-down in airplane—"

"Don't start," she said quickly. "I hate those stupid adolescent Confucius-say jokes of yours."

"Sorry," I said. "About the dog . . ."

Julie stood, gathered up the bags and cans and waxed paper from our lunches, and tossed it all into the waste basket. "Caring for stray dogs is not in my job description," she said. "And it's not negotiable."

"If I didn't know you better," I said, "I'd think you didn't want Henry to have a loving home."

She snorted a laugh out her nose, turned, and headed for the door.

"I'm leaving the office early," I said. "We've got no appointments. Why don't you take off for the afternoon?"

She turned and frowned at me. "I don't care if you double my salary," she said. "I'm still not taking the dog."

"He's really a sweet dog," I said.

"Yes, he seems to be. You two are destined for each other."

"No, huh?"

"No."

I flapped my hand. "Take the afternoon anyway."

"Thank you," she said. "I believe I will."

After Julie left, I made sure Henry's water dish was full and locked him in the office. If he made a mess, the cleaners who came in at night would just have to take care of it.

It was a fifteen-minute walk to the Emerson College registrar's office on Tremont Street. I took the elevator to the fourth floor and got the attention of a pretty young woman behind the long counter.

"Help you?" she said.

"Are you the registrar?" I said.

"Me?" She smiled. "Not hardly."

I took out a business card and put it on the counter. "I need to talk to the registrar."

She peered at the card, then looked up at me. "A lawyer, huh?"

I nodded.

"Did somebody do something wrong?"

"Yes," I said.

She cocked her head at me, then smiled. "Well, it wasn't me. Hang on."

A minute later a fortyish man in horn-rimmed glasses came to the counter. He had my card in his hand. "Mr. Coyne?"

I nodded.

"I'm James Connors. I'm the registrar here. Were you threatening Jamie?"

"Nope. I wasn't threatening anybody. I need your help."

"What kind of help?"

"The father of one of your students died last night. I need to get ahold of the boy."

"That's a shame." James Connors shook his head. "Classes ended nearly a month ago. The students have all gone home."

"I know where he lives," I said. "He's not there. I thought

maybe I could look up his friends, see if they might be able to help."

"Who's the student?"

"Ethan Duffy. He's studying screenwriting."

"WLP," he said. "Writing, literature, and publishing. That would be his department. Hang on."

He disappeared around the corner. I waited about five minutes, and then he came back with a computer printout. "This is the class roster for his freshman screenwriting seminar. My best guess would be that he'd have friends in this class. Otherwise, I wouldn't know how to help you."

I looked at the printout. There were sixteen names on it, including Ethan's. "You wouldn't have phone numbers for these kids, would you?"

He reached under the counter, pulled out a thin paperback book, and slid it toward me. On the cover it said, "Emerson College Directory."

"No hometown numbers in there," he said. "Many of the students have apartments here in Boston. Some stay in the city for the summer. Others hang around for a while after classes end. I imagine a lot of them have gone home, but I'm not comfortable giving you their family information."

"This is a big help," I said. "I assume Ethan's somewhere in the city, probably staying with one of his friends. Thank you."

Henry was glad to see me. I scooched down on the floor, and he leapt upon me, braced his front paws on my shoulders, and licked my face.

I let him do that for a while. Then I stood up and went

to my desk. Henry looked at me for a minute, then came over and curled up under my feet.

I tried the number of every student in Ethan's freshman screenwriting seminar, starting at the top of the list James Connors had given me. I left messages on the five voicemails that answered, saying the same thing: I was Ethan Duffy's family friend, I had important news for him, if you see him please have him call me, or if you know where he is, call me yourself. I left my name and phone number.

Seven of the phones had been disconnected.

Three students answered, two boys and a girl. All of them knew Ethan, but none of them admitted to being his friend. They all volunteered that he seemed to be a good guy but kind of a loner, and they had no idea where he might be.

I asked them to have Ethan call me if they happened to run into him. They said they would, but they didn't expect to run into him.

After I hung up from the last call, I pushed myself back from my desk, lit a cigarette, and stared out the window.

Ethan. Where the hell are you?

I hauled out my big Boston-Cambridge Yellow Pages and looked up Vintage Vinyl. I picked up the phone, then put it down and glanced at my watch. It was a little after four.

"Hey, Henry," I said. "Let's get the hell out of here."

I turned off the electric coffeemaker, rinsed out the pot, snapped on Henry's leash, picked up the sweatshirt he'd been lying on, and went across the street to the parking garage. I spread my sweatshirt on the backseat and told Henry that was his place. He hopped in, sat on the sweatshirt, and pressed his nose against the window.

I hooked onto Mass. Ave. and crossed the Charles River

on the Harvard Bridge. It was another glorious June day, and the river was dotted with sailboats and one-man sculls and kayaks and canoes. I spotted a couple of bass boats with men chucking spinning lures toward the banks. Seeing them reminded me that I hadn't been fishing in a couple of weeks. I'd give Charlie McDevitt a call, see if he could free himself up for a day over the weekend.

I needed to go fishing. Fishing, I'd discovered over the years, was an excellent antidote to the bleakness I always felt when somebody I knew died.

Vintage Vinyl, the record shop where Ethan worked, was on Mass. Ave., and I spotted it on the left outside of Central Square just past City Hall. Finding a place to leave my car was a greater challenge.

I finally slid into an empty space on a side street. I hooked Henry to his leash, locked the car, and the two of us strolled over to the record store.

The storefront was just wide enough for a door and a display window. A hand-painted sign in the window read: "Old LP's and 45's Bought and Sold." A dozen or so album covers sandwiched in protective plastic covers were on display—Frank Sinatra, looking boyish and skinny the way he did in *From Here to Eternity*, Nat King Cole holding a cigarette, *Cheap Thrills,* the Janis Joplin breakout with Big Brother and the Holding Company, Fats Domino, Chuck Berry, Johnny Mathis, the Beatles' White Album. I wondered if record album collectors valued the sleeves the way bibliophiles prized mint-condition book jackets. I was willing to bet that they didn't actually play the records.

Henry and I went inside. Joan Baez was singing "Baby Blue" over the speakers. Both walls were lined with shelves packed with record albums, and a long narrow table stood in the middle. It held boxes of 45's.

A pale, lanky man with a receding hairline and a ponytail and rimless glasses was sitting at an ancient rolltop desk in the corner beside the door. He was talking on the telephone, and when he spotted me, he held up a finger.

I riffled through the 45's. "Oh Gee" by the Crows. Vintage 1953. "Come Go with Me," the Del Vikings. A couple of years later, I seemed to recall. Before I was even born.

The guy at the desk hung up and came over. Up close I saw that he was younger than I'd thought. Thirty, maybe.

When he noticed Henry, he scooched down and rubbed the dog's head. "It's old Henry. How you doin', man?"

Henry lay down and rolled onto his back.

The guy looked up at me and grinned. "He loves to have his belly scratched. You must be a friend of Ethan's, huh?"

I nodded and held out my hand. "Brady Coyne."

He shook my hand. "I'm Phil," he said. "So how come you got Henry? Ethan brings this mutt to work with him sometimes. Nice dog. Knows how to behave. Customers like him."

"Are you the owner?" I said.

"Of this place?" He rolled his eyes. "Nah. Not me. I couldn't afford it. We don't make any money here. Conrad, the guy who owns it, he collects this stuff. I think the store is some kind of tax thing. We get a dozen people in here in a day, we've had a good day, and most of 'em don't buy anything. Conrad sells some stuff on the Internet, I guess. Mainly, this is his collection. You lookin' for something?"

"I was hoping to catch Ethan," I said. "Return Henry to him."

"Ethan works nights," said Phil. "Comes on at six."

"Is he scheduled to be here tonight?"

"Not tonight." He shrugged. "He was supposed to be here last night, but he never showed up."

"No?" I said. "What happened?"

"Well, shit, man, I don't know what happened. He just didn't show up. I was here. I can't leave 'til Ethan gets here, you know? I waited 'til close to seven, and no Ethan. So I called Conrad—that's the owner, Conrad Henshall—and finally he came in so I could go home."

"Does this happen a lot?"

"What, Ethan not showing up?"

I nodded.

"No. He's pretty reliable usually."

"Did he call in last night, do you know?"

"He didn't call me," said Phil, "and Conrad didn't seem to know anything about it." Phil adjusted his glasses and frowned at me. "You must know what's going on. I mean, you're taking care of his dog, right? So what's up with Ethan?"

"I just want to return his dog," I said. I fished one of my business cards from my wallet and gave it to Phil. "If you hear from Ethan, tell him to give me a call, will you?"

Phil took my card and looked at it. "Lawyer, huh?"

I nodded.

"Ethan in some kind of trouble?"

"He's in trouble with me," I said. "I'm getting sick of taking care of his dog."

"Aw," said Phil, "Henry's a good old pooch."

"You want to watch him for a while? He's all yours."

Phil held up both hands. "Hey, not me, man."

I nodded. "That's what everybody says."

Outside the store I paused to light a cigarette.

Then I heard a soft voice say, "Sir?"

I turned. A large man wearing yellow-tinted glasses and an expensive-looking gray suit was standing there. He seemed to have emerged from the alley beside the store. He was squinting at me through his glasses.

"Can I help you?" I said.

"I don't believe so," he said. "Perhaps I can help you. My name is Conrad Henshall."

I nodded. "You own this place?"

"That I do."

He held out his hand, and I shook it. "My name is Brady Coyne. I'm a lawyer. I'm looking for Ethan Duffy. I understand he works here."

"Mr. Duffy no longer works here," he said.

"Oh? Your man in there, Phil, he told me—"

"Philip is the employee. I am the owner. I don't make it a practice to confide in my employees."

"Did Ethan quit, or did you fire him?"

"May I ask you what difference it makes?"

"Ethan's father died last night."

Henshall looked at me from behind his yellow-tinted glasses, as if he expected me to elaborate.

Instead, I said, "Have you been in touch with Ethan since yesterday?"

"As I told you, sir," he said, "young Mr. Duffy no longer works for me."

"Does that mean you haven't talked with him?"

"It means I'd have no reason to talk with him."

"And this is what you told the police?"

He smiled. He had a small, rather unpleasant mouth, and his smile suggested neither humor nor good will. "If I had told the police something different, it would mean I was lying either to you or to them, wouldn't it?"

I nodded. "I guess it would." I fished out a business card and gave it to him. "If you talk to Ethan, ask him to call me, will you?"

He put the card into his pocket without looking at it, then dipped his head at me. "If I can be of any more service to you, sir, don't hesitate to call on me."

"You can count on it," I said.

Seven

The Thursday afternoon traffic out of Cambridge was typically tangled, and by the time I took the West Concord exit off Route 2, it was close to six o'clock. I stopped at the little grocery store by the train station and bought six cans of Alpo and a bag of dry dog food. Then I went to the liquor store across the street and picked up two bottles of Merlot.

I don't know anything about wine. Those bottles cost twenty bucks apiece. How bad could they be?

Evie lived in a condominium complex that had been carved out of an old orchard. Many of the fruit trees had survived the bulldozers, so the area bloomed lavishly—and aromatically—in the springtime. A brook meandered through the grounds, and the developers had dammed it up in several places, forming a series of interconnected little ponds. Hundreds of mallards, once wild but now tame, lived there year-round, as did a resident flock of Canada geese. The birds thrived on handouts, and they weren't shy about soliciting strangers.

I parked in the visitor's lot, released Henry with instructions not to run away, and watched while he checked out the shrubs, peed on most of them, squatted awkwardly for a massive dump, and then resumed snuffling the bushes. When I called him, he came. I told him he was a fine, obedient animal, snapped on his leash, tucked my bag of groceries under my arm, and we headed for Evie's townhouse.

About halfway there, a flock of webfoots materialized behind us. They gabbled and quacked, hissed and honked, and Henry nearly yanked me off my feet trying to get at them. I stamped my foot at them, and Henry growled. The dumb birds just stood there with their heads cocked, looking at us.

Evie enjoyed her flock of tame waterfowl, even if they did litter the lawns and parking areas and pollute the ponds. Evie was an amateur ornithologist. When she went fishing with me, she brought her binoculars and prowled around the banks of my beloved woodland streams looking for birds, while I waded in the water looking for trout.

Once, a few months after Walt Duffy's accident at Quabbin I took her in to meet him. They talked about birds, and he showed her his collection of decoys and carvings. Evie collected bird carvings, too. Walt flirted outrageously with her, and she flirted right back at him.

Afterward, she told me he was a seriously depressed man.

I rang Evie's bell. Henry sat on the stoop expectantly.

When she opened the door and smiled at me, I felt a little shiver, the way I always did when I first saw Evie after not having seen her for a few days. Evie Banyon was slender and tall—only a couple of inches shorter than me—and her hair was the color of high-grade maple syrup, halfway between amber and gold. Now she had it pulled back in a ponytail, and it cascaded down her back nearly to her waist. She was wearing cutoff jeans and one of my old blue dress shirts knotted over her midriff.

She wrapped both arms around my neck and kissed me hard and long on the mouth. I reciprocated her kiss with equal enthusiasm, but since I had bags of wine and dog food under my arms and a dog on a leash, I couldn't hug her tight against me the way I wanted to. No need. She pressed herself against me anyway.

Suddenly she pulled away. "Something's lapping my leg." She looked down. "Oh. Well, hello there."

"Meet Henry," I said. "He's an orphan."

Evie squatted down and stroked Henry's head. He lapped her face, and Evie giggled. "He's a friendly fellow, isn't he?"

"He loves you," I said. "Hard to blame him."

She stood up. "His name's Henry?"

"Yes. His full name is Henry David Thoreau Duffy. He's Walt Duffy's dog. Actually, you met Henry that time."

She nodded. "You told me that Mr. Duffy . . ."

"Yes. Walt died."

She frowned and nodded. "Are you okay?"

I shrugged. "Not really." I wanted to tell her that Walt had apparently been murdered, but Detective Mendoza had instructed me not to. It was hard to keep any kind of secret from Evie.

She put her arm around my waist and laid her cheek against my shoulder. "I'm so sorry," she said.

I turned and kissed the top of her head. "Shit happens, I guess."

"That it does," she said. "So what's with the dog?"

"How'd you like to adopt a loving, well-behaved Brittany for a few days?"

"You've got to be kidding."

"No. I'm serious. Henry would love it here, with all your tame mallards for entertainment. Brittanies are excellent bird dogs, you know."

"Brady, for heaven's sake, I can't take care of a dog."

"You can take care of a dog better than I can," I said. "At least you live on the first floor, and you're out here in the country, practically. If Henry shits on the lawn, nobody will even notice with all the duck and goose turds around. Me, I live on the sixth floor in the middle of the damned city. No place for an outdoorsy dog like Henry. So it seems to me . . ."

Evie grinned and shook her head.

"I don't get it," I said. "Nobody wants him. He's a great dog. It would probably only be for a few days. Until Ethan shows up."

"Ethan?"

"Walt's son."

"Where's Ethan?"

"I don't know. That's another story. Right now, I've got to figure out what to do with Henry. He's taken over my life."

"So put him in a kennel."

I looked down at Henry, who was sitting there on Evie's stoop looking up at us. "I can't do that. He'd hate it in a kennel."

"Well," said Evie, "bring him inside, anyway. It looks to me like you brought us some wine. Let's open one of those bottles, let it breathe for a few minutes, then have some."

"I also brought dog food."

"So we'll feed the dog, too. Come on."

We went in. Henry wandered through the downstairs, sniffing the furniture, then lay down in the middle of the living-room carpet where he could keep an eye on things.

I went upstairs to Evie's bedroom, where I kept a few changes of clothes, and got out of my suit. When I got back to the kitchen, Evie had one of the wine bottles uncorked, and Henry was eating from a mixing bowl.

"You fed him," I said.

"Yes. And I'm going to feed you pretty soon, too. But first, you strike me as a man who could use a nice, soothing massage."

An hour later Evie and I were lying naked under the sheets in her bed sipping wine. Henry had followed us upstairs to the bedroom. He was asleep on the floor by the door.

"I was thinking," said Evie.

"Oh, oh," I said.

"I was thinking maybe it's time you moved. Find someplace where you can keep a dog. You love dogs. You've been in that place in the city ever since you got divorced. You keep saying it's temporary, and it's been, what, ten years?"

"Eleven," I said.

"So what are you waiting for?"

"I don't know. It's inertia, that's all. I have no reason to move. I mean, it would be one thing if you and I were going to move in together, but . . ."

"We've talked about that," she said. "It would put too much pressure on us. Neither of us is ready. We agreed on that, remember?"

"Speak for yourself."

She sat up and frowned at me. "What are you trying to say, Brady?"

I shrugged. "When I'm not with you, I miss you. When—when bad things happen, I feel like I need you to be with me. Talking on the phone is great, but it's not the same thing."

She nodded. "I feel that way, too."

"So maybe we should think about it some more."

"Living together?"

I nodded.

She lay back and gazed up at the ceiling.

After a minute, I said, "What are you thinking?"

"I'm trying to imagine it," she said quietly.

"Living with me?"

"Yes."

"And?"

She turned her head and looked at me. "Are you serious?"

"I'm serious about thinking about it some more, anyway. I don't know. It's a big step."

"You're damn right it's a big step," she said. "I, for one, don't move in and out with people willy-nilly. If we decided to live together, that would be it."

"That's how I feel about it, too," I said.

"It would be a commitment."

"Yes."

"Scary," she said.

"Very scary," I said.

When we were at my place, I did the cooking. At Evie's place, she did it. This time, she said she was in the mood for a big salad and fresh bread. So I sat at the kitchen table and watched her dump stuff into her big wooden salad bowl. Bibb lettuce, spinach greens, slivers of Bermuda onion, cherry tomatoes, cucumbers, scallions, green peppers, shiitake mushrooms, green olives, ripe olives, chickpeas, raisins, a can of baby shrimp, a can of tuna fish, a can of crab meat. She splashed on some vinaigrette dressing, tossed it with wooden spoons, sprinkled on some chopped chives, took a pass over it with the pepper mill, and put it on the table.

I snaked out a green olive with my fingers, sucked out the red pimento, then ate the olive.

She brought over a loaf of French bread on a cutting board and handed me a serrated knife. I sliced the bread.

I was thinking how much fun it would be if Evie and I took turns making dinner every night. I kept that thought to myself. It was, indeed, scary.

After we ate, we cuddled on her sofa, watched an old Hitchcock movie on her TV, and finished the Merlot.

Henry slept on the cool flagstones in Evie's foyer.

Around eleven, we took Henry out for a ramble around Evie's yard. I didn't bother leashing him. He'd proven he would come when I called him.

Frogs were grumbling from the ponds, and some night birds were swooping around, snagging mosquitoes. The ducks and geese had apparently bedded down for the night, but Henry still found many fascinating things that needed to be snuffled.

We wandered over to my car. I called Henry and told him to jump into the backseat. Then I leaned back against the door. Evie put her arms around my waist, pressed herself against me, and tucked her face into my shoulder. "If you lived here, you'd be home now," she whispered.

I kissed her hair and nodded.

"We can think about it some more, if you want," she said.

"Let's."

"Not here, though. And not your place. If we ever decided to, um, cohabit, it should be someplace new for both of us. Our own place. Not yours or mine. Does that make sense?"

"Yes," I said. "That makes excellent sense."

"Someplace with a yard. Maybe we could raise some vegetables. Fresh salads every night."

"I don't want a big lawn," I said. "I hate to mow the lawn."

"We could hire somebody."

"I'm perfectly capable," I said. "I just hate it."

"Sure," she said. "It would have to be perfect for both of us. I'd want to feed the birds in the winter. Feeders right outside the kitchen window, so I could watch them."

"No tame ducks, though."

"I was thinking of wild birds." She kissed my cheek. "Go now. Drive carefully."

I kissed her, climbed into the car, and rolled down the window. "I was thinking about going fishing one day this weekend," I said. "I kind of need to go fishing."

"Then you should most definitely go fishing," she said. "A day of fishing always gives you a better outlook."

"Want to come along?"

"We'll see. Mary and I talked about doing something."

"Maybe I'll give Charlie a call."

She smiled. "Do what you want, Brady. Be happy." She bent to the window and kissed me again. "Good night. Love you."

"Me, too," I said.

When I got home, I realized I'd left Henry's dog food at Evie's. I'd have to scrounge up something from my refrigerator for his breakfast.

I found an old sweatshirt and dropped it on the floor beside my bed. Henry sniffed it suspiciously, pushed it around until he got it the way he wanted it, then curled up on it, let out a long snuffling sigh, and went immediately to sleep.

He'd had a hard day.

The light on my answering machine was blinking. I hoped it was Ethan, telling me he was okay and wanted his dog back, or maybe one of his classmates telling me where I could find him.

There had been three calls, all hangups. I hit star-69, which would give me the number of the last call.

But the recorded voice informed me that I could not reach the number by that method. Whatever that meant.

EIGHT

When I woke up the next morning, Henry was straddling me, licking my face. I rolled onto my belly and buried my face in my pillow. Henry poked at my head with his nose. When I told him to cut it out, he jumped off the bed, sat on the floor, and whined.

I looked at my alarm clock. It was a little after five-thirty.

I sat up on the edge of the bed and rubbed my face. "I can't do this," I told him.

He went over to the door and poked it with his nose, then turned and whined at me.

"Do they have litter boxes for dogs?" I asked him.

He wagged his tail.

So I pulled on my jeans and sneakers, got Henry on his leash, took the elevator down six floors, and we went to my neighborhood park, a lovely little strip of greenery—a sort of miniature Boston Common—along Commercial Street. There were paths and trees and gardens and bushes and benches. Kids sometimes rollerbladed there, but mostly it was a place where folks from nearby business establishments ate lunch on a nice day and nearby residents went for an evening stroll. I unleashed Henry there and let him snuffle around and take care of business, while I sat on a bench and smoked a cigarette.

Henry stayed close by, and when I spoke to him, he lifted his head and perked up his ears. "Don't go away," I told him, and he sort of nodded and resumed snuffling around.

I'd been there a few minutes when a pretty college-aged blond woman approached me. A golden retriever was leading her around on a leash.

"You should keep your dog leashed," she told me.

"Henry won't go anywhere," I said.

"Well, he could get run over, you know."

"I told him not to do that."

She shrugged. "Anyhow, you're supposed to take care of his poop."

"Take care of it?"

"Clean it up, bring it home."

"Bring it home," I said. "Then what?"

She smiled. "I guess that's up to you. Just so you don't leave it here."

Her dog had eyes for a bed of irises, and she allowed herself to be hauled in that direction. She smiled at me over her shoulder, and I waved.

This young woman seemed to have her hands full with that one golden. There were city people, I knew, who kept many dogs in their apartments. Some of them owned five or six dogs. They walked them several times a day, their whole gang of dogs on leashes. It was a big responsibility.

I liked Henry. But I didn't like the idea of scraping up his leavings and carrying them home with me, and I profoundly disliked waking up at five-thirty in the morning.

Mainly, I didn't like responsibility.

We walked to my office, I in my lawyer suit with my briefcase in one hand and Henry's leash in the other, and Henry trotting along beside me.

When we got there, he was exhausted. He curled up in the corner and went to sleep. I was pretty tired myself.

In the middle of the morning, I called Detective Mendoza's cell phone.

"It's Brady Coyne," I said when she answered.

"Mr. Coyne," she said. "What've you got for me?"

"Nothing. Unless I can talk you into a dog."

"No Ethan Duffy, huh?"

"I was hoping you—"

"You talked to the guy at the record store," she said. "You talked to Ethan's mother. You talked to the registrar at Emerson College. You've been busy."

"You've been keeping tabs on me."

"I'm a cop," she said. "It's my job. Snooping around isn't your job, though."

"Walt Duffy was my friend," I said. "Mostly, I want to return this dog to its rightful owner. You haven't found Ethan, then?"

"Not yet. We're keeping an eye on his place on Mt. Vernon Street, and we've got the Sudbury cops watching his mother's place. We know our business, Mr. Coyne."

Friday is generally a slow day at my office, especially during trout season. Julie schedules no appointments, and unless I've got to be in court, we use the day to catch up on phone calls and paperwork. Often we quit early on Friday afternoons, and that was our plan for this pretty Friday in June.

I had Julie dig out Walt Duffy's file for me. As I'd remembered, aside from his collection of books, manuscripts and artwork, which he'd bequeathed to museums, Walt had left everything to Ethan. All that really amounted to was his townhouse on Mt. Vernon Street and whatever was in his bank accounts—which I knew wasn't much. Every time Walt got some money, he spent it on his collection.

I was staring out the window trying to imagine Ethan whacking Walt on the back of the head with a brick when the phone buzzed.

When I picked it up, Julie told me it was Benjamin Frye. She said he sounded agitated.

I hit the blinking button on my console and said, "Ben. What's up?"

"*You*, goddamn it. You sicced the pigs on me."

"Did you say pigs?"

"The cops. The police. I hate the police. The police hate me."

"Have you done anything wrong, Ben? Need a lawyer?"

"Maybe I've got a baggie or two in the bottom drawer of my file cabinet. That's not the point. They always treat you like you're a fucking criminal, make you feel guilty whether you did anything or not. Why'd you have to give them my name?"

"Walt Duffy died," I said. "They were asking me about it. I told them about the Meriwether Lewis letters."

"Yeah," he said. "Sorry about Duffy. Crabby bastard, but he knew his stuff. Anyway, it's hard to hate a guy who likes birds, you know? What happened to him?"

"The police didn't tell you?"

"Tell me?" He laughed quickly. "Cops don't tell you anything. I think they thought I already knew about it. As if I was going to cross myself up, let it slip."

"He fell and banged his head on the bricks," I said. "He died in surgery."

"They think somebody pushed him or something, huh?"

"I guess so," I said. "So what about those letters?"

"Well," he said, "they wanted me to hand 'em over. When I refused, they threatened me."

"Why did you refuse?"

"You kidding? Those things are fucking priceless. You ever see a police evidence room? You want two-hundred-year-old letters from Meriwether Lewis to Alexander Wilson collecting dust and cigar smoke and mouse turds on some shelf in a police evidence room?"

"I'd say you showed good judgment," I said. "How did they threaten you?"

"In that nasty, suggestive way that cops do it that you can't really put your finger on but you know they're doing it. That Mendoza, she's a nasty one. I surmise she pulled my sheet."

I found myself smiling. Ben Frye had been arrested many times when he was younger, and he was quite proud of it. He'd spent nights in American jails from Birmingham to Chicago to San Francisco to Boston. He'd been convicted just once. That was when he lay down in the middle of Mass. Ave. in Harvard Square and went limp when they dragged him to a paddy wagon. The judge fined him a hundred dollars for disturbing the peace.

Ben always thought that was supremely ironic, since he'd been carrying a sign that read "Peace Now."

"So where are the letters?" I said.

"Oh, don't worry. I got 'em. Now I want the damn things off my hands. Come and fetch 'em."

"What about tonight? I'll buy you dinner, you can give me the letters. Remington's? Say six-thirty?" Remington's was a pleasant restaurant-bar on Boylston Street, just around the corner from Ben's office on Temple Place.

"You can buy me dinner," he said. "But that doesn't mean I'm gonna stop being pissed at you. I'll see you there."

It wasn't until I hung up that I remembered Henry.

What the hell was I going to do with Henry? I couldn't bring a dog into the restaurant.

He'd been with me for just two days, and already I felt like I had a cinder block chained to my ankle.

I went out to the reception area. Julie looked up at me with her eyebrows arched. "What?" she said. "You've got that look on your face."

"Please come in," I said. "We've got to talk."

She followed me into my office. I pointed at the sofa. "Have a seat."

She remained standing there. "You act like you're going to fire me."

"I'm thinking about it."

She smiled. "No you're not. Why don't you just tell me what's on your mind."

"Actually I was thinking of giving you a raise."

Julie looked up at the ceiling and sighed. "Come on, Brady. For heaven's sake, spit it out."

I went over to the sofa, sat down and patted the seat beside me. Julie came over and sat.

I cleared my throat. "I really need . . . I mean, I wonder if I could convince you to take Henry for the weekend."

She shrugged. "Sure. Okay."

"Please? It would—what did you say?"

"I said sure. I wouldn't mind taking Henry for the weekend."

"You wouldn't?"

"No. If it would help you."

Henry, who'd been sleeping in the corner, apparently heard his name mentioned. He stood up, stretched, came over to where Julie and I were sitting, lay down in front of us, and gazed up at her.

"Do you mean it?" I said.

"I sort of expected this, Brady. Megan will love it, and Edward likes dogs. I like dogs, too, of course. Henry seems like he'll be easy. Just for the weekend, though. You'll have to take him back on Monday."

"I thought Megan was allergic to animals."

Julie smiled. "I made that up."

"What if she falls in love with him?"

"That's the only thing that worries me," she said. "It's not like you can give him to us. He's not yours to give away."

"It feels like he's been my dog for years," I said. "He's running my life. He woke me up at five-thirty this morning."

"Thanks for the warning."

"You sure you want to do this?"

"Are you trying to talk me out of it?"

I reached over and gave Julie a hug. "You're amazing."

"True."

"I was prepared to order you to take him off my hands," I said.

"That would never work," she said.

Around four-thirty, Julie came into my office. "I turned off all the machines," she said. "I'm leaving." She went over to where Henry was snoozing in the corner, scooched down beside him, and scratched his forehead. "You ready to go?" she said to him.

He looked up at her and yawned.

"He likes three scoops of the dry stuff and half a can of Alpo at suppertime," I said, "plus a little smackerel of something in the morning. He likes to sleep on a ratty sweatshirt. I think he likes the smell of manly sweat. I bet Edward's got one he can spare. He'll wake you up by lapping your face sometime between five-thirty and six. You should let him off the leash so he can ramble around the backyard. He needs all the exercise he can get. He'll come when you call him. He's really a very obedient dog. He loves to be scratched between his ears. Oh, and don't forget . . ."

I stopped. Julie was grinning at me.

"What?" I said.

"You sound like a new parent, giving instructions to your very first babysitter."

"Hell," I said, "it's just a dog."

"Don't worry about Henry. We'll be fine."

"Worry? I'm not worried."

She smiled.

"It'll be a relief," I said. "Not having that damn dog running my life."

"I'll have him back to you on Monday."

I waved my hand. "Keep him as long as you want."

Henry was lying there with his chin on his paws watching us. His eyes snapped back and forth to our faces as we talked.

I handed his leash to Julie. She clipped it onto his collar

and stood up. Henry pushed himself to his feet, arched his back, then waddled over to me.

"You're with Julie," I said to him. "She's the boss now. Please behave yourself. You're going to a loving home. You'll have a great time."

He looked up at me and wagged his tail.

I reached down to pat his head. He licked my hand.

"Look," I said to him. "It's just for the weekend, okay?"

"Maybe this is a bad idea," said Julie.

"Go," I said. "Now. Please."

Julie started for the door. "Come on," she said to Henry.

He cocked his head and looked at me.

"For God's sake, just go," I told him.

After they left, I sat down on my sofa, put my feet up on the coffee table, and lit a cigarette. Free at last, Lord. A glorious weekend ahead of me. No responsibility, no obligation, no dog whining at me.

I called Evie at her office and asked her if she'd decided whether she wanted to come fishing with me tomorrow. She said she'd made a plan with her friend Mary. They were going to meet at the Arnold Arboretum, stroll around looking at the trees and shrubs, then have an early dinner at one of the sidewalk cafes on Newbury Street before Mary headed back home. Evie said she intended to come to my place for a Saturday-night sleepover afterward, if that was okay by me.

That was terrific by me. I told her to let herself in and make herself at home if I wasn't there. I was going to be off fishing, and she might get there first.

After I hung up with Evie, I called Charlie McDevitt. He

couldn't go fishing, either. One of his kids was in a weekend soccer tournament in Connecticut, and Charlie had volunteered to be one of the chaperones.

I tried Doc Adams, but he and Mary were heading off to their place on the Cape.

Well, the hell with my friends. They were tied down with kids and wives. Me, I didn't even have a dog to tie me down. I could go fishing any time I wanted. I didn't mind going alone. I thought I'd head for the Squannacook River out in Townsend. It was a nice little trout stream, and I hadn't fished there for a couple of years. It was only a little more than an hour's drive from the city. I could fish 'til dark and still have my Saturday night with Evie.

The best of all possible worlds.

I got to Remington's a little before six-thirty and found an empty booth near the bar. Ben Frye ambled in a few minutes later. He slid in across from me and slapped a manila envelope down on the table.

"The letters?" I said.

He nodded. "Now you got 'em. Now they can stop harassing me. But I'm still pissed at you."

"So are they authentic?" I said.

Frye shrugged. "I didn't have a chance to test the ink and paper. That's very delicate work, not something I do in my office. I go to a lab for that. I didn't even take the letters out of their plastic sleeve. I heard about Duffy before I got around to that, decided I better just give 'em back to you. But the handwriting, the syntax, the sketch, it all looks like Meriwether Lewis to me. They could be forgeries, but I don't think they are. Anyway, they're yours now."

The waiter appeared. I ordered a gin-and-tonic. Ben asked for scotch. "So what happened to Duffy?" he said after the waiter left.

"What I told you on the phone," I said. "He fractured his skull. I found him out in his patio. He was unconscious when I got there. They tried to operate, but he died on the table."

"*You* found him?"

I nodded. "He asked me to come over. Said he had something he wanted to talk about. When I got there, he was lying on the bricks."

"So what'd he want to talk about?"

"He didn't say."

Ben shook his head. "You never know, huh?"

I nodded.

Ben looked up. Our waiter put our drinks in front of us and asked us if we were ready to order.

Ben glanced at his watch and nodded. "I've only got about an hour. Gotta get back to the office."

"On a Friday night?" I said.

He shrugged. "You do business when you can. I got a guy coming in at eight."

I ordered the 14-ounce Porterhouse with a baked potato, hold the sour cream, and Ben had a Greek salad. I'd forgotten that he was a vegetarian.

After the waiter left, Ben said, "That accident out at Quabbin changed Duffy. It pretty much destroyed his life."

I nodded.

"The man goes everywhere, does everything," he said. "Then the next thing you know, he's paralyzed, can't leave his house. And now he falls down and dies in his own backyard?" He shook his head. "Life is full of ironies, isn't it?"

Walt had been murdered, of course. But Detective Mendoza had forbidden me to tell anybody.

When our food came, I told Ben that I'd have to get Walt's collection appraised in order to settle his estate and was wondering if he'd do it. Ben, with no false modesty, reminded me that he'd traveled all over the country to appraise estates, that he was considered an expert on books, manuscripts and artwork pertaining to nature and wildlife in general and birds in particular, and that it would take him at least a week, so I should give him ample notice.

I told him that until Ethan showed up, there was nothing much to do, but I'd keep in touch with him.

After we finished eating, Ben looked at his watch and said, "I hate to eat and run, but . . ."

"No coffee? No dessert?"

"I've really got to get back."

He took out his wallet, but I held up my hand. "I got it. I'll charge it against Walt's account."

"Well, okay. I guess he can spare it now."

I held out my hand to Ben. "We'll be in touch," I said.

He shook my hand, then turned and shambled out of the restaurant.

I had a slab of lemon meringue pie and a cup of coffee, then walked home through the city.

When I got there, I watched the end of the ball game, then the news, which did not report on Walt's death. That left me feeling vaguely sad.

After the news, I went to bed and called Evie. We exchanged stories about our days and tried to talk dirty, but my heart wasn't in it, which Evie instantly picked up on. She said she loved me anyway.

I read a chapter of *Moby Dick*, turned out the light, and smoked the day's last cigarette in the dark.

I had to admit it. My place had been feeling empty lately. But without Henry sleeping on the floor beside me, it felt even emptier.

Nine

The ringing of the phone dragged me out of a deep black sleep. Ethan, I thought. I fumbled around in the dark, found the receiver on the table beside my bed, put it to my ear, and said, "Ethan? Is that you?"

A growly, muffled male voice said something that sounded like, "Boomer pierce ever."

"Huh?" I said. "Who's this?"

There was a hesitation. Then a click. Then nothing.

I sighed and put the phone back. The alarm clock on my bedside table read 3:50. The darkest hour. If it wasn't a dog waking me up, it was some crank phone call mumbling nonsense in my ear.

I lay there and smoked a cigarette in the dark. Two days had passed since Walt Duffy was murdered, and I still hadn't heard from Ethan. What the hell was going on?

I was sipping my coffee out on my balcony overlooking the harbor at eight o'clock the next morning, watching the gulls and terns wheeling over the water and the Saturday-morning fishing and pleasure craft cutting white wakes through it when I remembered that phone call, which, in turn, reminded me of the hangups I'd found on my voicemail the night before.

I went inside, picked up the telephone, and dialed star-69.

The mechanical voice said, "The number you are trying to call cannot be reached by this method."

Oh, well. Some drunk on a cell phone, probably. He'd mumbled his words. They made no sense. He—or she, maybe—had sounded like he was talking through a wet sock.

I refilled my coffee mug and went back out to the balcony. The day had dawned cloudy and still. The air tasted salty and felt damp on my face. It smelled like rain. I thought about bagging my plan to go trout fishing and spending a quiet Saturday at home. I could catch up on all the weekend paperwork Julie had stuffed into my briefcase, watch the ball game, maybe start that new Nick Lyons book and take a nap while I waited for Evie to show up. If Henry were here, we'd go for a few walks. Maybe I'd try to teach him something new. He wasn't that old.

The truth was, Walt Duffy's murder and Ethan's disappearance felt, somehow, like my responsibility. A day of fishing struck me as frivolous. It seemed as if I should do something more useful with my time than wading in a trout stream.

In the end, of course, I decided I better go fishing. The gods don't give a man a completely empty Saturday in June very often, and to squander it would surely offend them.

I got to the Squannacook a little before eleven. The river more or less followed Route 119 in Townsend, but there were several stretches where it bent away from the road.

These were places that most fishermen considered too inaccessible to bother with. They were the places I liked, for that very reason.

I parked in a little pull-off on a side road near the state forest. As I'd hoped, no other cars were parked there. I quickly tugged on my waders and strung up my rod. Then I set off through the woods, guided by the gurgling sound of water flowing around rocks and over gravel.

When I reached the riverbank, I sat on a log, lit a cigarette, and watched the currents glide past me.

Pocket water. This section of the stream was studded with boulders, and it ran quick and relatively shallow. Up close, a discerning angler such as I could identify the little eddies and holes and slicks and riffles—the pockets where trout liked to lurk.

A few yellowish mayflies fluttered over the water. Mosquitoes and blackflies, too. I rubbed some insect repellent on my arms, face and neck.

I sat there looking for feeding fish. In that quick-moving, broken water, the rings of their rises dissipated instantly. You needed to see the splash or the trout's little nose when it poked through the surface.

I forced myself to stay seated for the length of time it took me to finish my cigarette, even though I spotted two or three spurty little rises against the far bank. Then I tied on a bushy white-winged dry fly, stepped into the water, and began casting. I picked my targets—the little chute between two boulders where the current quickened, the riffly place that spilled into deeper water, the slick, shadowy, slow-moving current under the hemlocks against the bank . . . and almost instantly my mind was absolutely focused on studying the water, locating my targets, dropping my fly onto them, and watching it bob along on the currents, and all thoughts of Walt Duffy's murder, of Ethan's disappearance, of Henry and Ben Frye, of Julie and Evie, of my sons and my ex-wife and my old girlfriends, of my clients and my cases, of taxes and mortgages, of debtors and creditors, of friends and relatives living and dead, of the time and the season and the year, of hunger and thirst, of age and illness—all of those earthly preoccupations were entirely gone.

I was fishing.

Non-fishing friends sometimes tell me, "Oh, I'd like to try fly-fishing sometime. It looks like fun. I just don't think I have the patience for it."

In fact, patience is no virtue for the serious angler. Concentration, intensity, focus, imagination. That's what fly-fishing for stream trout requires. But I don't tell my friends that. I just nod and say, "Oh, yes. You've got to have plenty of patience." There are too damn many fishermen cluttering up the prettiest parts of the world already.

Sometime toward the end of the afternoon a misty rain began to filter down, and a short time later small olive-colored mayflies appeared on the water, and trout began to sip them. I tied on the right fly, as the fish quickly told me, and for an hour or so I caught and released trout more or less continually. They weren't particularly large, and I knew that most of them had been born in a cement trough at a state fish hatchery, but still, they were trout and they demanded a fly that looked and behaved like the real ones they'd decided to eat, and by the time the hatch petered out I felt happy and triumphant and replete.

I'd fished my way a couple of miles upstream when I decided it was time to quit. It was a long wet walk through the woods back to my car, and by the time I got there it was nearly dark and the misty rain had turned into a drizzle.

My mind was still full of trout and mayflies and those subtle sippy little strikes that had made my fly disappear in a bubble, and it wasn't until I was in my car with the windshield wipers going that I started looking forward to seeing Evie.

I hoped her day with her friend at the Arboretum hadn't been ruined by the rain.

And then my mind turned to Walt and Ethan, and I felt guilty for not thinking about them while I'd been fishing.

By the time I got back to the city, a steady rain was falling, and my apartment was dark and empty and altogether gloomy. Nine o'clock, and no Evie. Not even a dog to greet me at the door.

I checked my answering machine. No messages, from Ethan or from Evie or from one of my sons or from some mumbling drunk. No messages from anybody.

I shucked off my wet clothes, took a long steamy shower, and pulled on a clean T-shirt and a pair of jeans, and just about the time I'd settled myself on the sofa with a glass of Rebel Yell in one hand and the TV remote in the other, I heard a key scratching in the door.

I got there in time to help Evie slip off her raincoat. She bent her head forward and pulled her hair to the side so I could kiss the back of her neck. That, she'd taught me, was a special place. Then she turned in my arms, pressed against me, kissed me hard on the mouth, and grabbed my hand. She led me directly to the bedroom, sat on the edge of the bed, and reached out to unbuckle my belt.

I started to protest that I'd just gotten dressed, but I figured that would not deter her.

Sometime later I got up, found my drink where I'd left it on the coffee table and brought it back to the bedroom, and Evie and I passed it back and forth and exchanged stories of our days. I thought mine had been a lot more eventful than hers. She hadn't caught a single trout all day.

I, on the other hand, hadn't gotten twenty percent off a new Coach shoulder bag at some shop on Newbury Street.

We talked for a long time, lying there on our backs with our heads on our bunched-up pillows. When we both started yawning, I got up, loaded up the electric coffeemaker, and turned off the lights. By the time I got back to the bedroom, Evie was asleep.

I woke up abruptly with the panicky certainty that Evie was gone.

I found her out on the balcony. She had pulled on one of my old sweatshirts and was bent forward with her forearms braced on the railing. She had my binoculars pressed against her eyes aiming toward Logan Airport on the other side of the harbor.

I saw instantly what she was looking at. A big fire was blazing over there on the edge of the water in East Boston.

I leaned on the railing beside her.

"I heard a kind of thumping noise," she said softly. "It woke me up. Here. Have a look." She handed me the binoculars.

Across the misty water I saw the blue and red lights of

firetrucks and police cars flashing around the edges of the fire. On the harbor, fireboats were shooting high arching spouts of water at the flames.

"One of those old warehouses, probably," I said. "Or maybe a fuel storage depot. Those big LNG tankers offload over there."

I went inside, found my cigarettes, and brought them out to the balcony. It had stopped raining, but the air was moist and a layer of fog lay over the harbor, so that the fire and the lights looked blurry half a mile away.

"I hate fires," said Evie softly. "Ever since . . ."

"I know," said. "Me, too."

We watched the fire burn for quite a while. When we went back to bed, it was still blazing over there across the harbor.

I woke up early and slipped out of bed without disturbing Evie. I plugged in the coffee machine, then turned on the little television on the kitchen counter.

I had to scan several channels before I found some early Sunday-morning news, and I had to wait nearly to the end before they mentioned the fire. The warehouse, they reported, was owned by some big French conglomerate called Beau Marc Industries. It was located on Pier Seven on the Boston Harbor in East Boston. They were estimating the damage at two million dollars, and they had not ruled out arson.

It took a couple of minutes for it to sink in.

Beau Marc. Pier Seven.

Boomer pierce ever.

Jesus!

That phone call that had awakened me in the dark hours

of Saturday morning. He was predicting that fire. He was telling me about it. That it was going to happen.

Who the hell would do that?

Then I thought: *Why me?*

When Evie woke up, I was sipping my second cup of coffee out on the balcony and scanning the site of the fire through my binoculars. She poured herself a mugful, brought it out, and sat beside me. She was wearing one of my T-shirts and a pair of my sweatpants. They fit her quite nicely, except the pants were a little long for her.

"What do you see?" she said.

"Not much. I'm going to go over, take a look. Want to come?"

"Why?"

"Why would you want to come with me?"

"Why would *you* want to go?" she said.

I told her about the phone call and the news report.

"That's way spooky, Brady," said Evie.

I nodded.

"Would you mind if I didn't go with you?" she said. "I really hate fires. They're too depressing. I'd rather just curl up with the Sunday paper."

I kissed her forehead. "I don't want you to be depressed. I won't be long."

It took about fifteen minutes in the sparse Sunday-morning traffic to zip through the Callahan tunnel and wend my way through the streets of East Boston to the side street that led down to the water. On this side of the harbor, the air was thick and the sky dark. Particles of white ash accumulated on the hood of my car.

I parked a block from a couple of fire engines, got out of

my car, and walked toward the standing brick walls and the blackened piles of rubble that had been a warehouse the previous day. Curls of smoke still rose here and there from charred rafters, and the smell of burnt rubber hung heavy and acrid in the damp air.

The entire area was circled by crime-scene tape.

I stood there a respectful distance from what was left of the building. A little clot of elderly men wearing baggy pants and cardigan sweaters came along and stood next to me. They weren't saying much. Just looking. I wondered what they were thinking about this big fire in their neighborhood.

After a few minutes, a fireman with wet sooty smudges on his face came trudging toward us, heading for the parked vehicles. His eyes were red, and he was looking at the ground. I guessed he'd been up all night.

"Excuse me," I said to him after he ducked under the tape.

He looked at me and blinked.

"I was wondering who's in charge here," I said.

"Why?"

"I might have some helpful information."

"Helpful how?"

"It's complicated," I said. "Look. I live across the harbor. I saw the fire last night."

"You saw something you think is helpful?"

"If it would be easier, you could have somebody call me," I said. "I know you guys are busy."

The fireman squinted at me for a minute, then nodded. "Man in charge is Lieutenant Keeler. He's the PD arson investigator. You should talk to him."

"Can you point him out to me?"

"Wait here," he said. He turned, ducked under the tape, and headed back to the standing walls with the empty windows and the piles of brick and blackened wood that had once been the Beau Marc warehouse.

A few minutes later, the fireman reappeared. With him was a tall rangy man wearing a yellow hardhat, a blue T-shirt, blue jeans, and rubber boots. The letters BPD were stenciled on the hardhat. He had a clipboard in one hand, and a cell phone was clipped to his belt. The fireman pointed to me, and the tall guy nodded and came toward me.

"I'm Lieutenant Keeler," he said. He took off his hardhat and wiped his forehead with his wrist. He had close-cropped red hair. His eyes and face were red, too. He looked about forty. "You got something for us?" he said.

I told him about the phone call I'd received around four A.M. on Saturday morning, and how I lived directly across the harbor from the warehouse.

"You didn't recognize the voice, huh?" he said.

"No."

"You thought it was just some crank call?"

I shrugged. "He sounded drunk. His voice was muffled. I figured it was a wrong number."

"But he said Beau Marc Industries? Pier Seven?"

"I didn't recognize those words when he said them," I said. "But when I heard them on the news this morning, I realized that's what he said."

"When did you say this was?"

"Friday night. Early Saturday morning, actually."

Keeler shook his head. "What do you make of it?"

"I don't know," I said.

"I mean," he said, "why you? Who'd call you about a fire he was going to set the next night, right where you'd be sure to see it?"

"I don't know," I said. "This was an arson fire, then?"

He nodded. "And it sounds like you talked to the arsonist. So why would he want to tell you about it, have you see it?"

"The only thing I can think of . . ." I shook my head. "It makes no sense. I don't see how there could be any connection."

"What?" said Keeler. "Connection with what?"

I told him about Walt Duffy's murder and how Ethan had gone missing. "Does that make any sense?"

Keeler shook his head. "Nope. But the fact that it makes no sense might only mean we're not seeing it. If there is no logical connection, then it's a damn strange coincidence, isn't it?"

I nodded. "It is. That's why I thought I should tell you about it."

"You did the right thing. Thank you. I expect I'll want to talk with you some more. Right now things are pretty hectic here. How can I get ahold of you?"

I gave him one of my business cards. He looked at it, then looked up at me. "Lawyer, huh?"

I nodded.

"Lawyers deal with a lot of weirdos, don't they?"

"Some lawyers do," I said.

"You ever deal with any arsonists, Mr. Coyne?"

I shook my head. "I don't think so."

"Well," he said, "there's always a first time." He raised his hand and touched his forefinger to his brow in what might have been a salute. "Appreciate it, sir. We'll be in touch."

He fitted his hardhat back onto his head, turned, and trudged back to the rubble.

I picked up some muffins at Dunkin' Donuts on the way home, and when I got there I told Evie about my conversation with Lieutenant Keeler. It was her opinion that I'd misunderstood the phone call, that the caller had, in fact, been a drunk with a wrong number, just as I'd originally thought, that Walt Duffy's death had overwrought my imagination, and that I should stop perseverating on it.

I didn't agree with her. But I didn't pursue it. I figured it would only upset her.

We ate muffins and drank coffee and read the Sunday *Globe*, and when the sun came out in the afternoon, we walked along the waterfront and ended up in the North End. We decided to have an early supper at one of the little restaurants there. We drank red wine and ate pasta and listened to the Italian opera they piped in through the speakers, and we didn't talk about arson fires or the deaths of friends or missing college boys.

When we got back to my place, Evie said she guessed she'd head for home. I went down to the parking garage with her. She climbed into her car, rolled down the window, and stuck her face up at me for a kiss, which I readily delivered.

"Given it any more thought?" she said.

"Shacking up, you mean?"

She smiled. "Couldn't we call it something else?"

"I saw you studying the real estate section."

"I figured you were so engrossed in the sports you wouldn't notice."

"I noticed," I said. "See anything?"

"I saw a lot." She started up her car. "Maybe a picnic this week?"

"I'd like that. I'll probably have a dog with me."

"Good. I like Henry." She reached out and touched my cheek. "Are you okay?"

"I'll feel better when Ethan Duffy shows up." I hesitated, then said, "I'd feel a lot better if you weren't leaving."

She nodded. "Me, too. But that's how it is right now. Call and tuck me in, okay?"

I watched Evie pull out of the garage. Then I got into the elevator and went up to my apartment.

I was thinking: I'd had several fairly serious relationships since I split with Gloria. For a while it seemed that Alex Shaw and I had a chance of making it. I know I loved her. But with Alex, our "weekend marriage," as she called it, felt just right to me. She lived in southern Maine, more than a two-hour drive from Boston, and I didn't mind being apart from her Monday through Friday. I liked spending the weekends with her, but I liked missing her during the week when we didn't see each other, too.

With Evic, I didn't like missing her during the week at all. I wanted to be with her all the time.

Scary.

TEN

When I got to the office Monday morning, Henry came bounding over from Julie's desk. I squatted down to rub his ears, and he licked my face and wagged his entire hind end.

"How'd it go?" I said to Julie.

"Megan cried this morning when I told her I was bringing him back to you. She played with him the entire weekend. He slept on her bed."

"On the bed, huh?"

"I told her he could sleep in her room provided he stayed on the floor. When I went in the next morning, he was curled up beside her with his chin on her shoulder. I bawled her out. She claimed he must have snuck up there after she went to sleep."

"At least he didn't crawl under the covers."

She smiled.

"You better get Megan a dog."

"That's what Edward says. We'll see."

When I went into my office, Henry followed me. When I

sat at my desk, he slipped around my legs and curled up under them. I liked having him there by my feet while I talked on the telephone and read legal documents.

Julie buzzed me a little before noontime. "There are two people here to see you," she said.

"Who?"

"Detective Mendoza and Lieutenant Keeler. I told them you only had a minute." That was for their benefit, I knew. Julie likes to promote the illusion that I am busy and in-demand.

"I've got many minutes," I said. "Tell them to come on in."

A minute later, the door opened and Detective Saundra Mendoza came in, followed by Keeler, the tall redheaded arson cop I'd met Sunday morning at the scene of the fire. Keeler looked tired. Mendoza looked angry.

Henry scrambled out from under my desk and went over to sniff them. Each of them gave him a perfunctory pat on the head.

I told Henry to come back, and he did, reluctantly. I pointed at the floor and told him to lie down. He did that, too.

"You got him trained," said Mendoza. She was wearing black leather pants, black boots, and a red short-sleeved jersey.

"The offer's still open. You want a dog?"

"Not me," she said. "My sister's cats don't like dogs."

"What about you?" I said to Keeler. "You want a dog?"

He smiled quickly and shook his head.

I shrugged. "Too bad. He's a nice dog. Did Julie offer you folks coffee?"

"Yeah," said Mendoza. "We declined. We're pretty hassled, and you and us, we've got to talk."

"Seeing the two of you together, it makes me suspect that what I've been thinking isn't far off the mark."

"What have you been thinking?" she said.

"That there's some connection between Walt Duffy's murder and that fire the other night. Am I right?"

She shook her head. "Not exactly. It's about Benjamin Frye."

"What did Ben do?"

"He died."

"*What?*"

Mendoza nodded.

I blew out a long breath, then pointed to my sofa. "Let's sit."

The two cops sat on the sofa, and I took one of the chairs across from them.

"So what happened to Ben?" I said to Mendoza.

"That fire?" she said.

I nodded.

She turned to Keeler. "You tell him."

Keeler cleared his throat. "We found Mr. Frye's body in there," he said. "Took the ME's office all day yesterday to identify him."

"Jesus," I said softly. "I had dinner with Ben just the other night. He was in that building?"

Keeler nodded.

"What the hell was he doing there?"

"That's what we're trying to figure out. We were hoping you might help us."

"Me?"

"Well," said Mendoza, "just for one thing, you might've been the last person to see him alive."

"The last time I saw Ben was Friday night," I said. "We

had dinner at Remington's. That fire was Saturday night. I know he saw at least one person after me. He had to leave the restaurant before dessert to keep an appointment."

"Who was it with, did he say?"

I shook my head. "He just said he had to get back to his office to meet somebody at eight o'clock. Business thing, he said. Ben was a rare-book dealer and appraiser, you know."

Mendoza and Keeler exchanged glances. "Well, see, Mr. Coyne," said Mendoza, "we went to Mr. Frye's office and we found his appointment book. His last appointment was you. Remington's at six-thirty Friday, right?"

"Right. But he told me—"

"There was no appointment after you."

I shrugged. "So he didn't write it down."

"Did Mr. Frye say anything about East Boston or Pier Seven to you?" said Keeler.

"No."

"He happen to mention Beau Marc Industries?"

"No."

"What was Benjamin Frye's connection with Walter Duffy?" said Mendoza.

"They were friends. They both collected old books and documents. Both into birds and nature stuff. Walt had some old letters that I gave Ben to authenticate for him. I think I mentioned that to you the other day. That's why I met with Ben on Friday. He wanted to return Walt's letters to me. He complained about you hassling him."

Mendoza snorted. "Hassling? Jesus Christ."

Keeler touched her shoulder, then turned to me. "That's it?" he said.

"What, their connection?" I shrugged. "Far as I know, that's all."

"Not quite," he said.

"Oh," I said. "They're both dead, you mean. I don't know anything about that, I'm afraid."

"Except you got that phone call."

I nodded. "I don't know what to make of that."

Keeler frowned at me. Mendoza leaned toward him and whispered something. Keeler looked up at the ceiling for a moment, then shook his head.

Saundra Mendoza narrowed her eyes at me. "See, you're the connection, Mr. Coyne," she said. "Both of these men, they meet with you, and the next thing—I mean, the next goddamn *day*—they're dead. You're the one who finds one of the bodies. The other one's body turns up in a fire that you're telling us you knew was going to happen. An arson fire. We can assume that it was the arsonist who called you. The arsonist most likely is also the murderer. How can you say you don't know anything about that?"

I shook my head. "I didn't know the fire was going to happen. I didn't understand what that guy said on the phone until I heard about the fire on the news."

Mendoza rolled her dark eyes. "We're not stupid, Mr. Coyne," she said.

"Are you accusing me of something?"

"I can't figure out what to accuse you of," she said.

I narrowed my eyes at her. "Look—"

Keeler reached across the coffee table and touched my leg. "Take it easy, Mr. Coyne. We're just trying to get a handle on this."

I looked at Mendoza. "And I'm trying to help."

Her dark eyes glared at me for a moment. Then she shrugged. "Sure. Sorry." She didn't sound particularly sorry.

"What about those letters?" said Keeler.

I glanced at Mendoza, who was studying her boots. Then I turned to Keeler. "They were apparently written by Meriwether Lewis to an eminent ornithologist named Alexander Wilson right after Lewis got back from his expedition," I said. "They're about the birds he saw on the voyage. They belonged to Walt Duffy. Ben Frye was going to authenticate them."

"Where are they now?"

"I've got them."

"With you?"

I jerked my head in the direction of my desk. "They're in my briefcase, actually."

"Let's see them," said Mendoza.

"They're just old letters," I said. "But if they turn out to be authentic, they're very valuable. Priceless, in fact. They're part of Walt Duffy's estate." I frowned at her. "You think those two men were killed for these letters?"

"Could be, huh?" she said.

I shook my head. "Doesn't make sense. First off, the only people who knew Walt had them were Ben and me. Second, whoever killed Walt had the chance to steal a lot of other priceless stuff he kept in his house. Walt had a very valuable collection of old books and documents and artwork. But they didn't touch any of it."

"Just his computer and camera and cell phone," she said. "So what about the son? Ethan? He must've known about those letters."

I shrugged. "Maybe he did. I don't know."

"And you don't know who Duffy and Frye and the son told about them, either."

"No. I don't know."

"Could be dozens of people."

I nodded.

"When did Duffy get those letters?" she said.

"He picked them up in some little antique shop in the Poconos about ten years ago."

"But you didn't know about them before the other day?"

"No."

"Duffy never even mentioned them to you before that?"

I shook my head.

"And the truth is, we really have no idea how many people knew about them."

"I guess you're right," I said.

Saundra Mendoza looked up at the ceiling as if she were praying for patience.

"I'd like to look at those letters," said Keeler.

"Sure." I went over to my desk, took the manila envelope out of my battered old briefcase, and handed it to him. "Don't take them out of the plastic," I said. "They're two hundred years old, very delicate. The acid from your fingers would ruin them."

Keeler slid the plastic envelope out, held it gingerly by the corners, looked at it, shrugged, and handed it to Mendoza.

She started to open the plastic envelope.

"Hey," I said. "I told you, don't touch the letters."

She stared at me for a moment, then blew out an exasperated breath. "Dammit, Matt. This is evidence," she said to Keeler.

Keeler nodded. "Could be. If it is, though, we better not tamper with it."

Mendoza shrugged. "We're going to take this envelope with us," she said to me.

I remembered what Ben Frye had said about police evidence rooms. "Over my dead body," I said.

"Very funny," she said sourly. She turned to Keeler. "We got an arson fire and two dead people, and the lawyer here's worried about some old letters."

"Those old letters are priceless and irreplaceable," I said. "I intend to keep them safe. You want 'em, get a warrant. Which I promise you I'll contest."

"Sure," said Keeler. "That's what I'd do if I were a lawyer." He turned to Mendoza. "We've got to know a lot more than we know now before we could convince a judge. At least we know where they are if we need them."

Saundra Mendoza looked at him for a minute, then turned and narrowed her eyes at me. "The two men who had these letters in their possession got killed. Now you've got 'em. That okay with you?"

"I guess it'll have to be," I said.

She stood up. "Come on, Matt," she said to Keeler. "Let's get the hell out of here. We're not getting anywhere with this damn lawyer." She pronounced the word "lawyer" as if it were a synonym for excrement.

Keeler looked at me, shrugged, and followed her out of my office.

Eleven

After Mendoza and Keeler left, I took the envelope with the letters in it over to my office safe, which was cleverly hidden behind a black-and-white photograph of my two sons, Billy and Joey, when they were seven and five. Gloria, my ex-wife, took the photo fifteen years ago. She had it blown up and framed, and she gave it to me for Christmas. The boys were sitting side-by-side on the bow seat of a leaky old rowboat on a lake in Maine where we'd rented a cottage for a week in August. They were both holding fishing rods. They looked sunburned and mosquito-bitten and scruffy. One of those happy times in what was, for a while, a happy family's life.

Even then you could see the devil in Billy's eyes and the intensity in Joey's.

I wondered what a photo of Gloria and me, taken back then, would have revealed in our eyes.

The safe's six-number combination was the boys' two birthdays. I opened it and put the Meriwether Lewis letters inside next to the Smith & Wesson .38 revolver I kept there.

Ben Frye had been right. Whether or not the letters turned out to be evidence, they were considerably more secure in my safe than they'd be on a shelf in the Boston PD evidence lockup.

Henry, I noticed, was sitting meaningfully beside the door. I opened it, and we went out to the reception area. He waddled over to Julie, who was hunched over her computer, plopped his chin on her knee, and gazed up into her eyes.

"I think he wants to go out," I said to her.

"His leash is hanging over there," she said without looking up.

"He's asking you."

Julie patted Henry's rump. "Go ask Brady," she said to him.

Henry looked at me, then came over, sat beside me, and whined.

"Okay, okay," I said.

Henry and I strolled down Huntington Avenue and meandered around the grounds of the Christian Science Mother Church, where Henry lifted his leg on all the likely targets. Then we turned back up Boylston and stopped in the deli. Henry sat obediently inside the door. Manny, the counterman, didn't object, perhaps because Julie and I got takeout from him three or four times a week. Boston is a famously dog-friendly city. I got tuna sandwiches on whole wheat and Cokes for Julie and me and a roast beef on pumpernickel for Henry. I didn't tell Henry. It was to be a surprise.

The three of us ate at the coffee table in my office. Henry gulped down his sandwich in about three bites, then sat there watching me and Julie, following our hands intently as they moved our food up to our mouths. Finally Julie gave him a piece of her sandwich. He gobbled it, then turned his gaze upon me. I gave him a potato chip, which he seemed to enjoy, and offered him a bite of my dill pickle. He gave the pickle a sniff, glanced at Julie, then lay down at her feet. I'd insulted him, apparently.

"So what did those two officers want?" said Julie.

I told her about the fire Evie and I had watched burn, and how Ben Frye's body was found there.

Julie shook her head. "First Mr. Duffy has that accident," she said, "and now . . ."

I nodded.

"Detective Mendoza is with homicide," she said after a minute.

"Yes. They were both unattended deaths. They have to be investigated."

Julie smiled. "Meaning you can't talk about it, right?"

I nodded.

"And you're in the middle of it, of course."

"I guess I am."

"So what are you going to do?"

I shrugged. "I don't know. I wish Ethan would show up. He might know something. I just hope . . ."

"You hope what?"

"I hope nothing's happened to him."

I had office appointments with clients in the afternoon. Henry behaved himself while we conferred.

When the last one left around four, I called Ellen Bramhall, Walt Duffy's ex-wife and Ethan's mother, at her home in Sudbury.

She answered on the first ring. "Yes?"

"Mrs. Bramhall," I said, "it's Brady Coyne again."

"Oh, Mr. Coyne. Have you heard anything from Ethan?"

"I'm sorry, no," I said. "I was wondering if you had."

"No," she said. "I've talked with our police. They've been very kind. But . . ." She sighed. "I'm out here in my garden. Weeding, pruning, watering, mulching, tending my dear little plants, trying not to think about Ethan and what happened to Walter. I've got my telephone right here with me so I won't miss any calls. I was hoping . . ."

"I'm sorry," I repeated. "I was wondering if you and I might talk?"

"Talk?"

"About Ethan. About how we might find him. I guess we're both worried about him. And I think he might be able to help us understand what happened to Walt."

"Well," she said, "I've wracked my brain to no avail ever since I talked with you on Thursday. I don't know what good I can do. I feel so useless. Maybe talking with you will make me feel less useless. Do you want to come over to the house?"

"How about after supper tonight?"

"That would be lovely," she said.

She gave me directions and insisted I call her Ellen. She sounded like a frantic mother trying desperately to hold herself together.

Julie and Henry and I left the office together. I had Henry's leash in one hand and my briefcase in the other. I'd stuck Walt Duffy's file, including copies of his will and his divorce decree, into it with the intention of glancing at it before I met with Ellen Bramhall. I wanted to double-check my memory that she was not mentioned in it. Anyway, it made Julie happy to think I might spend some time at home catching up on my paperwork.

We stopped outside the parking garage across the street where Julie always left her car, and I held out Henry's leash to her. "Last chance," I said.

"Not today, Brady."

"Another time, then?"

She shook her head. "I don't know. I'm not sure it's a good idea. It was, to tell the truth, really fun having Henry around over the weekend. Megan loved every minute of it. But I don't want her to become attached to him. He's not our dog. He's not even yours."

"Getting attached to pets is part of growing up."

She nodded. "Then they're gone. They run away. They get old and die."

"That's part of growing up, too. Kids can take it better than we give them credit for."

She cocked her head and looked up at me. "So maybe it's me, then." She bent down and gave Henry a pat, then straightened up. "See you guys tomorrow."

Henry and I cut over to Commonwealth Avenue, where the sidewalks were wide and less congested than those on Boylston or Newbury at five o'clock in the afternoon, and we'd gone less than a block when a dark unmarked sedan pulled over to the curb in front of us. Lieutenant Matthew Keeler stepped out from the passenger door and stood there on the sidewalk.

Henry went up to him and sniffed his cuffs. Keeler bent down and patted his rump.

"You following me?" I said.

He smiled. "Mind if I walk with you?"

"What's up?"

He fell in beside me. "We parted kind of abruptly this morning. I thought you deserved an explanation."

"Detective Mendoza was the abrupt one," I said.

Keeler nodded. "Sandy Mendoza's got some things on her mind. I apologize for her. She tends to be rude with lawyers in the best of times."

"She was a lot friendlier when I saw her the other day," I said. "I was a lawyer then."

He smiled. "You shouldn't take it personally."

"It's okay. Lots of people don't like lawyers. Especially cops. I don't take it personally except when they're asking for my help."

"It's not really that," he said. "She'd probably kill me for telling you, but I figured after the way she acted, you've got a right to know." He hesitated. "See, Sandy just found out this morning that her sister's got a brain tumor. They don't know if it's operable. It hit Sandy pretty hard. Her sister's just a college kid. They live together. Both of their parents are dead. Sandy pretty much raised her."

I shook my head. "That's a rough one."

Keeler shrugged. "I feel for her. I lost my little girl two years ago."

"Your daughter?"

Keeler nodded. "Becky. Leukemia. She was nine." He smiled quickly. "Becky had a dog she called Bo-Bo. Seeing your dog there . . ." He blew out a breath. "Anyway, Sandy Mendoza is a good cop. She's just angry now. Kinda mad at the world, you know?"

"Sure," I said. "Hard to blame her. I'm sorry about your daughter. That's an awful thing."

"Yeah," he said. "You're never the same after something like that."

Henry seemed to have lost interest in the trees and fire hydrants and sign posts along Commonwealth Avenue. Apparently he'd finally emptied his bladder, and he was trotting along sedately between Keeler and me.

We walked in silence. The sedan was creeping along a discreet distance ahead of us. After a few minutes, Keeler said, "We didn't really finish our conversation this morning."

"What else is there?" I said.

"What we mainly wanted to know was if Benjamin Frye gave you any hint that might help us understand what he did between the time he was with you Friday evening and when we pulled him out of that warehouse on Sunday."

"He didn't say anything about his weekend plans. Like I said, he told me he had an appointment right after we ate. He didn't even stay for dessert."

"But he didn't say who the appointment was with?"

"No."

"Or what it was about?"

"Business was all he said."

"That was it?"

"Well, he pretended to be pissed off at me for giving Detective Mendoza his name. Ben didn't like cops."

"Pretended?"

I shrugged. "It was sort of a reflex with Ben. He practiced a lot of civil disobedience back in the sixties."

Keeler smiled. "So he didn't mention anything about East Boston or that warehouse or Beau Marc Industries?"

"No. I think I'd remember that."

"And nothing about Walter Duffy?"

I shrugged. "Just what I told you. He was upset that Walt had died. They'd known each other for a long time. We talked about the letters. That was about it."

Keeler stopped walking and touched my arm. "It wasn't the fire that killed Mr. Frye."

"What do you mean?"

"There was no smoke in his lungs. He was already dead when that warehouse went up." He hesitated. "The ME determined that he had a fractured skull."

"Fractured skull?"

Keeler patted the back of his head.

"Like Walt Duffy?" I said.

He nodded.

I stared at him. "So your arsonist is also a double murderer."

"Apparently."

"And he's the one who called me on the phone."

"Can't think of any other explanation," Keeler said.

"What's he want with me?"

"We'd like to figure that out," he said.

"Shit," I said. "Me, too."

The dark sedan had stopped at the corner where Commonwealth Avenue butted onto Arlington Street. When we got to it, Keeler stopped and handed me a business card. "My cell phone's on there," he said. "Call anytime."

I put the card in my shirt pocket.

"Look," he said. "The media are asking questions. We're not telling them everything."

"That's a bit unusual, isn't it?"

"This is an unusual situation."

"You can't expect them not to find out."

Keeler smiled. "If they do, Mr. Coyne, we better not learn it was from you."

Twelve

After Keeler drove off in the dark sedan, Henry and I crossed Arlington Street and strolled through the Public Gardens. When we got to Charles Street, Henry veered off to the left. I gave his leash a tug, but he dug in his heels. He was aiming for Mt. Vernon street, I figured. He wanted to go home.

I had intended to continue diagonally across the Common to Boylston Street, my usual route to my apartment from my office. But this was a better idea. Maybe Ethan would be there.

So I told Henry what a smart dog he was, and we crossed Beacon Street to Charles, then went up Mt. Vernon. Henry led me into the alley behind Walt's townhouse and pressed his nose against the door in the brick wall that opened into the bird garden.

My note to Ethan was still wedged under the latch, and the big X of yellow crime-scene tape was still plastered over the door. That tape was a stark reminder that Walt had died on the other side of the door. It had happened less than a week ago.

Correction. Walt had been murdered.

"Come on," I said to Henry. "We can't go in there."

We retraced our route back to Mt. Vernon Street. When we turned to continue up the hill, I saw a tall, elegant-looking white-haired woman with two greyhounds on leashes coming down the sidewalk toward us.

Henry tugged at his leash and whined. The greyhounds approached us. They were whining, too. They all seemed happy to see each other.

"Now, boys," the woman was saying. "It's just Henry. You be nice to Henry."

The greyhounds sniffed Henry fore and aft, and Henry sniffed them. All three tails were wagging furiously.

"You must be a friend of Mr. Duffy," said the woman. She appeared to be in her late seventies or early eighties. She wore sneakers, baggy blue jeans, a short-sleeved white shirt with the tails flapping, and a Red Sox baseball cap.

I smiled at her. "Yes, I am."

"Taking care of Henry, then?" She had sharp blue eyes and a sun-creased face. Her white hair hung in a braid halfway down her back.

I nodded.

"Terrible thing," she said. "Poor man. First that awful fall that left him all crippled, and now this. We used to walk with Mr. Duffy and Henry all the time. Spite and Malice think Henry's about the nicest little doggie on the Hill. We'd let them off their leashes on the Common, and the three of them would have the grandest time chasing each other."

I smiled. "Spite and Malice?"

"This," she said, pointing to one of her greyhounds, "is Spite. And this saucy fellow is Malice. Spite and Malice is a card game I used to play with my husband. I rescued these boys from Wonderland after Win passed away. They were racers. My name is Gladys. Gladys Whyte. Whyte with a y."

"I'm Brady Coyne," I said. "Coyne with a y." I put down my briefcase and held out my hand, and she shook it.

The greyhounds were circling Henry, who had decided to lie down on the sidewalk. The three leashes had become hopelessly tangled.

Gladys Whyte jerked her head at Walt's front door. "That tape. Was there some kind of crime? I heard Mr. Duffy fell down and hit his head."

"He was alone," I said. "Unattended death, the police have to investigate."

"Ethan wasn't there when it happened, then?"

"I guess not," I said.

She nodded. "I would've expected Ethan to be walking Henry today."

I pointed at Walt's front door. "They won't let anyone in there for a few days. Henry's staying with me until Ethan can move back in."

"That poor boy must be devastated. Such a shock, losing his father that way."

I nodded.

"I thought it odd," she continued, "not running into Ethan and Henry since . . . since Mr. Duffy's accident. Is Ethan staying with his friend, then?"

"Which friend do you mean?"

"The big fellow. What was his name?" She frowned, then nodded. "Connie. That's what Ethan called him. Connie. Very well-mannered gentleman. Somewhat older than Ethan.

They often walked Henry together, Ethan and Connie."

"I don't think I've met Connie," I said. "What's his last name?"

She shrugged. "I'm not sure I ever heard." She smiled. "They made quite a pair, Ethan and Connie. That Connie fellow is always dressed nicely. Well groomed. Conservative, you might say. And Ethan with his shaved head and his earrings and all." She smiled. "Quite a pair."

"You said Connie is older than Ethan?"

"Oh, my, yes." She narrowed her eyes at me. "You are in your mid-forties, am I right?"

I nodded. I hated it when people did that. I still thought of myself as a young man.

Gladys smiled. "Connie would be, oh, five or six years younger than you, if I'm any judge. Around forty. I'm surprised you've never met him."

"Maybe I have," I said. "Is his actual name Conrad? Does he own the record store where Ethan works?"

"I wouldn't know anything about that. I try not to pry, you know."

"Of course," I said. "Do you know any of Ethan's other friends?"

She shrugged. "It's my impression that Ethan does not have a lot of friends. He was very devoted to his father, you know."

I nodded. "What about Walt's friends?"

"Mr. Duffy had a lot of visitors," she said, "especially after his accident. I always thought it was lovely that his friends came to spend time with him."

"Do you remember any of them?"

She shook her head. "I never paid that much attention. They always used the garden entrance. I'd glimpse them heading down the alley." She smiled. "I do remember you in your expensive suits. You visited him quite often."

"The others didn't wear suits?"

"Ethan's friend Connie, he often did. The others?" She shook her head. "I guess not. I notice nice clothes." She looked at me and frowned. "Why are you asking me these questions?"

"Gladys," I said, "the truth is, I haven't been able to get in touch with Ethan in the past few days. In the, um, confusion when Walt died, I neglected to ask him where he'd be staying. You don't recall any mention of where his friend Connie lives, do you?"

"No," she said, "I'm afraid I don't. I would surmise it's not within walking distance."

"Why is that?"

"Well, the two of them were always driving off in Connie's car. Connie would park it up on the curb when he came calling. Sometimes they'd take Henry with them."

"What kind of car is it?"

"Oh, lord," she said. "I don't know one thing from another when it comes to vehicles." She narrowed her eyes and looked up at the sky. "It's a nice car. Dark blue? Maybe green." She shrugged. "Could be black, I suppose. Expensive-looking. Big. Quite new, I'd say. That's about all I can tell you."

Now all three dogs were lying down. The greyhounds, Spite and Malice, lay on their sides. They appeared to be sleeping. Henry had his chin on his paws and was watching the other two warily.

"They've made a mess," said Gladys. "Perhaps they'll lie still so we can disentangle them."

After we got the dogs' leashes straightened out, she said,

"Well, we're headed for the Common so my boys can visit with their friends. Are you going our way?"

"No," I said. "I live in the other direction." I rummaged around in my briefcase, found one of my business cards, and handed it to her. "If you think of anything that might help me catch up with Ethan, I'd appreciate it if you'd give me a call."

She looked at my card. "You're a lawyer?"

I nodded.

"Of course," she said. "The briefcase, the nice suit. Mr. Duffy's lawyer?"

"Yes. And his friend."

"Well," she said, "I'd be happy to call you, of course. But I don't believe I'll think of anything I haven't told you already."

"You might notice Connie's car in the neighborhood or something like that. Maybe somebody else coming to visit." I smiled at her. "If you run into Ethan, please ask him to call me. Henry misses him."

She reached down and patted Henry's head. "Of course he does," she said. "Let's go, boys," she said to her dogs. She waved and smiled at me, then started down the hill toward Charles Street.

Henry and I went in the other direction. We continued up Mt. Vernon, turned right on Joy Street, down the hill and across Beacon and diagonally through the Common to Boylston, and we ended up at Skeeter's, where Henry and I both ordered medium-rare cheeseburgers. A slice of Bermuda onion for me, no onion for Henry. Onions make dogs sick. Skeeter gave Henry a bowl of water. I had coffee.

At Henry's request, we visited the park on Commercial Street on the way home. I let him off the leash, and it turned out to be a productive visit. I used a stick to scrape his production into a paper bag I found in a trash barrel and dutifully took it home with me.

The first thing I did when we got up to my apartment was flush Henry's production down the toilet. Then I checked the answering machine. No messages, ominous or otherwise. No hangups, even.

I changed out of my suit and into a pair of Dockers, cotton shirt, and moccasins, grabbed my briefcase, leashed up Henry, and ten minutes later we were in my car heading for Sudbury.

THIRTEEN

Ellen Bramhall lived in a newish eight-room colonial in a neighborhood of newish eight-room colonials in one of those typical 1980's suburban developments on a pleasant tree-shaded street that wound through what once had been an even more pleasant tree-shaded forest.

I sorted out the Bramhall colonial from the others—hers was one of the gray ones, distinguished from the others by the name "Bramhall" on the mailbox out front—and pulled into the driveway.

Henry, who had been snoozing on the backseat, scrambled to his feet and pressed his nose against the window when I stopped the car.

"You've got to stay here," I told him. "I won't be long."

He sat down and allowed his ears to droop and his eyebrows to furrow. Disappointment was written all over his face.

"Sorry, pal," I said. "I'll make it up to you."

That seemed to satisfy him.

I made sure all the windows were cracked open, grabbed

my briefcase, and went to the house. I rang the bell, and a minute later the door opened. A fiftyish man stood on the other side of the screen. He had a thick neck and bulky shoulders and a small, snarly mouth. He wore dark suit pants, a pale blue dress shirt, and a striped necktie snugged at his throat. Behind his rimless glasses his eyes were narrow and suspicious.

"What do you want?" he said.

"I'm Brady Coyne," I said. "Mrs. Bramhall is expecting me."

He glanced down at my briefcase. "You Duffy's lawyer?"

"I used to be. Walt is dead."

"So?"

"So I want to talk to Ellen. She's expecting me."

He pushed open the screen door and stepped out onto the porch. "Why don't you just stop bothering us?" he said, in what I think was intended to be a fierce growl. He was half a head shorter than me, and he had to look up in order to glare into my face, which made his fierceness less daunting.

"I certainly don't mean to bother you," I said. "I don't even want to talk to you. I'm here to see Ellen."

"You're already bothering me," he said.

"Is that because I'm a lawyer?" I said. "Or because I'm taller than you?"

He shook his head. "Jesus," he mumbled. He stared up at me for a moment, then shrugged and went back inside, letting the screen door slam shut behind him.

A minute later, a plump woman with curly brown hair and large brown eyes came to the door. She'd put on weight and added a few wrinkles since I'd met her at Walt's divorce ten years ago. Hadn't we all.

"Mr. Coyne," she said, "please come in."

She held the screen door for me, and I stepped into the flagstone foyer.

She held her hand out to me. "We met once. In court."

I took her hand and smiled. "Yes, I remember. It's nice to see you again."

She leaned toward me. "I apologize for my husband," she said softly.

"No need."

"Anything remotely connected to Walter, and he . . ."

I smiled. "Sure. I understand."

She peered over my shoulder. "Did I see a dog in your car?"

"Yes. It's Henry. Ethan's dog."

"Walter's dog, actually," she said. "Ethan's very fond of Henry. He can't be very happy, cooped up in the car."

"He'll be all right."

"I was thinking it might be nice to sit out on the back deck, maybe have some lemonade while we talked. The bats should be out pretty soon. It's fun watching the bats." She smiled. "Do you like birds the way Walter did?"

"I like birds," I said. "But not the way Walt did. Walt was an expert on birds." I didn't mention the fact that bats weren't birds. I wasn't sure she'd intended to imply that.

"Ethan likes birds," she said, "but he's no expert, either. Which Walter never let him forget." She shook her head. "Why don't you go get Henry and meet me around back."

"Sounds good."

I went to the car, liberated Henry, let him pee on a couple of shrubs, then told him to heel, and we went around to the rear of the house. The yard backed up on dense woods. It was bordered all around with well-tended flower gardens. I recalled the attention Walt had lavished on his little bird garden. Perhaps gardening was a passion that he and Ellen had shared when they were married.

Ellen was sitting at a glass-topped table on the deck. "Come on up," she said with a wave.

Henry and I went up onto the deck. I told him to lie down, and I sat across from Ellen.

A pitcher of lemonade and two glasses sat on the table. She filled them, handed one to me, and pointed at my briefcase, which I'd put on the floor. "Are you here to transact some sort of business?"

I shrugged. "I have Walt's file in there. A copy of his will. I didn't know whether you . . ."

"I'm not mentioned in it, am I?"

"No."

"I didn't think so. No reason why I should be." She waved the back of her hand at my briefcase. "I don't care about that. Walter doesn't owe me a thing. Right now, I'm more concerned about Ethan."

"Me, too."

"Are you serious about finding him?"

I nodded. "I guess I am."

"I was thinking I should file a missing persons thing with the police," she said. "What do you think?"

"I've already talked to the police," I said. "I guess it wouldn't do any harm, but I know they're on the lookout for him. And so am I."

"You're a lawyer," she said. "It's not your job, finding people."

"Well," I said, "there are times when it seems to be."

"You think something's happened to my son, don't you?"

"Not necessarily."

"Sometimes weeks go by and I don't hear from Ethan," she said. "He's a good boy and a loving son, but he's, well, thoughtless, the way boys can be. I try not to make a fuss. I don't want to be one of those naggy mothers." She took a sip of her lemonade. "I just thought, given what's happened, he would've at least called."

I nodded.

"I guess it wouldn't occur to him that I might be worried." She turned and looked at me. "But I am."

"I'm sure there's a perfectly logical explanation," I said lamely.

"Ever since we talked this afternoon," she said, "I've been trying to think of something that might help us find him."

"Did you come up with anything?"

She shook her head. "Not really. I don't even know his friends anymore."

"Did you ever meet Connie?"

She frowned. "Connie?"

"One of the neighbors on Mt. Vernon Street told me that Ethan has a friend named Connie. A man named Conrad. Conrad Henshall."

She looked up at me. "Never heard of him."

"He owns the record store where Ethan works. I'm just trying to come up with people that Ethan might get in touch with, somebody who might let him sleep on their sofa for a few nights."

"Well," she said, "if this Conrad man . . ."

"Yes," I said. "I'll talk to him. But if not him, what about relatives or old friends?"

"That's what I've been trying to think of. Ethan didn't have many friends in high school. He's always been kind of a loner. I have a sister, but she's in California. Ethan has a couple of cousins, but they've never been close. There are no relatives on Walter's side."

I jerked my head toward the inside of the house. "What about your husband?"

Ellen shook her head. "Ethan and Jonathan barely speak."

"That must be hard for you."

"It's not how I hoped it would be. But it is what it is." She shrugged. "Jonathan is the anti-Walter. A less adventurous man you couldn't imagine."

"What does he do? For work, I mean."

Ellen smiled. "He's a tax accountant. He never goes anywhere. Works out of his home office here so he can keep his eye on me."

I arched my eyebrows.

She waved a hand. "Oh, I don't mean that literally. He goes off to meet with clients now and then. Jonathan is very attentive, put it that way. It's quite a change from Walter. Walter mostly ignored me. And Ethan."

"You're saying that Jonathan is jealous?"

"I guess possessive would be the word. Lord knows he's got nothing to be jealous of." She smiled. "After Walter, it's a bit of a shock. But I suppose it's what attracted me to him. A man who actually noticed me."

"And Jonathan and Ethan . . . ?"

"Jonathan is a very precise man," she said. "He was a bachelor for a long time. He likes things done in particular ways. He calls them 'the rules of the house.' Ethan is . . . well, he's a teenager."

"Teenage boys," I said. "How well I know."

We gazed off into the backyard for a minute. Then Ellen said, "Have you thought of checking with the college?"

"I tried calling some of his classmates," I said. "No luck. The term is over. The students are off on their own."

She sighed. "What are we going to do?"

I gave her a big smile. I was sure it looked phony. "Oh, he'll turn up. I don't want you to worry."

"Well, I'm afraid I can't help it."

I reached over and patted her hand. "I'll find him."

"Will you?"

"Yes."

Darkness had come seeping out of the woods and into the backyard, and pretty soon the bats came out. They flapped around over our heads snagging mosquitoes. We watched them in silence and sipped our lemonade.

After a few minutes, Ellen said, "When Ethan was growing up, it was as if Walter was this—this superhero. Bigger than life, as far as Ethan was concerned. He worshipped that man. Of course, Walter was always off on one of his great expeditions to some remote and dangerous corner of the globe, to hear him tell it. It's easy to worship somebody if you don't know them. Ethan had a big map of the world on his bedroom wall, and he put thumbtacks on the places where Walter went. When Walter was home, which was rarely, he was distant and preoccupied. I don't think he was ever a real person to Ethan." She paused and sipped her lemonade. "Until his accident." She laughed softly. "Suddenly there was this—this giant of a man, hobbling around on crutches, brought crashing down to earth, quite helpless. What happens to a boy when his hero turns out to be just a man? A crippled, broken man at that."

I shrugged. "I guess the boy sees his chance to win his hero's love by taking care of him."

"Yes," said Ellen. "That's what I think." She shook her

head. "I never thought it was a good idea, Ethan moving in with him like that. But Ethan insisted. As far as I know, Walter never once in his whole miserable life told his son he loved him. He was just a grouchy, mean, self-centered, ungrateful . . ."

I realized that Ellen was crying. I reached across the table and touched her hand.

She looked at me and tried to smile. "I never stopped loving that man," she said softly. "I didn't like him very much, but I loved him. What is the matter with me?"

I gave her hand a squeeze and said nothing. I had no wisdom for her.

Fourteen

I pulled into the parking garage under my apartment building a little before eleven. I grabbed my briefcase off the front seat, then got out, opened the back door, and snapped Henry's leash onto his collar. "Okay," I told him. "Let's go. No peeing on the automobiles."

Normally Henry waited for me to leash him up and then bounded out, happy to be liberated and eager to explore. But this time he stood there stiff-legged on the backseat.

"Come on," I said. When I gave his leash a gentle tug, he dug in his heels and growled.

"What the hell's the matter with you?" I said. I bent into the backseat to give him a nudge. "Come on. Let's get—"

At that moment, the car door smashed against my back. It knocked me off balance and threw me forward, and my head crashed against the door frame.

A sudden white light flashed behind my eyes, and I ended up sprawled facedown on the cement floor of the garage beside my car. I was distantly aware of somebody close behind me. Then I felt a sudden sharp weight between my shoulder blades. He was kneeling on me. It knocked the wind out of me, and I felt him groping in my hip pocket.

Henry let out a fearsome growl and leaped over my prostrate body. The man on my back grunted, "Ow. Shit!" and Henry yelped, and then the man was gone.

Henry's leash, which was looped around my wrist, yanked my arm backward. I instinctively held onto it, and Henry barked and growled and raced back and forth and leaped against the leash so that it ended up tangled around one of my ankles.

I blinked away the pain in my head and got to my hands and knees in time to spot a running figure dodge around one of the cement pillars and disappear behind a row of parked cars. In the dim orange light I saw that he was dressed in dark pants and a dark shirt. He was carrying something in his hand.

His running footsteps echoed, then faded away.

I told Henry to sit, which he did, reluctantly, and I managed to get us untangled. Then I sat back against the side of my car and let out a long breath.

Henry sat beside me, growling in the back of his throat.

"Shh," I told him. "Sit down and be quiet. He's gone, and I'm not going to let you chase him."

I reached up to feel where I'd banged my forehead. My hand came away wet. I fished out my handkerchief and pressed it against my wound.

I gave Henry's muzzle a scratch. "You tried to warn me," I said.

He licked my face.

I patted my hip. My wallet, of course, was gone.

"God*damn*it," I muttered. I carried maybe a hundred dollars in cash, a couple of credit cards, an ATM card, my phone card, my driver's license, my fishing license, my membership card for Trout Unlimited, my gun permit—the usual stuff. Everything except the cash could be replaced, but at the exorbitant cost of a dozen calls to telephones that answered with automated menus where you ended up on hold for a half hour listening to violins play Beatles tunes and a recorded voice periodically broke in to thank you for your patience and to tell you how important your call was to them.

Well, it could've been worse. Henry and I were alive.

I stood up, closed my eyes against the quick, stabbing pain in my head, and leaned against the side of the car—and that's when I realized that my assailant had made off with my briefcase, too.

I felt bad about losing that briefcase. It wasn't that there was anything valuable, top-secret, or in any way irreplaceable in it. The papers Julie stuffed into my briefcase were photocopies of documents that were safely filed in our office. I did a quick inventory from memory. Walt Duffy's will. That was public record. A couple of legal journals. Boring junk. Copies of the drafts of some letters I was supposed to look over before we mailed them—technical stuff, legal posturing that only another attorney could appreciate. That was all. Nothing that contained any information worth stealing. Nothing I needed. Nothing of any value whatsoever to anybody else.

I remembered the Meriwether Lewis letters, and how nervous I'd felt carrying them around the evening Walt Duffy asked me to deliver them to Ben Frye. Thankfully, they were tucked securely away in my office safe.

But the briefcase itself—that was a different story. My father had given it to me when I graduated from Yale Law

School, and I'd carried it with me ever since. It was one of those big clunky dark-leather briefcases, scraped and stained from use and abuse. It had a wide flat bottom and opened like an accordion. The flap closed with a big brass locking clasp, the key to which had been lost long before the briefcase came to me. It was about eighty years old. The initials "HFS" were engraved in gold on its side. It once belonged to Harlan Fiske Stone, who was the twelfth Chief Justice of the United States Supreme Court. My father had clerked for him. When Stone died in 1946, he bequeathed the briefcase to Dad.

Without documents testifying to its provenance, that briefcase would be worth nothing to an antique dealer or a pawn broker, never mind to some low-life mugger. But it was priceless to me. Dad had always hoped I'd carry it with me the first time I argued a ground-breaking civil liberties case before the Supreme Court.

Well, I'd never gone before the Court, and as my career had evolved, there was good reason to believe I never would. But if somehow that occasion should come to pass, it looked like I'd have to do it without my Harlan Fiske Stone briefcase.

Dad would be rolling his eyes and groaning in his grave. "Heedless, Brady," he'd be saying with a wag of his finger. "You can be so heedless, my boy."

I'd disappointed the old man again.

I pushed myself to my feet. I staggered for a moment. I felt a little dizzy, and my head hurt. I took a deep breath, told Henry everything was all right, and we followed my mugger's escape route out of the parking garage. I vaguely hoped I'd spot my wallet and my briefcase where he'd decided to drop them along the way. But no such luck.

When he felt safe, of course, he'd take the cash and the credit cards from the wallet, and he'd empty out the briefcase and discover that it held no packets of cocaine, no rolls of thousand-dollar bills, no diamond necklaces. Then he'd heave it into a Dumpster somewhere, and that would be the end of my Harlan Fiske Stone briefcase.

Damn. I loved that briefcase.

When we got up to my apartment, I headed straight for the bathroom and looked in the mirror. There was a gash at my hairline and quite a bit of blood on my face and the front of my shirt. I took off my shirt, washed my face, and sprayed some Bactine on the gash. It wasn't much of a wound, considering how much it had bled.

I covered it with a Band-Aid, then went into the kitchen, poured some Rebel Yell into a glass, and added a few ice cubes. I took my drink into the bedroom and flopped down on the bed. I still felt a little woozy.

After a few minutes, I sat up, sipped my drink, lit a cigarette, and called Evie.

When I told her what had happened, she said, "What did the police say?"

"I didn't call the police."

"Why not?"

"What can they do?"

"Brady," she said, "you were mugged. That's a crime. You're supposed to report crimes. Otherwise, how do you expect the police to capture the criminals?"

"I don't expect them to," I said. "A hundred people get mugged every night in Boston. All he got was my wallet and an eighty-year-old briefcase full of worthless papers."

"That's hardly the point."

I sighed. "I know. I'm more pissed at the security around

here. This isn't the first time someone's been mugged in my garage. It's why I always walk down with you when you're leaving."

"Call the police, okay?"

"Sure," I said.

"I mean it," she said. "At least if somebody finds your briefcase, they'll know who it belongs to. Can you identify the guy, do you think?"

"Not in a million years. Dark clothing. That's it. Never saw his face."

"Did he say anything?"

"He just said 'shit' when Henry went after him. I think he hit Henry."

"Oh, I hate that man. Is Henry all right?"

"He's not complaining."

"How big was the guy?"

"I couldn't tell. Average sized, I guess."

"Could it have been a woman?"

"Me? Mugged by a woman?"

She laughed. "Silly me. Did you take something for your headache?"

"Rebel Yell and a cigarette."

"Take some aspirin."

"Yes, Doctor."

"Put an ice pack on your head."

"Right."

"Call the cops."

"Okay."

"Promise?"

"I promise."

"Don't forget to cancel your credit cards."

"Yes, ma'am."

"And get some sleep."

"Sure," I said. "I'm fine."

"I wish I were there to take care of you."

"Me, too."

After I hung up with Evie, I called the local precinct and reported what had happened. The woman who took the call asked perfunctory questions, and I gave her perfunctory answers. She didn't promise to send somebody over right away, and I didn't ask her to. I made sure she wrote down a description of my briefcase. She asked me what it was worth. I told her it had loads of sentimental value.

She reminded me to cancel my credit cards, too.

Somewhere along the way, Henry snuck up onto the bed. He lay on his side with his back pressed against my leg. He was sound asleep.

"Dogs," I told him, "are supposed to sleep on the floor."

He twitched and sighed.

I didn't have the energy to press the issue.

When the phone rang, I was instantly awake. The green glow-in-the-dark numbers on my digital alarm clock read 4:09 A.M.

"Yes?" I said when I got the phone to my ear. "Who is this?"

"Fawrivah." It was that same muffled voice.

"I didn't catch what you said," I said. "Say it again. Who are you, anyway?"

He hung up.

I pushed myself into a sitting position and turned on the light. Henry, who was still sprawled on my bed, lifted his head, blinked at me, and went back to sleep.

I hit star-69 on the telephone and was told that the number I was trying to call couldn't be "reached by this method." As expected.

I lit a cigarette. "Fawrivah," the voice had said. I repeated it aloud a couple times until I thought I had it. Then I called Lieutenant Keeler's cell phone.

He picked up on the fourth ring and grumbled, "Yeah. Keeler."

"It's Brady Coyne," I said. "I just had another phone call."

"Christalmighty," he said. "A phone call? Oh. A *phone* call. Another fire, you think?"

"I don't know. It was the same voice."

"You recognize it?"

"No."

"Well, what'd he say?"

"Fall River, I think." Fall River was an old down-on-its-luck fishing city near the Rhode Island border on the Massachusetts south shore.

"What do you mean, you think?"

"His voice was muffled, like last time. Like he had the receiver covered. It sounded like he said Fall River."

"You try to retrieve his number?"

"Yes. No luck."

"Okay," said Keeler. "Thanks. Got it. Go back to sleep."

"Wait," I said.

"What?"

"I thought you might be interested to know I got mugged tonight."

"Any buildings burn down?"

"No. He pushed me from behind and I banged my head. Took my wallet and my briefcase."

"So why're you telling me? I'm arson. Call the cops."

"I did. They didn't seem very interested."

"What do you want me to do?"

"That wasn't my point," I said. "I just thought, first Walt Duffy gets murdered, then Ben Frye dies in a fire, and these phone calls, and I've been lugging those Meriwether Lewis letters around, and—"

"He got those letters?"

"No. They're in a safe place."

"So what did he get?"

"Nothing that matters, really. Some cash. Credit cards. Except my briefcase. My father gave it to me."

"No documents in it?"

"Just photocopies of stuff. Nothing of any interest to anybody."

"This mugger . . ."

"I didn't get a look at his face," I said.

"Well," said Keeler, "this is something for the local cops, you know."

"I just thought it all might be connected," I said lamely.

"You have any idea how many people get mugged in Boston?"

"Sure, but . . ."

He was silent for a moment. "Okay," he said. "Maybe it is connected. Maybe you're lucky you didn't get the back of your head smashed in, too. Right now, though, I'm more interested in that phone call. Fall River? That was all he had to say?"

"That was all. He said it once and hung up."

"Well," he said, "let's see if we can nail somebody setting fires in Fall River, shall we?"

"I hope you do," I said. "These phone calls are ruining my sleep."

"Mine, too," he said. "Don't forget to cancel your credit cards."

Fifteen

I lay there in the dark, waiting for sleep to return. I kept hearing that voice on the telephone, muffled and obviously disguised. "Fawrivah," he'd said. Fall River. I was sure it was the same voice that had whispered "Boomer pierce even" to me the night before the Beau Marc warehouse on Pier Seven in East Boston went up in flames with Ben Frye inside.

So why tell me about it?

My head throbbed. Where I touched it, there was a big, tender bump. I staggered out of bed, went into the bathroom, and swallowed three ibuprofen tablets. I peeled off the Band-Aid, and when I looked in the mirror, I saw that the bump on my forehead wasn't all that big. A little scab had formed over it. I didn't figure I was a candidate for cosmetic surgery.

When I turned back to the bedroom, Henry was standing there in the doorway with his head cocked to the side and his little tail wagging.

"What do you want?" I said to him.

He went over and sat beside the front door.

"Do you know what time it is?" I said to him.

He perked up his ears.

"It's quarter of five in the morning," I told him.

That information seemed to please him.

So I got dressed, hooked up Henry's leash, and started to open the door. Then I went back into the kitchen, found an old spatula and a plastic zip-up bag. I shoved them into my pocket, and Henry and I went down the elevator, out onto the sidewalk, and headed for the park down the street.

By the time Henry finished his business—and I'd finished scooping it into the plastic bag—the sky had begun to turn silvery in the east, and overhead, the stars were winking out one by one.

Back home, I got undressed and went back to bed. Smoked a cigarette. Slogged through half a chapter of *Moby Dick*. Turned off the light. Stared up into the semi-darkness.

After what seemed like a very long time, I finally started to drift off . . . and that's when my alarm clanged. I reached over and shut it off without even opening my eyes.

When the phone woke me up, the sun was streaming through my bedroom window. Judging by its angle, it was the middle of the morning.

I picked up the phone. "Yeah?"

"Where are you?" It was Julie.

"I'm here. Obviously."

"You don't need to be crabby," she said. "I mean, why aren't you here? Mr. Alberts's appointment is in an hour."

"Oh, shit. What time is it?"

"It's after ten, Brady. Are you all right?"

"Actually, no," I said. "I've got a terrible headache. I slept lousy. Must've turned off the alarm. See if you can reschedule Herm Alberts, will you?"

"You never have headaches," she said skeptically.

"I fell and banged my head last night. It bled all over me. Now I've got a goose egg. I'll be fine."

"Take some aspirin."

I sighed. "I did."

"Put ice on it."

"Yes," I said. "Good idea."

"I'll call Mr. Alberts," she said. "What time will you be here?"

"What've we got this afternoon?"

"No appointments. We need to go over that paperwork I gave you."

"Oh," I said. "That."

She hesitated, then said, "What do you mean, 'Oh, that'?"

I told her about getting mugged and banging my head and having my wallet and my briefcase stolen.

"Your Harlan Fiske Stone briefcase?"

"Yes."

"You love that briefcase," she said.

"Ycs, I do."

"What about all that paperwork I gave you?"

I sighed. "What do you think?"

"Gone, huh?"

"Gone."

"Hm," she said. "So what did the police say?"

"They thanked me for reporting it." I cleared my throat. "I think I'm going to take the day off. See if I can go back to sleep, get rid of this damn headache."

"Well, sure," she said. "Certainly if you're not feeling well . . ."

"I feel lousy," I said.

It reminded me of lying to my mother when I was a kid, pretending to be sick because I didn't want to go to school. I felt a little guilty about it.

I figured I'd get over it.

After I hung up with Julie, I called to report the theft of my credit cards. As expected, it took longer than it should have, and the headache I ended up with had nothing to do with whacking it against the door frame of my car.

So I went back to bed.

I woke up a little after two o'clock in the afternoon, feeling fuzzy-headed and disoriented and vaguely depressed. A pot of coffee, sipped slowly, one mug at a time out on my balcony, helped.

After Henry and I returned from another tour of the park, I fried some bacon, scrambled four eggs, made some toast, and he and I had brunch.

Around six I told Henry I was going out for a while and he shouldn't bother waiting up for me.

He went over and sat by the door.

"No," I said. "I'm going. Just me. You're staying here."

He cocked his head and looked at me for a minute, then went to the sofa, hopped up on it, twirled around a couple of times, lay down, sighed, and closed his eyes.

"You're not supposed to get up on the furniture."

He ignored me.

"Well, don't chew anything," I told him.

He opened his eyes, glared at me, then shut them again.

"I'll only be a couple of hours, for Christ's sake," I told him. "You can't come everywhere with me."

I left Henry sulking on the sofa.

By the time I got to Central Square and found a parking space, it was after seven o'clock. A "Closed" sign hung in the window of Vintage Vinyl, but there were lights on inside.

I tried the knob, and the door opened. When I stepped inside, I recognized Benny Goodman's clarinet playing over the speakers.

There appeared to be no one in the store, but I saw an open door in the rear. I went back there and peeked in. Conrad Henshall was sprawled in a reclining desk chair with a keyboard on his lap. He was staring through his tinted glasses at the large computer monitor on his desk, and his fingers were flicking at the keys. He was wearing chino pants with sharp creases, a starchy white shirt, and a bow tie.

I knocked on the door frame. He glanced up at me, said, "Sorry, sir. We're closed," and returned his attention to the computer screen.

I stood there for a minute, and when it became apparent that he intended to ignore me, I said, "I'm Brady Coyne. We met the other day. I was looking for Ethan Duffy. I still am."

He didn't shift his eyes from his computer screen. "I am occupied and my shop is closed. That sign is hanging in the window to deter people from entering."

"The door was unlocked."

"My mistake." He looked up at me and jerked his head toward the front of the store. "Lock it on the way out for me, if you'd be so kind." He turned back to his computer and hit a couple of keys.

"I need to talk to you," I said. "About Ethan."

"This is not a good time, I'm afraid." He kept his eyes on his computer monitor. "Another day, perhaps."

I stood there for a minute. Henshall made a good show of

pretending I wasn't there. So I stepped into the room, reached around behind his computer, and yanked out a handful of cords.

Henshall yelled, "Hey!" and an instant later, without warning, someone slipped up behind me and clamped his forearm around my throat.

He wedged his arm up under my chin and yanked me back against him. His breath smelled of peppermint. He had the bony part of his wrist pressed against my windpipe. I tried to drag in a breath, and found I couldn't. Tears sprang into my eyes.

I stomped down on his instep with my heel and at the same time drove my elbow back into his ribs. I'd seen James Bond do that a dozen times, and it always worked.

It did this time, too. He grunted, and his grip on my throat loosened, and I twisted away from him.

When I turned to face him, I saw that it was the balding guy with the ponytail who'd been in the store on my previous visit. Phil was his name.

"Where the hell did you come from?" I said.

He was bent over rubbing his foot. "Fuck," he muttered. "That hurt."

Henshall was shaking his head. "Awfully inept, Philip," he said. "I appreciate the effort, however." He dismissed Philip with a backward wave of his hand.

Phil shrugged, frowned at me, and went limping back into the store whence, apparently, he'd come, although I hadn't seen him on my way in.

"If he's supposed to be your bodyguard," I said to Henshall, "you're in trouble."

He leaned back in his chair, and blinked at me. "If you don't leave right now," he said, "I'm going to call the police."

"Fine," I said. "I'll give you Detective Saundra Mendoza's number. She's with homicide. If you don't want to talk to me, you can talk to her."

"I don't want to talk to anybody," he said. "I just want you out of my store."

"I'm sorry," I said. "I'm not going to do that. Not until we talk."

He scowled at me. I scowled right back at him.

After a minute he shrugged. "I can't persuade you to leave, then?"

I shook my head.

"Even if I sic Phil on you?"

I smiled.

"You better not have broken any of those cords."

"I don't think I did," I said. "I just pulled out some plugs."

"That was unnecessary."

"I considered punching you in the stomach," I said.

He shrugged. "People have tried to intimidate me all my life. It doesn't work anymore."

"I just wanted to get your attention."

"Is that why you used the word homicide?"

"The word homicide should get your attention."

"I confess it did," he said. "So what about Ethan Duffy?"

"He works here."

"Worked. Past tense. I fired him, as I believe I told you the other evening. He just doesn't know it yet."

"Why not?"

"Because he hasn't showed up when he's supposed to for a week, and he hasn't called me, and he doesn't answer his phone, so I haven't had a chance to tell him."

"I understand you're not just Ethan's employer," I said, "but also a friend of his."

Henshall took off his glasses and looked at me. "What do you want with Ethan Duffy, sir?"

"He seems to have gone missing. His mother's worried about him."

"You work for the mother?"

"Who I work for is none of your business," I said. "Do you know where Ethan is?"

"No."

"Talked to him, seen him, gotten any message from him since last Wednesday?"

He shook his head. "I told you—"

"Any idea where he might go if he didn't want to be found?"

"Listen—"

"No," I said. "You listen. Ethan's in trouble, and I need to talk to him."

Henshall was shaking his head. "I'm telling you. I don't know anything."

I glared at him. He avoided my eyes. I felt sure he was lying. But short of beating him up, I didn't think I was going to convince him to tell me the truth.

I blew out a long breath. "Okay, Mr. Henshall," I said. "Here's what I want you to do. If you should happen to run into Ethan, talk to him on the phone, get an e-mail, anything, you tell him he should call Brady Coyne right away. Understand?"

He shrugged.

"It's important. Life and death. Do I make myself clear?"

"Life and death," he said. "Couldn't be clearer, sir."

"Tell him he can call me any time. He can call me at four in the morning and disguise his voice if he wants."

Henshall frowned at me. "What is that supposed to mean?"

"Never mind," I said. "If you think of something, you call me yourself, okay?"

He nodded. "All right."

I turned and headed for the front of the shop. Henshall followed me.

Phil was fooling around with a stack of record albums. He looked up at me.

"You better take some lessons," I said to him. "Before you hurt yourself."

He smiled quickly, then resumed poking among the records.

When we got to the door, I turned to Henshall. "What do you know about Phil?"

"What do you mean?"

"What's his background?"

He shrugged. "He's one of those Ph.D.'s who can't get a teaching job. He likes music. Comes to work on time. That's about all I know."

"What's his Ph.D. in?"

"History," he said. "American history. History professors are a dime a dozen."

"American history," I repeated. "Has he ever mentioned any interest in old documents, or the Lewis and Clark expedition?"

"Philip and I don't have those kinds of conversations."

"What kind of conversations do you have?"

He smiled. "To tell you the truth, I rarely have conversations of any sort with the help. They take care of the customers so I don't have to."

"How does Phil get along with Ethan Duffy?"

Henshall cocked his head and looked at me. "What are you getting at, sir?"

"Would you answer my question?"

He frowned for a minute, as if he were thinking deeply. Finally, he shook his head. "I don't have a good answer for you, sir. Ethan and Philip work here at different times. I never have more than one person out front at the same time. They know each other, of course. But I have no awareness of their relationship, or if they even have one."

I nodded and held out my hand to Henshall. He hesitated, then took it.

"I'm sorry if I came on strong," I said.

"Don't worry about it," he said. "Real experts have tried to bully me." He smiled. "For a lawyer, you're not that good at it."

"I'll take that as a compliment," I said. "Still, I kind of thought yanking those cords out of your computer . . ."

He shook his head. "Amateur hour."

"When I used the phrase life and death," I said, "I meant it literally and most sincerely."

"I believe you, sir."

I stepped outside. Henshall pulled the door shut from the inside, and I heard the lock turn and the deadbolt snap into place.

I was lying in bed waiting for Melville's heavy prose to put me to sleep when the phone rang. I glanced at the clock. It was a little after midnight.

I picked up the phone. "Yes?" I expected to hear that muffled voice again.

"It's me. Ethan."

"Ethan?" I said. "Jesus, son. Are you all right? Where are you?"

"I'm okay."

"So Henshall delivered my message, huh?"

"Is Henry all right?"

"I'm taking care of Henry," I said. I noticed that he didn't answer my question. "Your mother's worried sick about you."

"Tell her I'm okay, will you?"

"You tell her yourself. Give her a call, for God's sake. What the hell is going on?"

"There's nothing to worry about."

"Your father—"

"I know about that."

"Did you see anything?"

"I'm just calling to tell you I'm okay. You don't need to go looking for me or anything."

"It's the police who are looking for you. They want to talk to you."

"I know."

"Ethan, I'm a lawyer," I said. "I was your father's family lawyer, which, technically, makes me your lawyer. I'll help you, okay?"

"If you're my lawyer, you can't tell the police you talked to me if I tell you not to, right?"

"It's more complicated than that," I said. "But as your lawyer, I advise you to—"

"Please keep the police out of it."

I blew out a breath. "I can't do that. They're looking for you. So am I. Dammit anyway, Ethan. I've worn out two pairs of shoes looking for you. There's good reason to think people less friendly than I are also looking for you. Your father has been murdered. Ben Frye, too. Have I got your attention yet?"

He was silent for a moment. Then he said, "Yes."

"Good," I said. "Now listen to me. You've got to talk to the police, and I want to be with you when you do. Let's do it right now. Okay?"

"It's midnight, Brady."

"The cops are open for business all night."

"Who else is looking for me?"

"You don't know?"

"You're trying to scare me."

"You got that right," I said. "Where are you? Tell me where you are. I'll come get you."

"No," he said. "Not now."

"Dammit, Ethan—"

"I need more time, Brady. I'll call you again."

"Not good enough. You've got to—"

"It's the best I can do," he said, and then he hung up.

I put the phone back on the cradle, blew out a breath, and lit a cigarette.

Well, at least he was alive. That was a relief.

He said he was okay, whatever that meant. He hadn't sounded particularly okay, but it was hard to read somebody over the telephone.

On the other hand, his father had been murdered, and it was possible that he'd witnessed it.

It was possible he did it.

I snubbed out my cigarette, picked up the phone, dialed information, and asked the synthetic voice for the number for Jonathan or Ellen Bramhall in Sudbury.

It was close to twelve-thirty. Most people are asleep at twelve-thirty on a Wednesday morning.

Hell, if I were a worried mother, I wouldn't care what time I got a good-news phone call about my son.

Her husband answered. "Yeah," he grumbled. It sounded as if I'd awakened him.

I know I should have apologized for waking him up, told him who I was, reminded him that I was a lawyer, and indicated why I'd called in the middle of the night. But I'd found him to be an unfriendly sonofabitch, and Ellen didn't seem to like him much, either, so all I said was: "May I speak to Ellen, please?" He could think what he wanted.

"Who is this? What do you want?"

"It's Brady Coyne," I said, "and I want to talk to Ellen."

"Why?"

"None of your business."

He hung up.

I hit the redial button.

When he picked up the phone, Jonathan Bramhall said, "If you don't stop harassing us, I'm going to call the police."

"If you don't let me talk to Ellen," I said, "there will be a police cruiser in your driveway in ten minutes with its lights flashing for your neighbors to see."

I heard mumbled voices in the background. They sounded angry. Then Ellen said, "Brady?"

"I just talked to Ethan," I said.

"Oh, lord," she said. "I was worried that . . ."

"He's okay. He's staying with a friend. He made me promise to call you right away."

"Well, thank you," she said. "He could've called me himself."

"And I expect he will."

"Where is he?"

"He didn't tell me. He's upset about what happened to

Walt. He's taking some time to sort it all out. The point is, he's fine, and you shouldn't worry about him."

She blew out a long breath, then said, "Well, thank you, Brady. If you talk to him again, please tell him that his mother would like to hear his voice."

"Of course," I said. "I'm sorry I upset your husband."

"I'm not," she said. "Thank you so much."

After I hung up, I smiled to myself. I had told Ellen two or three little lies. Not even lies, really. Extrapolations. The fact was, I didn't know where Ethan was staying, and I didn't know why he'd decided to go into hiding, and I had no confidence that he'd call his mother.

But they were benign lies, and I felt pretty good about them.

Sixteen

A little after ten on Thursday morning, Detective Roger Horowitz, my old friend and nemesis from the Massachusetts state police, showed up at my office. When Julie ushered him in, Henry, who was lying under my desk, got to his feet, went over, and sniffed Horowitz's shoes. Horowitz glanced down and said, "Go away."

Henry looked up at me, sort of shrugged, then returned to his place under the desk.

I asked Horowitz if he wanted coffee.

He shook his head.

"I've been besieged with cops lately," I said.

"So I hear."

I gestured to the sofa. "You want to sit?"

"No," he said. "You gotta come with me. I got a car waiting outside."

I arched my eyebrows. "What now?"

He sighed. "You're in the middle of something. They asked me to come get you. On account of the fact that you and I are buddies."

I smiled. "Buddies, huh?"

He shrugged.

"Walt Duffy and Ben Frye and arson fires, huh?"

"Bigger than that," he said. "Sandy Mendoza and Matt Keeler have got those cases."

"Bigger than homicides and arson fires?"

He gave me his familiar sardonic smile.

"So who's 'they'?"

Horowitz frowned. "Huh?"

"You said *they* asked you to come get me. I'm asking who 'they' are."

"You'll see. I'm not supposed to tell you anything. Come on. I already told Julie I was taking you with me."

"Can I bring my dog?"

"No."

A state police cruiser had its motor running at the curb around the corner in front of the library. I sat in back. Horowitz got in front beside the uniformed trooper who was behind the wheel.

Nobody said anything in the fifteen minutes or so it took us to hook out onto Storrow Drive heading inbound, exit at Cambridge Street, and stutter through the traffic to Scollay Square. I smoked a cigarette, and they didn't even tell me to put it out.

We pulled into the paved area behind Center Plaza, the wide curved building that had been built in front of the old Suffolk County courthouse. Horowitz led me down some steps and into One Center Plaza. He signed us in at the door, and we took the elevator to the sixth floor, where the Boston field office of the United States Federal Bureau of Investigation was housed.

So. The FBI.

We passed through a metal detector in the cramped reception area, and Horowitz spoke to a woman behind bulletproof glass. A door buzzed on our left, and I followed Horowitz down a corridor and into a conference room. Two men and two women were seated around a rectangular conference table. I recognized the two Boston cops—Homicide Detective Saundra Mendoza was one of them, and Lieutenant Matthew Keeler, the arson guy, was the other.

The second man wore a dark suit and a white shirt and a striped necktie. The other woman was dressed the same minus the tie.

The dark-suited man half stood when Horowitz and I stepped into the room. "Mr. Coyne," he said. "Thank you for coming."

"I wasn't given much choice," I said.

"I'm Agent Aaron Elliot," he said as if he hadn't heard me. "I'm with the Boston field office of the F.B.I. This—" he waved his hand in the direction of the dark-suited woman "—is Agent Pauline Randall, from headquarters." Randall was thumbing through a sheaf of papers. She didn't look up. "I believe you know the Boston officers? Saundra Mendoza, homicide? Matthew Keeler, arson?"

"We've met," I said. I nodded to them. Keeler gave me a quick smile. Mendoza nodded.

"Won't you sit down?" said Elliot. He didn't offer to shake hands, so neither did I.

I sat. It was a small room. There was a pale oak conference table with upholstered chairs gathered around it. The upholstering on the chairs matched the thick royal blue carpet, and the oak furniture matched the paneling of the walls. An American flag and a flag of the Commonwealth of Massachusetts stood on flagstands in one corner. A large map of the United States dominated one wall. There was a white dry-erase board on another wall. Nothing was written on it. A television and a computer sat on a table against another wall. There were bright fluorescent lights in the ceiling and two tall windows with vertical Venetian blinds. The blinds were shut.

The whole effect was austere, sterile, standard-issue. I was willing to bet that every FBI conference room in America looked pretty much like this one.

Agent Elliot cleared his throat. "You're an attorney, Mr. Coyne."

"That I am," I said.

"So I don't have to remind you that whatever might be said in this room is, um, sensitive."

"Oh," I said, "it's always a good idea to remind me."

I thought a smile twitched at the corner of Elliot's mouth, but he restrained himself admirably. He was a bulky guy. Not fat. Solid-looking. He had big shoulders, a round face, shrewd pale eyes, and thinning, blond-gray hair. He looked to be in his early fifties. He gestured at a carafe in the middle of the table. "Water, Mr. Coyne?"

I shook my head. I didn't notice any ashtrays. "You dragged me away from my law practice with no notice. I came willingly. You don't need to soften me up, or impress me with the gravity of the situation. Why don't you just tell me what you want."

Elliot glanced at Horowitz. Knowing Horowitz, he'd warned the agent that I was a smartass. I wasn't, normally. But Horowitz always seemed to bring out the smartass in me, and Elliot was doing the same thing.

"Okay," he said. "I'm going to turn this over to Agent Randall." Elliot nodded at the woman, then sat down.

Randall stood up. Her blond hair was cut short and no-nonsense, and her face was angular. She looked about forty. She had a thin, hard-looking body. "We want to talk with you about Walter Duffy," she said. There was a trace of the Smoky Mountains in her voice.

"Walt was my client," I said.

"Of course." Agent Randall nodded. "And we both know that client privilege does not extend postmortem." She arched her eyebrows at me, and I shrugged.

She glanced down at one of the papers in front of her. "You told Detective Mendoza that Mr. Duffy asked you to hand-deliver a parcel for him the day before he was murdered."

"That's right."

"And you delivered that parcel?"

"Yes," I said. "I gave it to Benjamin Frye."

"You told the detective that as far as you knew, the parcel contained old letters."

"I looked at them. They were letters from Meriwether Lewis to Alexander Wilson, written almost two hundred years ago. They were about birds. Apparently quite valuable."

"You looked at all of the letters?"

"No. They were in a plastic envelope. Walt told me not to touch them. Touching them could damage them. I looked at the top one."

"And how many letters were there?"

"I didn't count them."

"And where are these letters now, Mr. Coyne?"

"They're in the safe in my office. Ben gave them back to me after he looked at them."

"The evening before he was killed."

"Yes."

"Before you put them in your safe, where did you keep them?"

"I had them in my briefcase over the weekend."

"I understand," said Randall, "that on Monday night, your briefcase was stolen."

"That's right." I touched my forehead. The bump had shrunk, but there was a scab there. "I was mugged in my parking garage. He got my wallet and my briefcase."

"This was after you removed those letters and put them in your office safe?"

"Yes."

"Where they remain."

I nodded.

"Mr. Coyne," said Randall, "you claim that you've been receiving some, um, unusual telephone calls."

"I don't claim it," I said. "It's true. I've reported them."

"Of course," she said. "To Detective Mendoza and Lieutenant Keeler. Two calls, correct?"

"Yes."

"The first one came the night before Mr. Frye died in a fire," she said. "You told the officers that the person said the words 'Beau Marc Pier Seven.' "

"I didn't understand the words when I heard them," I said. "They sounded like nonsense syllables. The voice was muffled—disguised. But, yes, I think that's what he said."

"He was naming the building that was torched the following night," she said. "The building where Benjamin Frye's body was found."

"I guess so, yes."

"Telling you it was going to happen."

I shrugged. "Evidently."

"And then two nights ago you got another call."

"Yes."

"The same caller?"

"It sounded like it."

"And what did he say this time?"

"Fall River. I called Lieutenant Keeler immediately." I looked at Keeler. He nodded.

Randall picked up a remote control device that had been sitting on the table beside her. "Please take a look at the TV, Mr. Coyne," she said.

She hit the remote. The screen flickered, and then what looked like a child's charcoal drawing of an owl appeared. A few seconds later the owl picture flicked off and the big red letters S O L F took its place. They looked as if they'd been finger-painted on a piece of white cardboard.

There was no sound with the video. The camera wavered a bit. Handheld. Very amateur.

A moment later the scene switched to a long-distance shot of a square brick building. Beyond the building was water. The building appeared to have been built on a harbor.

Then came a close-up of a sign. It read "Fore River Container Company."

Then the picture switched to a night scene. It was poorly lit, but the silhouette of the building and the pewter glint in the background made it clear that this was a repetition of the shot of the same brick building taken from the same place.

The camera held on that shot for a long minute.

Then there was a sudden little burst of light from the front of the building. I watched as the burst of light grew larger and materialized into flames.

The camera held on the burning building for perhaps two minutes.

Then the same shot of the red finger-painted letters S O L F appeared.

Then came the primitive charcoal drawing of the owl.

Then the screen went blank.

SEVENTEEN

Randall flicked off the TV with her remote. The room was silent.

She turned to me. "Somebody dropped this videotape on the receptionist's desk at Channel Seven around eight o'clock this morning," she said. "It was in a large padded envelope with the name of the news director printed on it. We have been in contact with all of the local media. The news director knew enough to forward this tape to us as soon as he saw what it was. So what do you think, Mr. Coyne?"

I shrugged. "Whoever set the fire wants publicity."

Randall pushed back her chair, went over to the white board, picked up a marker, and wrote the letters S O L F on it. "Did those letters mean anything to you, Mr. Coyne?"

I shook my head. "No. I never saw them before that tape."

"You never heard of SOLF?" She pronounced it as if it were a word.

"No."

"What about the Spotted Owl Liberation Front?"

"No." I smiled. "What's that, some group of radical ornithologists?"

"Pretty close," she said. She went over to the wall map. I noticed that about two dozen red pushpins stuck out of it, and each pushpin held a little square of paper tacked to the map. Four or five of them were clustered in the Pacific Northwest. Half a dozen or so ran down the California coastline. There were a couple in Colorado, three or four scattered along the Mississippi River, a couple on the Florida peninsula, and one cluster on the northeast coast around Boston and Long Island.

"These," said Randall, pointing at the pushpins, "are sites of SOLF strikes."

"Strikes?" I said.

"Arson fires. Twenty-seven of them, including the one last night."

"The one on that tape?"

"Yes."

I nodded. "I thought he said 'Fall River.' But on that tape it was—"

"He must have said 'Fore River,' " she said. "The fire happened on the harbor near the old Fore River Shipyard in Quincy. Last night's strike, as you saw, was against the Fore River Container Company. They produce corrugated cardboard products. Beau Marc Industries, which they hit a few nights ago, you recall, is a French-based consortium of mining interests. One of the Beau Marc satellite companies has been lobbying to extract gold ore from a site in Montana near the Yellowstone River. Another one is negotiating for mineral rights in federally protected wilderness areas in Alaska. Do you see?"

"These, um, targets, they're destroying bird habitat. Is that it?"

"Originally, that was it. They cut down forests and filled in wetlands. In recent years, the targets have included alleged air and water polluters, toxic waste dumpers, HazMat disposal businesses. The Fore River Container Company manufactures glue. Beau Marc mining companies use a cyanide process for extracting gold from ore."

"And this SOLF, they're hitting back at them."

"Exactly. They've caused nearly a hundred million dollars in damage in the past ten years."

"And they kill people?" I said.

"Before last week, no," said Randall. "Mr. Duffy and Mr. Frye were the first. Before that, SOLF only hit places when nobody was there."

"Wait a minute," I said. "Walt Duffy was a famous bird lover. He photographed them for a living. Hell, he spent the last year of his life on crutches, feeding the birds in his little garden on Beacon Hill. And Ben Frye was a peace-loving old hippie pothead. Hardly what you'd call an enemy of bird habitat. Why would these people want to kill them?"

Randall nodded. "We are hoping you might help us figure that out."

"I don't know anything about it."

"Did Walter Duffy ever mention SOLF to you? Or express anger toward any particular industries? Or comment in any way about arson fires?"

"No," I said.

"Mr. Coyne," she said with infinite patience, "two men, friends of yours, are dead."

"Yes. I'm very aware of that. I never heard of SOLF—the

word or the acronym—before that video tape."

She narrowed her eyes at me for a moment, then shrugged. "If you say so."

The others in the room had been following Randall's interrogation of me with impassive faces. Horowitz looked bored, as if he'd heard it all before. Mendoza had her hands folded on the table in front of her. Keeler kept shuffling through his sheaf of papers.

"Aaron," said Randall to Agent Elliot, "give Mr. Coyne a copy of Document C, would you?"

Elliot, who seemed to be Randall's subordinate, pushed some papers across the table to me.

I looked at them. There were four pages stapled together. In capital letters across the top were the words: DUFFY, WALTER. ITINERARY 1992–2001. It was a list of places, and beside each place was a date. In the left margin, some of the places had asterisks typed in beside them.

I skimmed through the pages. Bend and Eugene, Oregon had asterisks, as did Olympia and Seattle, Washington. San Francisco, Oakland, Los Angeles, San Diego. Aspen and Denver. Chicago and St. Louis and New Orleans . . .

"What's your point?" I said to Randall.

"These are places Walter Duffy visited during the ten years before his accident, and the dates he was there."

I smiled. "I figured that much."

"The asterisks," she said, "are places where SOLF strikes occurred."

"And I suppose the dates match up somehow," I said.

She nodded. "Within two months after Mr. Duffy's departure, in each of those cases, SOLF hit something in the area."

"Walt had already left, so he couldn't have set any of those fires, right?"

"That's right."

I thumbed through the list. "He seems to have visited a lot of places where there were no SOLF strikes."

"That's true."

"Has SOLF hit any places that don't match up with Walt's travels?"

"Yes," she said. "Many."

I shrugged. "Then . . ."

"It's a pattern, Mr. Coyne."

"So," I said, "you're trying to say that Walt Duffy was involved with SOLF? That he had something to do with these fires?"

She nodded. "We have reason to believe he was, yes."

"Based on this?" I slapped the sheaf of papers with the back of my hand.

"Based on several things," she said. "Including that."

"Well," I said, "you know more about it than I do."

"Perhaps."

I looked at Horowitz. He grinned at me. When Roger Horowitz grinned, he looked like Jack Nicholson. His Nicholson grin had no mirth to it whatsoever.

"Let me ask you something," I said to Randall. "How come I never heard of this SOLF?"

"What they're after is publicity," she said. "They want to spread their message. They destroy property to draw attention to their message. We've been fairly successful in, um, convincing the media to keep SOLF out of the public's eye. We do not want a videotape such as the one we just looked at to be on the evening news."

Agent Randall went over to her chair, sat down across from me, put her forearms on the table, and leaned forward. "Let me tell you about SOLF," she said.

In 1990, Randall said, the northern spotted owl, a rare, reclusive bird that lived only in mature forests in the Pacific Northwest, was declared a threatened subspecies, and cutting timber in the birds' habitat was banned. Almost immediately, the spotted owl came to symbolize the conflict between conservationists and those whose livelihoods depended on harvesting the bounty of the earth—loggers, miners, farmers, ranchers. In that part of the country, at least, the decision to protect spotted owl habitat was wildly unpopular. Locals saw it as a conspiracy between liberal east coast politicians, self-serving bureaucrats, and radical environmentalists to destroy their old and honorable way of life. Bumper stickers with messages like "Kill a spotted owl, spare a woodcutter's child" began appearing in Washington, Oregon, Montana, and northern California.

Then in September of 1991 an out-of-work Oregon logger named Emil Pritchard announced to the Portland media that he was taking his chain saw into a restricted Oregon forest, and he was going to cut down some spotted owl houses. The TV cameras followed him into the woods that day, and so did a crowd of supporters, who cheered him on as he felled half a dozen big oak trees.

Emil Pritchard, to his disappointment, was not arrested. The local police sympathized with his plight, and the feds opted for discretion. Still, it was a big story in the local news.

Two nights later, Pritchard's house burned to the ground. Somebody called a local television station and claimed that the fire was the work of a group calling itself the Spotted Owl Liberation Front.

The TV station ran the story, and one of the networks picked it up. And that was the beginning.

Arson fires in several states, all, directly or indirectly, aimed at enemies of bird habitat, followed. All were claimed by SOLF.

Once it became an interstate matter, the FBI got involved. Their first move was to keep SOLF out of the media.

"For a long time," said Pauline Randall, "we believed they were just isolated little knots of local amateur environmental radicals. College kids. Hippies. Dropouts. Get-a-lifers. We caught a few of them. They wouldn't tell us anything. They all just spouted their propaganda, thrilled at the chance to be martyrs for their righteous cause. They didn't seem to have any organization, any plan, any leadership. No different from a lot of other fringe elements. Poor, aimless souls who thought they'd discovered a grand way to give meaning to their own pitiful lives. Ever read *The Monkey Wrench Gang*, Mr. Coyne?"

I nodded.

"These SOLF people were like them, we thought. Kooks. Every burned-down warehouse and factory was a message, a way to spread their gospel. They figured the righteousness of their mission would eventually convert a corrupt and misguided nation."

"True believers," I said.

Randall nodded.

"No publicity," I said, "no way to spread the gospel. Eventually it would dry up and go away."

"That's what we hoped," she said.

"So where did Walt Duffy come into it?"

"At first we thought we were dealing with isolated cells scattered across the country," she said. "Random, ad hoc groups of six or eight local people. Then we began to unearth some evidence that these cells were communicating with each other. Mainly by e-mail. They were very clever about it, and we couldn't trace the e-mails to their sources. But one e-mail that we intercepted used the phrase 'The Urban Birder' as what seemed to be a code name. That put us onto Duffy."

I nodded. "His column."

"Right. So we backtracked his travels—that's the document you have there—and cross-referenced them with fires that SOLF claimed credit for."

"And you found a correlation."

Randall shrugged. "Enough of a correlation to interest us, certainly. Where Duffy went, it seemed, SOLF fires soon followed. Walter Duffy was something of a hero to conservationists and environmentalists, you know."

"You're saying he was the ringleader?"

She nodded. "We think SOLF is a national organization. We think it's well-funded, well-organized, and very dangerous. We believe Walter Duffy coordinated it."

"From his little bird garden on Beacon Hill," I said.

"After his accident, yes," she said. "Mostly by e-mail and cell phone."

"That's hard to believe."

She shrugged. "I've been here in Boston for two weeks," she said. "Last Thursday—exactly one week ago—Agent Elliot and I planned to serve Mr. Duffy with a subpoena to hand over his paper records and his computers and to testify before a federal grand jury."

"Thursday," I said. "That was—"

"Yes. One day too late. He was murdered on Wednesday."

"To keep him quiet? Is that what you think?"

"Mr. Coyne," said Randall, "you told Detective Mendoza

that on the day you found Walter Duffy's body, he had called you and said he needed to talk with you."

"That's right," I said.

"But he didn't tell you what he wanted to talk about."

"No."

"You had no sense that he might want to consult with you about appearing before a grand jury, or that he was concerned about what we might find in his files or the hard drives of his computers?"

"He only had one computer," I said. "His laptop."

She nodded. "And?"

I shook my head. "He didn't say anything like that."

"Did he mention those letters?"

I thought for a minute. "No. All he said was he wanted to talk to me."

"Did he sound agitated?"

"Not that I recall. It was pretty clear that something was on his mind. He implied that it was important. I didn't have the feeling that it was urgent, though. I told him I'd drop by when I was done in the office, and that seemed okay with him."

"And when you got there . . . ?"

I nodded. "He'd been smashed on the head. That was a couple hours after he called."

"And his computer and cell phone and camera were missing."

"That's right." I leaned forward and looked at her. "Did you tell him you were going to serve that subpoena?"

She rolled her eyes. "Of course not. We'd never do that."

"You're saying somebody tipped him off? He got wind of that subpoena? You think that's why he called me?"

Randall sighed. "Duffy was a very smart man. He was in

touch with a lot of people. He had strong intuitions. Perhaps he sensed something. Or maybe he was just having second thoughts about the whole thing. Perhaps if you'd gone to see him when he called, instead of waiting a couple hours, he would have told you about his involvement with SOLF. You would have advised him to cooperate, of course, and he might still be alive."

"I've been feeling guilty about it for a week," I said. "I don't need your help."

She dismissed that sentiment with a quick backhanded wave. "Maybe Duffy anticipated our subpoena," she said, "either because he'd been specifically tipped off or because he knew I was in Boston and arrived at the logical conclusion. Or maybe he just decided it was time to put an end to it, to come clean, so to speak. In either case, he would logically want to consult with his lawyer. Right?"

"Sure," I said. "Walt would do that. He trusted me."

"But before you got there," she said, "somebody murdered him."

"And," I said, "the question is who."

She nodded. "We theorize that he mentioned the possibility of the subpoena and his intention to consult with you to a third party."

"Some SOLF person?"

"Yes."

"And you think that person got to him before I did and killed him and took his computer to protect the organization."

"Or that person told somebody else who did it," she said.

"So all you've got to do is interrogate every SOLF member you can get your hands on in Boston," I said. "One of them will surely spill the beans."

"Catch-22, Mr. Coyne," she said. "We don't know who these people are."

"How does Ben Frye fit into it? You think he was involved in SOLF, too?"

She shrugged. "We're trying to backtrack Mr. Frye's travels in the past year as we speak."

"Since Walt's accident. Since he couldn't travel."

"That's right. Frye never hit our radar screen. But he did travel a great deal. We think it's possible that he and Duffy worked together."

"So if you can nail one of these people in the act of setting a fire . . ."

She smiled. "Exactly. They're still doing it, apparently under new leadership. We think if we can get ahold of one of them, we should be able to untangle the whole thing. And that's where you come in."

"Me?"

"Pier Seven? Fore River?"

"Ah," I said. "Those phone calls."

"Why would someone from SOLF be alerting you about these fires, Mr. Coyne?"

I spread my hands. "I have no idea."

She arched her eyebrows skeptically.

"Really," I said. "I can't think of anybody."

"You'll let us know the next time you get one of those calls," she said.

I nodded.

"Try to hear it clearly. Try to get that person to say more to you. Ask for details."

"I'll try."

"These two men who were murdered, they were your friends."

"Yes, they were."

Pauline Randall held my eyes for a minute. Then she leaned back in her chair, folded her arms, and looked around the room. "Anybody want to add anything?" She arched her eyebrows at Horowitz.

He shook his head. "You about covered it."

"What about the arson end of it?" she said to Keeler.

He shrugged. "Firefighters' lives are at risk with every fire. The sooner we can nail these bastards, the better." He glanced at me. "I know Mr. Coyne's trying to help."

"Detective Mendoza?"

Saundra Mendoza had been looking at her fingernails. When Randall spoke her name, she looked up and said, "I have nothing to add."

Randall looked at Agent Elliot, who shook his head.

She turned back to me. "Any questions, Mr. Coyne?"

"You just want me to let you know if I have another phone call," I said. "Is that it?"

"Anything at all," she said. "We've shared some highly confidential information with you here today. Our intention was to bring you in on this, to elicit your help. If you hear anything, see anything, remember anything, think of anything—anything at all, however unlikely, that might be connected to SOLF or these fires and murders—I expect you to share it with us right away."

"Of course I will," I said. "It's my duty. I'm an officer of the court." I hesitated. "I'm surprised you don't want to tap my telephone or something."

"We discussed it." She smiled. "We didn't think you'd like it."

"You'd have to get my permission," I said, "and I wouldn't give it to you. My clients sometimes call me at home. I would never compromise their privacy."

"Oh," she said, "under the circumstances, I think we could go ahead without your permission."

"No judge would agree to it," I said. "You'd have to convince him that I'm engaged in some criminal activity."

Randall smiled. "We could probably do that."

"Now listen—"

She raised her hand. "Relax, Mr. Coyne. Nobody's accusing you of anything. Your phone's not tapped, and it won't be."

"Good," I said.

"We did do some checking with the phone company, however."

"Oh?"

"Both of those calls from the arsonist were made from a cellular phone."

"Did you get the number?"

She nodded. "The phone belonged to Walter Duffy."

I thought about that. "Walt's phone was stolen when he was killed. So the person who's calling me and setting those fires is the same guy who killed Walt."

Randall nodded. "So it would seem."

I looked at her. "Why me?"

"I wish you could tell us, Mr. Coyne."

EIGHTEEN

When Horowitz and I walked out of the building, I glanced at my watch. It was nearly two in the afternoon.

"Jesus," I said. "I've got to find a phone. Julie will be going batshit."

"Here," he said. "Use this." He handed me his cell phone.

I dialed my office number. "You told her it would be a couple hours," I said to him as it rang. "It was closer to four."

"Tell her it was the FBI," he said.

When Julie answered, I said, "The good news is, the FBI let me go."

"No," she said. "The good news is, I haven't quit yet."

"I couldn't get to a phone," I said. "Sorry."

"You've got responsibilities, Brady."

"Tell that to Special Agent Randall."

"I'm not impressed."

"I didn't think you would be," I said. "How's Henry?"

"That dog sure does love to pee, doesn't he?"

"He's a guy," I said. "It's a testosterone thing."

"As if I didn't get enough of that," she said. "Are you planning to do any work today?"

"I'm on my way. I'll probably pick up something to eat on the way. Want anything?"

"I'm all set," she said coolly. "Thank you."

I snapped the phone shut and handed it to Horowitz.

"Julie's pissed, I bet," he said.

"Of course she is," I said. "That's her job."

He smiled.

I lit a cigarette and squinted up at the sky. "Another glorious June day," I said. "Reminds me of a couple weeks I spent in San Diego back when I was with my wife, the boys were little. Every day was perfect. Same ideal temperature, same low humidity, same cloudless sky, same soft breeze wafting in off the Pacific. The people we were staying with, they kept saying, 'Oh, it's another beautiful California day.' I asked them if it ever rained or anything, and they said, 'Oh, no, hardly ever.' Proud as hell of their damn boring weather. After about two days of it I was climbing the walls. All I wanted was a cloud on the horizon or a shift in the breeze. Anything to remind me that time was passing. With that monotonous weather, years could go by and you wouldn't even notice."

Horowitz was shaking his head, whether in sympathy or irritation I couldn't tell.

"These last couple of weeks remind me of San Diego," I said. "Same beautiful damn weather, day after day. It's driving me nuts."

He shrugged. "It rained last weekend, didn't it?"

"Yes. Briefly. Wasn't it glorious?"

"I don't generally notice the weather," said Horowitz. "Weather doesn't interest me."

We started walking across the brick courtyard behind Central Plaza to where the state police cruiser was waiting. "That Randall," I said. "I'd hate to oppose her in court."

"Tough cookie, all right."

"So where do you fit in, Roger?"

"Me?" Horowitz shrugged. "They've got to touch all their jurisdictional bases, that's all. Local, state, federal. I'm state."

"But why you?"

"Because I'm good, of course." He looked sideways at me. "Also, I know you."

"Am I that important?"

He shrugged. "You were Duffy's lawyer. You're the one who found his body, and you were the last person to see the other murder victim alive. You're the one this firebug keeps calling. You're the one who's been snooping around. What do you think?"

"Snooping?" I snapped my fingers. "Ethan Duffy," I said. "Agent Randall never mentioned Ethan."

"Is that a question?" said Horowitz.

"An observation," I said. "She pumped me on everything except Ethan. She was waiting to see if I'd mention him, I'll bet. And she probably found vast significance in the fact that I didn't. That's it, isn't it? You're probably supposed to catch me with my guard down, right? Encourage me to talk. Report back to Randall anything I might let slip."

"Don't be so fucking paranoid, Coyne. We're just trying to solve some crimes here."

"You are looking for Ethan, aren't you?"

He nodded. "Of course we are."

"I talked to him last night."

He turned and narrowed his eyes at me. "He's okay?"

"So he says."

He blew out an exasperated breath. "So you know where he is, right? We're gonna go there now and grab him, right? What the fuck were you waiting for? We should've done this last night."

"I don't know where he is, Roger. He wouldn't tell me. He just called to say he was okay."

Horowitz rolled his eyes. "Jesus Christ, Coyne."

"It was the best I could do. I tried to put pressure on him, but he sounded . . . skittish. I was afraid I'd lose him."

"Lose him?" Horowitz gave me one of his cynical Nicholson grins. "You can't lose somebody that you never had in the first place."

"He said he'd call again," I said. "I'll do better next time."

"Oh, good," said Horowitz. "I am enormously comforted."

Around seven-thirty the next morning Henry and I, having returned from our first stroll of the day, were having coffee on my balcony. It was yet another glorious June morning in New England, and Henry was watching the gulls and terns wheel and glide on the thermals over the harbor when he suddenly darted back inside and began barking.

"Hey," I yelled. "Cut it out. You'll wake up the neighbors. Come back here."

When he didn't come, I got up and went in. Henry was pressing his nose against the door and growling.

"Sit," I told him.

He sat.

"Shut up."

He kept growling.

"I didn't know you were a damn watchdog," I told him.

He took that as permission to stand up again. He prodded the door with his nose and growled some more.

I opened the door. Nobody was there. Henry slipped out around my legs and trotted down the corridor with his nose vacuuming back and forth across the carpet. I snapped my fingers and hissed, "Come." He stopped, looked at me, thought about it, then sauntered back.

That's when I noticed the envelope at my feet. It was one of those padded ten-by-thirteen manila mailers. It must have been leaning against the door when I opened it.

I picked it up. The words "Brady Coyne" were printed on it with a black Magic Marker. Nothing else.

The phrase "letter bomb" passed through my mind.

The question "Who'd want to blow the hands off an inoffensive fellow such as I?" immediately followed.

I ran down a mental list of people who I figured didn't like me. It was a fairly long list, comprised mainly of some lawyers I had opposed and their clients. A couple of my own clients, too, come to think of it. I thought of a few women who might misguidedly believe I'd wronged them, though none recently, and a couple of guys who believed I cheated at golf, guys I hadn't been in touch with for a long time.

I gave up golf several years ago, and I believed I was a better man for it.

Not a likely Unabomber in the bunch.

I picked up the envelope. There was an object inside it. I took it inside, put it on the kitchen table, picked up the phone, and called the doorman downstairs. "Frankie," I said, "it's Brady Coyne in 6-E."

"Good morning, sir." Francisco Martinez was a thirtyish man who somehow supported four children and a pregnant wife on what he earned as a doorman and a part-time waiter. He was from the Dominican Republic, but no relation to Pedro Martinez. "Everybody named Martinez in the Dominican," he once told me. He was very popular among the tenants, because he was unfailingly polite and always smiling. He was a big Red Sox fan.

"Frankie," I said, "did you just send somebody up to my apartment?"

"Oh, no, sir. Never send anybody up without buzzing."

"Maybe somebody came in with another tenant?"

"No, sir. Only person come in so far this morning was you and your dog."

"Well," I said, "did anybody you didn't recognize leave within the past five minutes?"

"Nobody leave in last half hour, Mr. Coyne. Something wrong?"

"No, it's okay. Thanks, Frankie."

The underground parking garage, of course. Anybody—including muggers and burglars and slippery delivery people—could walk in and squeeze around the place where the bar automatically went up if you had the electronic device on your dashboard. Then you had the option of entering the building via the elevator or the stairwell. Once inside, you had the choice of several fire exits for getting back out without being detected.

I picked up the envelope again. I shook it gently. Something solid moved inside.

The hell with it. I held my breath and tore open the envelope.

It did not explode in my face.

I reached in and removed what was inside. It was a cellular telephone. I tipped the envelope upside down, and a plug and cord fell out. For keeping the batteries charged.

There was no note or any indication whatsoever of where the phone had come from.

It was one of those super-tiny models with a soft leather cover and a little lid you flipped open when you wanted to talk and a light that blinked green when it was turned on. I flipped it open, looked at it front and back, shut it, put it back on the table . . . and nearly jumped through the ceiling when it beeped.

I opened it, hit the "talk" button, and said, "Yes? Hello?"

"Mr. Coyne." It was that same voice. The voice that had said "Beau Marc, Pier Seven" and "Fore River" to me. Growly and muffled, as if he were trying to disguise it, but unmistakable.

A quick thought flashed in my mind: If he feels he needs to disguise his voice, he must be afraid I'll recognize it.

"If you want to say something to me," I said, "you've got to speak more clearly."

"Do you like your gift?"

"I hate cell phones."

"You'll like this one," he said. "Keep it with you at all times. You will be receiving important calls on it. It would be disastrous to miss a call. Be sure to keep the batteries charged. We wouldn't want your phone to go dead."

"Why don't you tell me what this is all about?" I said.

"All will become clear in good time, Mr. Coyne. Meanwhile, I must advise you not to contact any law enforcement agencies about your new cellular phone or about our communications on it, as you have about our previous exchanges."

"Why shouldn't I?" I said.

"You're going to have to trust me on that for the time being. If you don't do exactly as I tell you, you will, I promise you, profoundly regret it."

It occurred to me that if this man knew where I lived and how to get into my building, he probably knew where Evie lived, and Julie, too. "You're threatening me," I said.

"Of course I am."

"Okay," I said. "You've got my attention."

"You won't be able to trace my calls," he said, "so don't bother trying. It will probably occur to you to turn your new phone over to your law-enforcement friends, have their forensics experts dust it and trace it and take it apart. That would be a very bad idea. If they're at all competent, they will determine that it was stolen, they will find no incriminating fingerprints, and then they will refuse to give it back to you. So don't do it. You need to have it with you."

"Why?"

"This is between you and me, Mr. Coyne. Just the two of us. Understand?"

"It's not that complicated," I said. "Do I know you?"

"I'll be calling you again," he said. "You better answer."

"I wish you'd speak more clearly," I said. "I have trouble understanding you."

"Remember," he said. "Keep it with you twenty-four/seven. And be sure those batteries are charged up."

"All right," I said, "but—"

"Your new phone," said the voice, "formerly belonged to Walter Duffy. Bear that in mind if you're tempted to ignore my instructions." Then he disconnected.

NINETEEN

I got up, refilled my coffee mug, took it back to the kitchen table. Sat down. Lit a cigarette.

I looked at the cell phone. It was about the size of a half-empty pack of cigarettes. Its green eye kept winking at me. I wanted to poke it with a stick.

This was the phone that the voice had used to call me about the fires he was going to set. The phone he'd taken from Walt Duffy when he killed him.

His threat had been unmistakable. He'd murdered Walt Duffy and Ben Frye, not even to mention burned down at least two buildings. He was connected, unquestionably, to the Spotted Owl Liberation Front which, if this voice on the phone was to be believed, were not just a bunch of wayward, idealistic eco-freaks who thought they were the second coming of the Boston Tea Party.

I figured I had better take him seriously. But I had no idea what he wanted from me.

My first impulse, as a law-abiding citizen, a member of the bar, and a dutiful officer of the court—not to mention a man who'd been interrogated at length by an FBI agent and had promised to cooperate with her—was to call Roger Horowitz and turn the cell phone and the envelope it came in and the entire problem over to him.

My second, even stronger instinct was to take a deep breath and do nothing until I could give the entire situation some serious analysis.

I smoked another cigarette. Drained my coffee mug. Refilled it. Lit another cigarette.

Serious, focused analytical thought wasn't coming that easy to me. There was a tight, acidic ache in my stomach that kept getting in the way.

So I called J.W.

J.W. Jackson was a former Boston cop who got shot, retired young, took his pension, and went to live on Martha's Vineyard. He was a no-bullshit kind of guy, a Red Sox and Hemingway fan, a lover of the sea—everything I like and trust in a friend.

Once or twice every summer I fished the Vineyard beaches and jetties for striped bass and bluefish with J.W., and we got along well, even if he sneered at my little fly rod, called it a "toy," and disapproved of my practice of using sporting tackle and putting back the fish I caught. "Fish," he liked to say, "are the bounty of the sea. They should be respected. You disrespect them if you play with them after you hook them, because there's no reason to think they consider it play. If they can be caught, they should be killed and eaten, not thrown back. Throwing them back makes it a game that they don't participate in voluntarily. It's disrespectful. Eating them shows respect. Take me. I really enjoy shellfishing. But you don't see me throwing back a bushel of oysters after I've had all that fun gathering them, do you?"

We didn't agree on some things. But J.W. was a pretty smart man.

Zee, his gorgeous wife, answered the phone, and after I begged her to divorce J.W., abandon her children, and run off with me, and after she declined in such a gracious way that I almost believed she was tempted, she gave J.W. a holler.

A minute later he came on the line. "What's up? You comin' down? Blues have headed out to sea for the hot months, but the stripers have been hitting pretty good around Cape Pogue and Lobsterville. The kids keep asking when Uncle Brady's coming back. They expect you to sleep in their treehouse with them. They claim you promised last time you were here."

"I'd like to," I said. "Believe me. But that's not why I'm calling."

He hesitated. "What's this I'm hearing in your voice?"

"I got a problem."

"And you're calling me?" He laughed. "You call *me* with a problem, you got a real problem."

"I need a cop's perspective here."

"I am not a cop anymore," he said.

"That's exactly what I want. I can't talk about this with an actual cop. You don't have any duty to perform."

"None whatsoever," he said. "It's a grand lifestyle."

"Yeah, I envy you. You know that. Really, what I need is a friend's perspective. Okay?"

"Then, indeed, you came to the right place. Fire away."

So I told J.W. about the murders of Walt Duffy and Ben Frye, about the Meriwether Lewis letters, about the late-night phone calls and the fires, about getting mugged in my parking garage, about my session with Agent Randall, about the Spotted Owl Liberation Front.

And then I told him about how I got my new cell phone and the call I'd received on it. "I know I should get ahold of Agent Randall and dump it on her lap," I said. "But . . . ?" I left it as a question.

J.W. didn't say anything.

"I don't know what to do," I said finally.

"I can't tell you what to do," he said.

"I know," I said. "I've been trying to analyze it."

"Yeah," he said. "Sometimes analysis helps."

I laughed. "*Sometimes?*"

"Lemme ask you a question," he said.

"Ask away."

"When you analyze this thing, and when you conclude that you should turn the whole deal over to the FBI, how does it make you feel?"

"Feel?" I said. "It makes me feel . . . nervous. Jumpy. Unsettled."

"It doesn't feel right?"

"No, I guess not."

"You don't trust the cops, huh?"

"Oh, I guess I trust them. But . . ."

"But their priorities are different than yours," he said.

"This is the guy that already killed two people," I said. "He could kill anybody. Me, somebody I love . . ."

"A crazy person," said J.W. "Deranged."

"Oh, talking to him, he sounds sane enough. But he burns down buildings and kills people."

"That could be a pretty good definition of deranged," said J.W. "See, Brady, the problem with cops is, they're always looking for patterns and clues, trying to understand cause and effect, stuff like that. Rational stuff."

I found myself nodding. "I guess that's what's bothering me. It's not that I don't respect cops."

"They're not infallible," said J.W. "I oughta know. I was a cop myself. This guy who's calling you. He sounds smart and crazy. Nasty combination. You don't have any idea who it could be?"

"No," I said. "He seems to know a lot about me, though. And he disguises his voice. That probably means I'd recognize it if he spoke normally."

"He got into your apartment building. He was probably the one who swiped your wallet and your briefcase. He's studied up on you."

"I should do what he says, then," I said. "Leave the cops out of it. That what you're saying?"

"Is that what you want me to say?"

"Jesus, J.W."

"No, I mean it. You called me. What did you want from me?"

"Perspective, I guess."

"What if I told you flat out to call the cops, give 'em that cell phone, and wash your hands of the whole thing? Would you do it?"

I hesitated. "I don't know."

"Would you have regretted calling me in the first place if that's what I said?"

"Yeah, maybe."

"Because it doesn't feel right."

"I guess so."

"So you already know what you want to do, right?"

"I know how I feel," I said. "But I don't know if it's the right thing."

"Yes, you do," he said. "A very wise person once said to me: For most decisions, give it deep analytical thought, then do what your head tells you to do. But for really important decisions, you've got to listen to your heart."

"Do what feels right," I said.

"This is a pretty important decision, huh?"

"It sure feels like it," I said.

"Your heart's telling you to leave the cops out of it, right?"

"For now, at least. Yes."

"Then that's probably what you should do."

I blew out a long breath. "I don't know, man."

"Look," said J.W. "I'm not saying you shouldn't get some help. I'm just saying you've got to be damn careful whose help you ask for."

"I trust Horowitz."

"Yeah," said J.W., "except he's part of that FBI bunch. You say something to him, you can't expect him not to take it to that agent."

"I should just wait, then," I said. "Don't make a decision until I'm sure of it. Do nothing for now."

"Doing nothing is a decision, too," he said.

"It feels like the right decision."

"For what it's worth," said J.W., "if it was me, I think that's what my heart would be saying. I'd play it by ear. If this guy wanted to kill you, he'd've probably tried it by now. I studied up on these psychos when I was with the cops. For some reason, he's decided you're a challenge. It's personal for him. He's playing with you. The way you like to play with fish on that little toy fly rod of yours. He's got you hooked, and he's enjoying it, him pulling one way, you thrashing around, pulling back. Why not string him along for a while, see what you can figure out."

"String him along how?" I said.

"Psychos like this guy," said J.W., "once they got you beat, reeled you in and you're flopping on the beach with your gills flapping, gasping for air, they're done with you. You've got to give him a tussle. Don't give in to him. Don't lose your temper. It's a fine line. You don't want to piss him off. Do what he says, but don't give in to him. He wants to beat you mentally. That's his power game."

"It sounds like an extremely fine line," I said.

"Sure," he said. "You're angling for time, so to speak. Try to figure out where he's headed with all this. When the time comes to call in the cavalry, you'll know it."

"How will I know?"

"Keep paying attention to your heart," he said. "It's hard-wired to your subconscious. It picks up on all the subtle vibes, the tiny little nuances and clues that don't quite register with the rational part. Your heart knows things that your mind doesn't know."

"So who is the wise person who explained that to you?" I said.

"Zee," he said. "Wisest person I know. Listen. When this is over, you and Evie come down for a weekend. We'll catch us a keeper-sized striper, and if they're not biting, we'll rake some quahogs, dig some clams, make a pitcher of martinis, have us a feast from the sea."

"You're on."

"You better be careful," he said. "Zee would kill me if something happened because I gave you bad advice."

Henry and I walked to the office. I had the damn cell phone in my pants pocket. I was acutely aware of it. It was just a sliver of a thing and weighed about as much as my car keys, but it felt like I was lugging around a hand grenade that might explode at any minute.

Julie was sitting at her desk when we got there. She made a big point of looking at her watch.

"Don't start on me," I said.

"I didn't say anything."

I poured myself some coffee and took it into my office. Henry followed me.

I took the cell phone out of my pocket, put it on my desk, and sat down. I hoped I wasn't making a mistake, not telling Horowitz about it.

I lit a cigarette and called Evie at her office. When she answered, I said, "Your place tonight, right? Usual time?"

"Hi. Yes. Kinda busy here, Brady."

"Do you mind if we stick close to home this weekend?"

"Well, okay," she said. "But I thought . . ."

Earlier in the week we had talked about piling into my car on Saturday morning, cranking the sun roof open, loading up the CD player with a lot of good ol' rock 'n' roll, and spending the weekend driving the back roads of Vermont, finding an out-of-the-way bed-and-breakfast, prospecting for old hand-carved decoys in village antique shops, maybe stopping to cast a fly on one of those lovely little Vermont trout streams that spill out of the Green Mountains and seem to meander along the edge of every pasture and pass under every dirt road on their way to the Connecticut River.

"I got some things going on," I told her. "I'll explain when I see you."

"Fine," she said. "See you tonight. Gotta go."

I hung up. That was easy.

The damn cell phone sat there on my desk with its little green light blinking at me. I felt as if the man with the muffled voice was watching me through that green eye.

I tried to concentrate on the stack of papers Julie had left for me. It was slow going. I couldn't get that voice out of my head.

J.W. said the man with the voice was playing with me, enjoying it. Crazy, deranged, unpredictable, J.W. had called him. He killed people.

What did he want with me?

Julie came into my office around noon. When she came over to my desk to collect the papers I'd piled into the out box, she recoiled as if a weasel had poked its head out of its hole and snapped its teeth at her. "What the hell is *that*?" she said. She pointed at the cell phone.

"Oh, that," I said. "It's a telephone."

"It's a cellular phone," she said. "You hate cellular phones. Is it yours?"

"Sort of."

She grinned. "Well, finally. I never expected you to enter the twenty-first century. But I'll be darned if you haven't at least crawled into the twentieth. Congratulations."

"I haven't. Not really."

"Do you realize how much easier this will make my life?" she said. "I've been begging you to get a cell phone. What a lovely surprise."

"Julie," I said, "this is not for business."

"What are you talking about? That's exactly what cell phones are for."

"It's not really my phone, and I can't say any more about it."

"Are you carrying it around with you?"

I nodded.

"Well, give me the number."

"No. I can't do that."

"Why not?"

"Please," I said. "Forget about the cell phone. I didn't mean for you to see it."

She narrowed her eyes at me. "You're serious, aren't you?"

"Yes."

"You don't want to receive any calls on it?"

"No, I don't."

"Will you at least use it to make calls?"

"Absolutely not."

"Let me get this straight," she said. "You're carrying around this phone, but you're not going to use it? You intend to continue waiting in line at pay phones in courthouse lobbies? You will continue to be entirely out of touch when you're out walking or driving your car or off fishing somewhere? Is that it?"

"That's it," I said. "I like being out of touch. We've talked about this a hundred times."

"It doesn't make any sense."

I shrugged.

She picked up the phone.

"Put it down," I said.

She hastily put it back on my desk, then lifted her hands in a gesture of surrender.

"I'm sorry," I said. "I can't explain it to you."

Julie shook her head. "Sometimes you are a profound disappointment to me, Brady Coyne."

"Sometimes," I said, "I'm a profound disappointment to me, too."

TWENTY

The cell phone sat silently on my desk with its little green light winking, and after a while I stopped thinking about it. I spent the day catching up on phone calls and plowing through paperwork, and around four in the afternoon Julie tapped on my office door.

I called, "Enter," and she entered.

She dropped a stack of papers beside my elbow. "This is your weekend homework. Machines are shut off. Except the coffee. I made a new pot for you on the assumption that, since you took one day off and missed the better part of another day this week, you were planning to stay and get caught up."

I tapped the new stack of papers. "I don't have a briefcase," I said. "Can't bring this stuff home."

"That's a good one, Brady," she said. "Ho, ho. Do it before you leave, then."

I gave her a salute, and she rolled her eyes. She knew I wouldn't do any such thing.

After Julie left, I tried to return my concentration to my paperwork. Julie was right. It had piled up during the week, and if I were a conscientious attorney, I'd either stay there at my desk until it was done, or I'd bring it home with me and clean it up over the weekend. That's what conscientious attorneys did.

I flipped through the stack of papers. There was nothing urgent. Nothing that couldn't wait 'til Monday.

I hadn't worked hard all my life because I wanted to end up being a conscientious attorney. I'd expended all that effort and energy so that I could become a lazy attorney, and I'd succeeded rather well.

I stuck it out until five, then said the hell with it. I straightened out the corners on those stacks of papers, stood up, stretched, went out to the reception area, turned off the coffee machine, and rinsed out the pot.

Then I went back into my office, picked up the cell phone, and slipped the damn green-eyed albatross into my pants pocket. I stood there for a minute. I recognized a familiar tension in my gut.

Listen to your heart, J.W. had said.

I listened, and my heart told me to go over to the safe behind the framed photograph of Billy and Joey. So I did. I pushed the photograph aside, spun the dial, opened the safe, reached in around the envelope that held Walt Duffy's Meriwether Lewis letters, and took out my Smith & Wesson .38 revolver.

Once upon a time I killed two men with that gun. They were both evil men, murderers who would have killed me and the women who were with me, and in both cases I pulled the trigger and shot those men in the chest at point-blank range, and I did it without compunction or hesitation or regret.

If I ever confronted the man with the muffled voice, the man who had killed Walt Duffy and Ben Frye and who set off explosions in buildings, I guessed I could shoot him without compunction, hesitation, or regret, too.

I always kept my .38 loaded with the hammer down on an empty cylinder. If I cocked it, the cylinder would rotate. If I then pulled the trigger, the hammer would fall on a live cartridge.

A .38 hollow-point from point-blank range makes an impressive hole in a man's chest.

I stuck the gun in my jacket pocket, and its comforting bulk seemed to neutralize the barely noticeable weight of the vile little cell phone in my pants pocket. Yin and yang.

I locked up, and Henry and I headed home. We took my favorite route down Newbury Street, across Arlington, through the Public Garden and across Charles Street, and we were approaching the duck pond on the Common when a little beep sounded in my pants.

I glanced around. It was five-thirty on a pretty June Friday afternoon, and the Boston Common swarmed with people. As usual, there were clumps of Japanese tourists snapping pictures of each other, college-aged kids playing Frisbee, secretaries and loan officers striding along in their short skirts and high heels, investment bankers and lawyers lugging home their weekend briefcases, dog owners allowing themselves to be tugged around on leashes, homeless men tossing popcorn to the pigeons and drinking from bottles in paper bags.

Maybe it was my imagination, but it seemed that all of them—except the bums—had a hand pressed against an ear.

They all seemed to be frowning and gesticulating with their empty hands and talking intently, as if they were very important people and the fate of the world depended on the words they chose to yell into their cellular phones.

My pants beeped again. I reached into my pocket, fished out the little phone, and flipped it open. "Yes," I said.

"A lovely afternoon for a stroll on the Common, isn't it?"

The sonofabitch was watching me!

I looked around. Dozens of men were talking on cell phones. Any one of them could have been the voice.

"Why don't you come over here," I said, "so we can talk face-to-face."

He chuckled. "All in good time, Mr. Coyne. I simply called to wish you a happy weekend."

"Thanks."

"You'll be hearing from me again," he said. "Be sure to keep those batteries charged."

"You bet."

"Oh," he said, "and when you get home, why don't you take a peek under your car."

"What do you—?"

But he'd disconnected.

I walked the rest of the way home peering over my shoulder with my hand in my jacket pocket cradling my .38.

Henry and I took the stairs down into my parking garage. I kept my hand in the pocket with my gun and went over to my car, which was parked in its reserved slot against the green concrete wall. Even in the middle of the day, the garage was lit only by dim orange bulbs high in the ceiling, so that it always seemed like nighttime down there.

I wondered if the voice had attached some kind of bomb to the undercarriage of my car. He blew up buildings. I figured he could blow up an automobile if he wanted to.

But why tell me about it?

I knew the answer: To show me he could do it. To impress me with his control over me. To harass me, to confuse me, to frighten me.

But why would he want to do that?

Well, I figured sooner or later I'd get my answer. I'd have to wait. For now, he was in charge.

I knelt down on the concrete floor and peered underneath my car. I saw instantly what was there.

It was my briefcase, tucked behind the left rear tire.

I slid it out, brushed it off, and put it on the hood of my car. My treasured Harlan Fiske Stone briefcase.

Maybe the bomb was in the briefcase.

Well, the hell with it. I couldn't live my life wondering if everything I touched would explode.

I held my breath, popped the latch on the briefcase, and peered inside. It was full of papers. I took them out and riffled through them. Photocopies of legal documents. All the stuff that had been there when I was mugged. As near as I could tell, nothing had been added and nothing had been removed.

When I started to put the papers back, I saw that my wallet was in the bottom of the briefcase. I opened it. There was cash in it. I didn't bother counting it, since I didn't know how much had been there in the first place. Credit cards, membership cards, other cards—all there.

Hm.

Henry and I took the elevator up to my apartment. I dropped my briefcase in its usual spot just inside the door, and went directly to the kitchen, where I poured a double shot of Rebel Yell into a square glass. I added two ice cubes and took it into my bedroom.

Henry came along behind me and flopped down on the floor.

I put the cell phone and the revolver and the glass on my bedside table, peeled off my office clothes, and pulled on a pair of jeans and a T-shirt.

Then I lit a cigarette, bunched up the pillows, and lay back on my bed. I balanced my drink on my chest and alternated sipping and smoking until I decided what I had to do.

I picked up my regular plug-in portable phone and hit the speed-dial number for Evie.

She answered on the fourth ring. She sounded a little breathless.

"Hi, baby," I said.

"Oh, Brady. You caught me just stepping into the shower. I'm gonna be all clean and squeaky and sweet-smelling. You're on your way, I hope?"

"I've got to call off our weekend, honey."

She was silent for a moment. Then she said, "Well, okay."

"I'm sorry," I said.

"You mean the whole weekend?"

"Yes."

"What's wrong, Brady?"

"I can't explain it right now."

"It's not that you—that you don't want to see me, is it?"

"Not hardly. I want desperately to see you."

"Because," she said, "if that's it, you've got to tell me. We've agreed about that."

"That's not it. I love you."

She laughed softly. "Well, me, too."

"I'm really sorry," I said again.

"I know."

I hung up the phone, drained my glass, picked up the cell phone, hefted it in my hand. I had to fight the urge to fling it against the wall.

God *damn* him.

I took my glass to the kitchen, hesitated, and put it in the sink. I figured that was enough booze for one evening. I wanted to remain alert.

I was eating a fried-egg sandwich out on my balcony, watching darkness gather over the harbor and feeling lonely and angry and frustrated and altogether sorry for myself, when Henry, who was sitting beside me making eyes at my sandwich, started growling. I told him to shush, and when he did, I thought I heard a soft scratching sound coming from the front door.

I went in, paused to listen, then picked up my .38 from the kitchen table where I'd left it and tiptoed to the door.

Henry poked it with his nose and growled. I told him to go lie down, which he did, reluctantly.

There it was again. The scratching sound. It was coming from the other side of my door.

Someone was trying to get in. Picking my lock.

I held the revolver behind my back with my right hand. With my left, I slowly turned the knob.

Then I yanked the door open.

Evie was standing there with her key in her hand. She had a big carryall slung over her shoulder, and she was wrapped in a trenchcoat.

"Hi," she whispered.

"Honey," I said, "I thought I told you—"

"Banyon's Escorts, at your service." She gave me a half-lidded smile and opened her coat.

She appeared to be clean and squeaky and sweet-smelling all over.

Twenty-one

I glanced up and down the hallway, then grabbed Evie's arm and tugged her inside.

She leaned back against the door with her trenchcoat hanging open.

"Jesus," I said. "You're naked."

"Yes," she said. "But I am discreet." She saw Henry sitting there and closed her coat. "Stop peeking," she said to him.

"You shouldn't be here, honey," I said. "I told you that."

"It sounded to me like you had a problem."

I shrugged.

"You've got to share it with me," she said. "That's our deal." She reached out her hand, then jerked it back and pointed. "What the hell is *that*?"

I realized I had my .38 dangling from my hand. "It's my gun."

She frowned at me. "That bad, huh?"

"I don't want you involved."

"I am involved," she said. "I'm involved with you. Put the gun down, okay?"

"I thought you were somebody trying to break in." I went into the living room, put the gun on the coffee table, and sat on the sofa.

Evie sat beside me. "It wasn't that long ago," she said, "when I was the one with the problem. I kept telling you to stay out of it. You refused, if you recall. You said my problems were your problems. Share the good stuff, share the problems, you said. That's what loving each other means. Remember?"

I nodded. "But this is different."

"Why, because you're a big strong independent man and I'm just a weak flighty girl? Girls need help but men don't? Is that it?"

I shook my head. "It's dangerous."

"Most problems are dangerous in one way or another." She leaned her head on my shoulder and put her hand on my leg. "I do believe you're frightened," she said.

"I'm not sure that's the word for it."

"Anxious?"

"Definitely."

She put her arms around my neck and kissed me on the mouth. "I bet you could use a nice massage, hm?"

"I don't remember calling for an escort," I said.

She was nuzzling my throat. "A friend sent me," she murmured.

"How much?"

"It's on the house, baby. You couldn't afford me." She leaned back and looked into my eyes. "Leave the gun, though, huh? I don't do kinky."

An hour or so later, Evie and I were lying on my bed passing a cigarette back and forth. Henry was curled up on the pile of clothes I'd left on the floor.

"I'm sorry, honey," I said.

She kissed my bare shoulder. "Nothing to apologize for."

"I'm a dud."

"You're my sexy man."

"Usually, the minute I see you . . ."

"It happens," she said. "Really. Forget about it."

"You think I'm getting old?"

She chuckled. "I think you've got something on your mind. You're holding it in."

"Holding it in, huh?" I said. "Thank you, Dr. Freud."

"You've got to let it out. Come on, sweetie. What is it?"

"I don't want to involve you."

"I'm already involved," she said. "I'm with you, and I'm not going away. Talk to me."

So I took a deep breath and told Evie about the man with the muffled voice, the murders and the fires, my hunt for Ethan Duffy, my encounters with Detective Mendoza and Lieutenant Keeler, my session with the FBI, the Spotted Owl Liberation Front, the mysterious appearance of the cell phone, and my conversation with J.W. Jackson. I told her how the cell phone rang while I was walking across the Common, how the voice knew where I was, and how he was the one who'd mugged me, taken my wallet and my briefcase, and then returned them.

"See," I said, "he's watching me. He knows what I'm doing. Like J.W. said, he's toying with me. He gets off on it. He probably knows you're here now. That's why I wanted to keep you out of it. He's dangerous, unpredictable, probably psychotic. I don't want anybody else to get drawn into this. Especially you." I hesitated. "I feel like he's watching us right now. Maybe that's why . . ."

"That's impossible," said Evie.

"I know," I said. "But it's how I feel."

Evie took my cigarette from my fingers, dragged on it, and blew a plume of smoke at the ceiling. "J.W. was wrong," she said softly. "You should turn the whole thing over to the police."

"No," I said, "I think J.W. was right. Somehow, this guy would know it the minute I talked to the cops. He'd certainly know if I didn't have that damn cell phone with me. If he called and I didn't answer? It would infuriate him, and there's no telling what he'd do. This way at least he feels like he's in control. He's having fun with it. He's bound to make some kind of slip. That's what I'm waiting for. Meanwhile, I'm trying to be really careful."

"Like canceling our weekend together," she said.

"It seemed prudent, yes. It still does. You should leave."

"No way," said Evie.

We lay there quietly for a few minutes, looking up at the ceiling.

Then Evie said, "We really are all alone here, you know. Just big strong you and little old bare-naked me."

"And Henry," I said. "Don't forget Henry."

"We've been alone with Henry before," she said. "His presence has not deterred us. Do you feel any better?"

"I guess so," I said. "Telling you about it, sharing it with you, getting it off my chest, it's kind of a relief. I don't like holding things back from you."

Her hand slid up the inside of my bare leg. "Oh, my," she whispered. "You *do* feel better."

I was slogging through the murk of a bleak senseless dream about rain and mud when Evie prodded me. "Hey," she said. "Hey, wake up."

"What?"

"Your phone."

"Huh?"

"Your cell phone. It's ringing."

"Shit. I don't hear anything. Where is it?"

"You left it on the coffee table to recharge it, remember?"

"What time is it?"

"Quarter of six."

"Let it fuckin' ring," I grumbled.

She poked me again. "You better get it."

I squeezed my eyes shut for a minute, then blinked them open. "Yeah, okay."

I stumbled my way into the living room. The phone's green light was a beacon. It beeped again.

I picked it up, flipped the lid, and said, "What do you want?"

"Rise and shine," he said.

"I'm up."

"I'm waiting for you to thank me."

"What'm I supposed to thank you for?" I said.

"Returning your wallet and your briefcase."

"Oh, right," I said. "Thank you so much."

"You're entirely welcome," he said. "Now get dressed and go down to your car."

Then he was gone.

I put the phone down and went back into the bedroom. Evie was sitting up in bed rubbing her eyes. Henry opened his eyes, but didn't bother uncurling.

"I've got to go out for a little while," I said.

"What's going on?"

"Go back to sleep. I won't be long."

"Where are you going?"

"I don't know."

"What do you mean?"

"I'm supposed to go to my car. That's all I know."

"I'm coming with you."

I kissed her. "Absolutely not. You stay here. I'll be all right."

"That man again?"

"Yes."

She brushed her hair off her face. "I'm not going to let you go by yourself."

"Please don't argue with me," I said. "Stay with Henry."

"Brady, damn it—"

"Tell you what," I said. "I'll leave Horowitz's number with you. If I'm not back in—" I glanced at my watch "—in four hours, and if you haven't heard from me, call him. That would be about ten-thirty. Okay?"

"I don't like this," she said.

"Me, neither. I'd rather snuggle back in beside you. I'll be all right. Don't worry."

"Of course I'll worry."

"I know you will. That's why I wish you'd stayed home this weekend." I kissed her again. "Make sure to lock up behind me."

Evie watched while I pulled on my jeans and a T-shirt and my sneakers, then followed me out into the living room. I wrote Horowitz's cell phone number on a piece of paper and gave it to her. I found my windbreaker in the closet and put the phone in one pocket and the .38 in the other. Then I poured some of yesterday's coffee into a car mug, gave it a minute in the microwave, made sure I had a full pack of cigarettes, and turned to Evie. "I'll be back."

She nodded.

"Don't worry, okay?"

"Fat chance," she said.

I kissed her, went out, waited to hear her lock the door behind me, then took the elevator down to the parking garage.

I went to my car, unlocked it, and slid into the front seat.

Now what?

I'd smoked half a cigarette and taken a few sips of coffee when the cell phone beeped. "You in your car?" he said.

"Yes."

"Alone?"

"Yes."

"Good. Can you find your way to Storrow Drive by yourself."

"Yes."

"Do it, then." And he disconnected.

There were virtually no other cars on the streets at seven on this Saturday morning. I swung around Commercial Street to Causeway, took Cambridge to the rotary, and less than fifteen minutes after I'd pulled out of my garage I was heading outbound on Storrow Drive with the Charles River on my right. A few carefree little sailboats were skidding across the water, and swarms of early-bird joggers were bouncing along the paths that traced the shoreline.

The phone beeped.

"You're at the Esplanade," he said, not as if it were a question, but something he knew.

"Passing it now."

"Take the Harvard Bridge across the river." He clicked off.

Was he tailing me? I glanced in my rearview mirror. I saw just one car, a dark SUV about fifty yards behind me. I slowed down to see what it would do.

It passed me, moving fast, and kept going. A newish Explorer, dark green, Massachusetts plates. I caught only the first two numbers and got just a quick glimpse of the driver. He was wearing a baseball cap. It could have been a short-haired woman.

Up ahead was the Harvard Bridge. The Explorer didn't turn onto it.

I did, and just as I was crossing the river, the phone beeped again. "Don't hang up 'til I tell you to," he said. "Stay on Mass. Ave."

"Okay," I said.

He said nothing. I kept the phone to my ear, trying to hear something significant in his silence—ambulance sirens, church bells, train whistles, construction noises, music from a car radio, some telling background sound that in a spy movie would turn out to be a plot-turning clue. But all that came through the phone was soft ambient static.

"You still there?" I said.

The voice chuckled. "I'm here." Another minute of silence, then, "Up ahead on the right you can see a Dunkin' Donuts."

"I see it."

"Take the drive-through. Buy yourself a large black coffee and a donut. What kind of donuts do you like?"

"Jesus Christ," I said.

"Plain, I'll bet. You strike me as a plain donut kind of guy. Get yourself a plain donut, too. We want you strong and alert. Disconnect now."

I did as I was told, and just as I was pulling away from the drive-through window, the phone beeped.

"Did you eat your donut?"

"Not yet."

"Eat it while you drive," said the voice. "Pull back onto Mass. Ave. Go right. Check your odometer. In one-point-four miles you'll come to a brick Catholic church on your right. St. Lucia's. After you pass it, find a place on the street to park. Now disconnect."

I put the phone on the seat beside me, took a bite of my donut, and continued on Mass. Ave.

When I came to the church, I realized where we were going. Vintage Vinyl, Conrad Henshall's record shop, was almost directly across the street from St. Lucia's Catholic church.

I found an empty space on the street, pulled into it, and turned off the engine. I finished my donut, lit a cigarette, sipped some coffee.

The phone beeped.

"I'm here," I said.

"It should look familiar to you. Keep me on the line while I tell you what I want you to do. Get out of the car and cross the street."

The voice was still too muffled and distorted to recognize. I wondered if it belonged to Conrad Henshall himself.

I felt ridiculous, crossing Massachusetts Avenue near Central Square in Cambridge early on a Saturday morning with a cell phone pressed against my ear.

"Okay," I said. "I've crossed the street."

"You're in front of the record store?"

"Yes."

"To the left of it you see an alley. Walk down there. At the end, go right. In back of the store you'll see a door. Stop there. Don't disconnect."

It was a narrow alley, barely wide enough for me to pass around the trash barrels. I kept one hand in my pocket, gripping my .38. Where the alley ended, it intersected with another somewhat wider alley. I turned right onto it and came upon a doorway with a little wooden stoop under a small overhang.

"I'm here at the door," I said into the phone.

"Enter, Mr. Coyne. It's not locked. Ascend the stairs, open the door at the top, and go ahead inside. Don't disconnect."

I turned the knob on the door and went in. The stairway was steep and lit only by the dirty glass window on the door. It smelled faintly of cat piss. As near as I could tell, it led to a room directly over the record shop.

I took my gun out of my pocket, cocked the hammer, and climbed the stairs. At the top, I pushed open the door, held my gun at my hip pointing ahead of me, and went in. I was standing in a kitchen. Peeling brick-red linoleum floor, refrigerator that had once been white but now was yellowish, matching gas stove, sink with some pots and pans in it, rickety wooden table with four spindly wooden chairs around it.

The place appeared to be deserted. I let down the hammer on my revolver and put it back into my pocket.

"You there, Mr. Coyne?"

"I'm standing in the kitchen."

"Close the door."

When I turned to close the door behind me, I saw that a poster was tacked on its inside. I'd seen that poster before. It was a childish drawing of an owl with the big red letters S O L F under it.

"Is this Conrad Henshall's apartment?" I said into the phone. "Are you Henshall?"

"I could be anybody, couldn't I?" he said. "Look on the table, Mr. Coyne. Tell me what you see."

I went over and looked. "I see a videotape. Also a sugar bowl and salt and pepper shakers."

"Guess what we're interested in?"

"I'd guess the tape," I said, "but maybe there's a prize in the sugar bowl."

"Pick up the tape," he said, "and take it through the doorway in front of you. You'll see a television set. It's very important that you do exactly what I tell you, Mr. Coyne. Are you with me?"

"I'm with you." I went into the other room. "I see the TV."

"Please play the tape. Then you'll receive your next instructions. Isn't this fun?"

Don't lose your temper, J.W. had said. *Don't give in to him. He's toying with you, like a fish on a hook. Don't let him wear you down.*

I took a deep breath. "I've had more fun, I've had less fun," I said. "This is mainly annoying."

"It gets better," he said. "Play the tape. Keep me on the line."

I was in a tiny living room, maybe twelve by twelve. One sooty window looked across the alley to someone else's sooty window. The television sat on a table against one wall, and across from it was an overstuffed chair with a wooden coffee table in front of it.

I put the phone on the table, went over to the TV, turned it on, slid the tape into the VCR, hit the "play" button, and sat in the chair to watch.

There was a minute of fuzz. Then the owl image appeared on the screen. Then it switched to a picture of the front page of the Boston *Globe* sports section. The headline read, "Manny Helps Sox Over Tigers, 8–3." The subhead said, "Sox open homestand on high note."

The date was Saturday, June 27. That was today's date. I guessed it was the bulldog edition, the one that hits the streets at about three in the morning.

As I looked, the camera slowly pulled back until I could see that somebody was holding up the newspaper. It kept pulling back until the person's face was revealed.

It was Ethan Duffy. His eyes were covered with a strip of duct tape, but it was unmistakably Ethan.

I caught just a glimpse of the bare wall behind him before the red letters S O L F filled the screen.

Then the fuzz returned.

The entire show lasted no more than two minutes.

I picked up the phone. "You've got Ethan?"

"As you see, Mr. Coyne."

"What do you want?"

"All in good time. I want you to stop the tape and rewind it. Do it now."

When I hit the stop button, a Roadrunner cartoon appeared on the television screen. The tape took about ten seconds to rewind. "Now what?" I said.

"Hit the record button."

"To erase the tape."

"Naturally."

I did what he said. "It's recording Wile E. Coyote and the Roadrunner," I told him.

"Appropriate, don't you think?"

"Beep-beep," I said. "Tell me what you want with me. I'll cooperate. Let Ethan go."

"Be patient, Mr. Coyne. I'll contact you when the time comes. Now it's time for you to go home. I don't need to remind you that if any officers of the law come snooping around Vintage Vinyl this weekend, you will have young Mr. Duffy's fate on your conscience."

"If you'll just—"

But he was gone.

I shoved the phone into my pants pocket and made a quick survey of the apartment. A tiny bedroom with a single window looking out on the alley held a single bed and a chest of drawers. The blankets on the bed were thrown back, as if it had been slept in. The drawers were empty.

In the bathroom there was a half-empty tube of toothpaste on the side of the sink and a bath towel draped over the shower rod. I sniffed the towel. It was dry and smelled faintly sour.

I went out to the kitchen and looked in the refrigerator. A cardboard carton of orange juice, a couple of apples, a hunk of cheddar cheese, some leftover pizza wrapped in aluminum foil. The juice had not gone bad, and neither the cheese nor the pizza had grown mold.

Somebody had been staying here recently.

Ethan Duffy, I assumed.

He wasn't here any longer. He was somewhere else, and he had duct tape over his eyes.

Twenty-two

When I walked into my apartment, I found Evie and Henry sitting out on my balcony watching the boat traffic on the harbor. I lifted Evie's hair and kissed the back of her neck, then sat in the aluminum folding chair beside her.

"Did you give Henry some breakfast?"

"Yes," she said. "And we took a long walk. Now tell me where you've been, what's going on."

"Ethan's been kidnapped."

"*Kidnapped?*"

I nodded.

She grabbed my arm. "Oh, Brady. What happened?"

I told her.

"Duct tape over his eyes?" she said when I finished.

I nodded.

"But that's good, isn't it?" she said. "Doesn't that mean the kidnapper doesn't want Ethan to see his face? That he's going to let him go?"

"I don't know," I said. "It might mean that. It might just be to keep him under control."

"And you haven't figured out who this person is?"

I shook my head. "I thought it might be Conrad Henshall, the guy who owns the record shop. If so, he's got a lot of balls, sending me to the apartment right over the shop. But I can't recognize the voice. Maybe it's nobody I know. Maybe it's just some SOLF crackpot. Or maybe it's got nothing to do with SOLF."

"But why? Why kidnap that boy? And why drag you into it this way?"

I sighed. "I don't know."

"What are you going to do?"

I shook my head.

"You can't—"

"I know," I said. "J.W. said I should listen to my heart. Now both my heart and my head are telling me I should call Horowitz."

"It's about time."

"If I do this wrong," I said, "Ethan's doomed."

"What's this person want out of you?"

"I don't know. Maybe he's just enjoying his game. Maybe when he gets sick of it, or when he thinks he's won, he'll kill Ethan."

"Call your friend Horowitz," said Evie. "He'll know what to do."

I went inside, got my portable telephone from the bedroom, took it to the sofa, and dialed Horowitz's cell phone.

He answered with his usual grumpy, "What?"

"I've got to talk to you."

"What about?"

"Murders. Fires. Spotted owls. Kidnapping."

"Huh? Kidnapping?"

"Ethan Duffy."

"How do you know?"

"Trust me, he's kidnapped."

"Okay. I'll call Randall, we'll get together at One Central Plaza in an hour. I'll send a car around for you."

"No good," I said. "I'm being, um, monitored. This has got to be just me and you."

"Christ, Coyne, I can't do that. I'm supposed to—"

I hung up on him, put the phone on the coffee table, lit a cigarette, and waited.

Five minutes later he called me back. "Okay, you got my attention. How do you want to play it?"

"No FBI. Not until you and I agree that they can safely be brought into it."

"Yeah, okay. I knew you were gonna say that. So I lose my job. Fuck it. What's going on?"

"Yesterday morning my dog barks at the door," I said. "I open it. On the floor there's a big padded envelope with my name on it. I bring it inside and open it. There's a cellular phone inside. Then it rings. It's that same guy."

"The one who called you about those fires? He's got the Duffy kid?"

"Yes. He tells me to carry this phone with me all the time. Says it used to be Walt Duffy's, which means he's the one who killed Walt and has been calling to tell me about the fires he's going to set. He keeps calling me on it, telling me what he wants me to do. Yanking me around. Bastard's having fun with it. I'm pretty sure he's following me around. He seems to know where I am, what I'm doing, all the time. So this morning—"

"Okay, Coyne. That's enough."

"But—"

"Shut up," he said. "Lemme think."

I shut up.

Horowitz was silent for a minute. Then he said, "How about a ball game this afternoon? The state cops have season tickets at Fenway. Four boxes right by the Red Sox dugout. Nice seats. Detroit's in town."

"Can you get us into those seats?"

"Lemme get back to you," he said, and then he hung up on me.

He called back about an hour later. "Section seventeen," he said, "row three, seats one through four. First pitch at one-oh-five. Wakefield's on the hill. There'll be two tickets waiting for you at the window. Bring Evie. I'm bringing my wife."

"I better not see Randall or Elliot there," I said, "or Mendoza or Keeler, either."

"Don't worry," said Horowitz. "But I wouldn't worry about being seen."

"Why not?"

"Game's sold out. Standing room only. Your friend can't get in."

"That's no consolation," I said. "This guy seems to be everywhere, know everything. We've still got to be careful."

"Oh, I'll be careful," he said. "You're the amateur. You're the one I worry about. Bring your cell phone with you."

Evie and I decided to walk to Kenmore Square, take advantage of the damn San Diego weather while it lasted. We left my apartment a little after noon. When I told Henry he couldn't come to the ball game with us because we didn't have an extra ticket, he climbed up on the sofa, closed his eyes, and pretended to ignore us.

I carried the cell phone in my pants pocket. I left my .38 home.

We had just walked through the Public Garden and crossed Arlington Street when the phone beeped. I fished it out. "I'm here," I said.

"Where are you going?" said the voice.

"Red Sox game."

"Nice day for it," he said, and disconnected.

I glanced over my shoulder. "Sonofabitch is around here somewhere," I muttered.

"He wanted to know where we were going?"

"Yes."

"He thought you'd be home waiting for him to call," she said, "all worried and frightened. Instead, you're going to a ball game with your girlfriend. You've got him off balance."

"You think that's a good thing?"

"Let's hope so."

The streets and sidewalks around Kenmore Square were jammed with Red Sox fans descending on Fenway from all over New England. Men with pushcarts hawked boiled hot dogs and roasted unshelled peanuts and Italian sausages and Red Sox memorabilia at prices that were, they claimed, half of what you'd pay inside the park. There were whispering scalpers, too, with tickets you could buy for twice their face value.

I bought official Red Sox caps for Evie and me. We'd need the visors. The afternoon sun would be in our faces sitting on the first-base side. Evie wanted peanuts, so I bought us each a bag. We'd get our beers inside.

Just a happy couple at the old ball game on a picturebook New England Saturday afternoon in June. That was us.

I picked up the tickets Horowitz had left at the window, and as Evie and I waited inside to pass through the turnstile, I slipped the cell phone to her. "Tuck it into your bag," I said. "If it beeps, give it to me."

I was about ten years old the first time I walked up the runway and got my first look inside Fenway Park. It was like the first time I saw the Grand Canyon. It gave me the shivers. The grass was as lush as an emerald carpet, mown in a geometric crisscross pattern and shimmering in the summer sunshine. The foul lines were absolutely white and perfectly straight, and the infield dirt was golden orange. And out there was the Green Monster, and the old-fashioned scoreboard where they posted the numbers by hand, and the flagpole in center field, and the bullpens in front of the bleachers in right, and Pesky's Pole in the corner. Legendary places, storybook places. The Babe had won a World Series for the Red Sox here, and Ted Williams, who'd done everything else, hadn't.

When Evie and I walked up the ramp, I got the shivers all over again.

We stepped out into the sunshine. An usher asked for our tickets and led us down to our seats. Horowitz was sitting on the aisle with his wife, Alyse, beside him. The usher spoke to them, and they stood up to let Evie and me sidestep past them.

I went in first. Evie sat beside Alyse, putting as much distance as possible between Horowitz and me.

I decided to assume that the guy with the voice had bought himself a scalped ticket. I imagined that he had binoculars, and wherever he was in the ballpark, he had his eye on me.

Whether it was true or not, it was how I intended to play it with Horowitz.

I leaned my head to Evie and said, "That's Mrs. Horowitz beside you. Her name is Alyse. Say hi to her as if she were some stranger. Tell her to tell Roger that we should assume we're being watched."

While Evie spoke to Alyse, I said hello to the guy on my right. He had his son with him. It was their first-ever father-son trip to Fenway, he told me. The boy looked about ten. He had his glove with him, hoping for a foul ball. Reminded me of me, many years ago, with my father.

The groundskeepers were raking the infield. Some of the players were playing catch in front of the dugout. From where we were sitting next to the field, we could see their faces. They all looked too young to be millionaires.

"Roger," I said, keeping my eyes on the field.

"Talk to me," said Horowitz.

"Evie," I said, "pretend I'm talking to you, okay?"

She turned to me, smiled, and kissed my cheek. "This is deliciously clandestine," she said. "If it weren't so scary, it would be kinda fun."

Without once looking at him, I told Horowitz everything that had happened since the arrival of the cell phone. I paused while we stood for the national anthem, then continued after we sat down again.

"Evie," said Horowitz when I finished, "slip that damn phone to Alyse, okay?"

She did it so smoothly that even sitting beside her, I almost missed it.

At the end of the second inning Horowitz stood and walked up the aisle. He was back five minutes later with two beers. He gave one of them to Alyse.

"I checked out your phone," he said. "As I figured, he erased the old messages and the speed-dial numbers and the memory numbers. No bugs, fortunately. It's clean."

"Bugs?" I said.

"It occurred to me that he could've slipped one of those little listening devices into it somewhere. They're about the size of a dime. Used to be, only the FBI, CIA, those guys had 'em. Now you can get 'em on the Internet, for Christ's sake. Listen to everything you say whether you're talking on the phone or not."

"Christ," I muttered. "That would've been disastrous."

"Yeah," he said. "You should've thought of it. Alyse, honey, give this to Evie, huh?"

From the corner of my eye I saw Alyse hold the phone beside her leg. Evie took it, and it disappeared into her bag.

Horowitz sat back and sipped his beer. We watched the game. He didn't say anything.

"What now?" I said to him finally.

"Relax. We've got the whole ball game. You're worried this nutcake is watching us? Pretend you're having a good time."

The Red Sox scored a couple of runs in the sixth inning, and when we stood up to cheer, Horowitz said, "Vintage Vinyl? That's the name of that place, right? In Central Square?"

"Yes, but don't go near it. He'll know."

"I got the picture, Coyne."

"No cops dressed like exterminators," I said. "This guy's smart."

"You called me, remember?" he said. "Now you've got to trust my judgment."

"If anything happens to Ethan . . ."

He sat down and drained his cup of Fenway Park beer.

At the end of the inning, I stood up. "Gotta go pee," I told Evie. "Want something? They stop selling beer after the seventh inning."

"Just a Coke, please," she said. "Ballpark beer tastes like warm urine."

I sidled past Horowitz and started up the aisle. I was hoping he'd follow me and stand beside me at the porcelain trough that passes for a urinal in the Fenway Park men's rooms so we could talk some more.

But he didn't.

I returned with two Cokes. As I slid past Horowitz, I said, "What else can I tell you?"

"Nothin'," he said.

I sat down and handed a Coke to Evie. I leaned toward her and said, for Horowitz's benefit, "So now what happens?"

"Just do what you've been doing," he said. "He calls you, you call me. And don't say anything about this to anybody, understand?"

"Nobody?"

"Nobody," he said.

The Red Sox retired the Tigers in the ninth inning and the game was over, a satisfying one-run victory for the Old Towne Team. Everybody in the ballpark stood up to cheer as the players trotted off the field.

When Evie and I turned to leave, Horowitz and Alyse were gone.

TWENTY-THREE

That evening after supper, Evie and I took our coffee out onto the balcony. The sun was setting somewhere behind us, and over the harbor, the light was fading from the sky. The breeze had shifted. Now it was coming in off the water, and it tasted salty and moist. The bell buoy in the channel was clanging hollowly the way it does when the sea kicks up and the air becomes damp and heavy. Out toward the eastern horizon over the airport, dark clouds were boiling and churning and moving toward us.

"Gonna have some weather," I said. "Taste it?"

"Weather?" said Evie. "We always have weather."

"To us old-time New Englanders," I said, "weather means bad weather. Duck hunters, they always hope for weather. Wind, rain, cold, drop in barometric pressure. Weather makes the ducks restless, gets them flying."

"Makes me restless, too," she said.

We sat there silently, watching the airplanes take off and land at Logan Airport while the cloudbank moved in on us, like someone was slowly pulling a giant black blanket over our heads.

"You're worried, aren't you?" said Evie.

"Sure."

"About Ethan."

I nodded.

"Because that person hasn't called?"

"Yeah," I said. "I keep thinking I shouldn't have involved Horowitz. That the guy with the voice knows. I'm worried I blew it for Ethan."

"You did the right thing," she said.

"We'll see."

"Detective Horowitz will handle it. He knows what to do."

"I hope so."

"No matter how it turns out," she said, "you did the right thing, bringing him in on it."

"If it turns out bad," I said, "that will be no consolation."

A few minutes later, Evie said, "He's teasing you. The man on the cell phone."

"With his silence, you mean."

"Yes. Trying to spook you."

"He's doing a damn good job of it."

We watched the darkness close in on the harbor. The wind picked up. It was moist and salty, and as we sat there with our bare feet propped up on the railing, thunder began grumbling in the distance. A minute later a fat raindrop splatted on my ankle. Then a sudden bolt of lightning zigzagged across the dark sky, a quick flare that momentarily illuminated the gray wind-chopped water and the rocking boats at their moorings below us. The images remained in my eyes for an instant after the burst of light was gone. A few seconds later came a crash of thunder.

"Shall we go inside?" I said to Evie.

"No. I love thunderstorms."

"We'll get wet," I said.

She patted my bare leg. We were both wearing shorts and T-shirts. "So we get wet. It'll feel good."

She groped for my hand and held onto it, and we watched the rain come sheeting across the water and in on us. We were drenched instantly. The air temperature plummeted, and soon we were shivering. I stood up, and Evie did, too, and we hugged each other there on my little iron balcony, pressing close, sharing our warmth, blinking the rain out of our eyes.

Evie laughed against my shoulder, then stepped away from me. She held my eyes as she shucked off her soaking T-shirt, balled it up, and tossed it off the balcony. Then she wiggled her shorts down over her hips, bent over so gracefully it made my throat hurt, still looking up into my eyes, and slid the shorts off her feet. They went over the rail, too.

She laughed again, then put her arms around my neck, pressed her wet bare breasts against my chest, and kissed me on the mouth. I raised my arms over my head, and she peeled off my T-shirt and threw it over the side. Then she knelt in front of me and tugged down my shorts.

She stood up and hugged me hard while lightning zipped across the sky and thunder filled the air around us and the wind slapped rain against our bare bodies, and when I felt that I was about to explode in a billion megawatts of pent-up electricity, I picked her up and carried her into the bedroom.

Sometime in the night I woke up with my heart pounding. I sat up in bed.

Beside me Evie stirred, then said, "What is it?"

"I thought I heard the phone."

She reached out and put her hand on my back. "It didn't ring. I would've heard it."

The cell phone was sitting on the table beside the bed. Its green light was winking in the darkness. I picked it up and held it in my hand. It didn't ring.

I put it back. "I guess you're right," I said. I lay back and let out a long breath. "Why hasn't he called?"

"He's trying to get into your head," said Evie. "It's his game."

"Well, he's winning."

She rolled onto her side, put her head on my shoulder and her arm across my chest, and kissed my throat. "Go to sleep," she whispered.

I held onto her, and after a while I did.

When my eyes popped open, gray light was filtering in through the window. I looked at my watch. Six-thirty. Evie's head was on my chest and one of her legs was hooked over mine.

I eased myself out from under her and sat on the edge of the bed.

"Wha'sup?" she mumbled.

I patted her shoulder. "Nothing, honey. Go to sleep."

She groaned and flopped onto her belly.

I pulled on my jeans and a T-shirt, put the cell phone in my pocket, and padded barefoot into the kitchen. Through the sliders I saw that we had ourselves a drizzly June Sunday. So much for San Diego weather.

I got the coffee going, then took Henry for his morning walk down to the park. When we got back, I fetched the fat Sunday *Globe* from outside my door and brought it in. I gave Henry some breakfast, then took the paper into the living room.

Normally I start with the sports, but today I turned to the Metro section. No stories about the Spotted Owl Liberation Front or arson fires or FBI subpoenas or kidnappings there.

None in the national news, either. Agent Randall was doing a good job of media control.

It felt unreal. Twenty-four hours earlier, the voice on the cell phone had led me on a scavenger hunt to the apartment over the Vintage Vinyl record store in Central Square. I'd watched a videotape of Ethan Duffy with duct tape over his eyes holding up the morning newspaper. Then I erased the tape, got in my car, and drove home.

Brought Horowitz into it.

Went to a ball game.

Made love in a thunderstorm.

Now I had to convince myself it had all happened.

I got up, poured a mug of coffee, and took it out to the balcony. I leaned my elbows on the railing and looked up at the gray sky. The misty June rain dampened my face.

When I went back inside, Evie was pouring herself some coffee. She had one of my ratty flannel shirts wrapped around her.

I went over and kissed her forehead.

She smiled. "You're all wet."

"A lot of people have told me that."

We went over to the sofa and sat down. "What do you want to do today?" she said.

"Oh, I don't know. Read the paper. Watch a ball game. Rescue Ethan."

She touched my arm. "How are you doing?"

"To tell you the truth, I feel like I'm going to explode," I said. "What the fuck is he up to?"

"You've got to be patient, Brady."

"Patience is the least of my very few virtues," I said. "When there's something wrong, I need to be fixing it. Look at me. I'm not doing anything. I can't think of anything to do. It's driving me nuts."

"You're waiting," she said. "That's what you're doing."

"I hate waiting," I said. "You know that."

She smiled. "I know that very well."

"I keep thinking about Ethan."

She put her head on my shoulder. "I know."

"I'm trying to decide whether I should call his mother, tell her he's okay."

"You did call her, didn't you?"

"That was after he called me. That was before I found out he'd been kidnapped."

"You intend to tell her that he's been kidnapped? That some weirdo has got him with duct tape over his eyes? You think she wants to hear that?"

I shook my head. "I know. That doesn't sound too good, does it?"

"If it was me," said Evie, "I don't think I'd want to hear that."

"But it would give me something to do," I said. "It would make me feel useful."

"You can't be selfish, Brady," she said. "Anyhow, don't

forget, Detective Horowitz is working on it."

"Yeah," I said, "or screwing it up."

"He told you not to talk to anybody about it, didn't he?"

"Even Ethan's mother?"

She shrugged.

"So what am I supposed to be doing while I'm waiting for this bastard to make the next move?"

Evie picked up the magazine section of the newspaper. "Come on," she said. "Help me do the crossword."

The crossword puzzle didn't take us long. Evie was very good at crosswords. After we finished it, we read the paper, swapping sections back and forth.

Around eleven I fried some bacon and made a mushroom omelette. Sunday brunch, which we ate at the table that looked out the sliding glass doors to the harbor. The rain had stopped sometime in the morning. Now it was just one of those cool, cloudy June days in New England.

After Henry licked our plates and we cleaned up the kitchen, Evie spread out the real-estate section on the living-room floor, and we both got down on our hands and knees and made up stories about what our lives would be like if we lived together in some of the country properties we found. Billy and Joey would have their own bedrooms, and maybe they'd come and stay with us now and then. Hell, there would be plenty of extra rooms, so our friends could come for weekends. We talked about buying a horse and digging a trout pond and growing vegetables and fruit trees and having lots of dogs and cats who could roam freely in our woods and meadows. Evie wanted goats, and when I asked her why, she said she just thought goats were cute, and

I realized that it wasn't that scary, the idea of living with Evie, and for a while I managed to push Ethan Duffy and the Spotted Owl Liberation Front and the voice on the cell phone into a dark corner of my brain.

Then Evie sat back on her haunches and said, "Guess what?"

"I give up."

"I got a job offer."

I looked up at her, trying to read her face. The first thing that flashed through my mind, for some reason, was Chicago. The woman I loved would be leaving me. It had happened to me before.

"Hey, that's great," I said, trying to look pleased. "Where?"

She looked solemnly at me. "Beth Israel."

I know I grinned foolishly. "Beth Israel? Here in Boston?"

She smiled. "You didn't think I was going to move out of state or something, did you?"

I shrugged. "People do that all the time."

"Not me," she said. "My job is my job, not my life." She reached over, grabbed my hand, and peered into my eyes. "What if I told you this job was in, like, Los Angeles?"

"Truthfully?"

"Of course truthfully," she said.

"Truthfully, I'd be heartbroken. And I'd probably try to hide it from you, support you and your career." I bent toward her and kissed her neck. "I don't want you to move away from me. I'd rather you moved nearer to me."

"Beth Israel is nearer," she said.

"Yes it is. It's practically around the corner. Is it a good job?"

"Lots more money, lots more responsibility. Is that good?"

I smiled. "Not necessarily. You gonna take it?"

She shook her head. "I don't know. I've got a couple weeks to decide. They only made the offer on Thursday."

"But you've been negotiating for it for a while, huh? Sending in your résumé? Having interviews?"

She put her hand on my arm. "Don't be upset."

"You never said anything to me about it."

She shrugged. "I was afraid they wouldn't want me. It was like, if I told anybody, it would be bad luck."

"I bet you told Marcus." Marcus Bluestein was Evie's boss at Emerson Hospital.

"I had to tell Marcus," she said.

"What's he think about it?"

She smiled. "You know Marcus. He's my biggest supporter." She squeezed my hand. "My second-biggest supporter, I mean."

"So you're tempted by this job," I said.

"Tempted? Oh, yes. It's a really good job. But I don't know about commuting into the city every day from Concord, and the idea of moving again . . ."

We renewed our exploration of the real estate pages, looking for a place for Evie that would be convenient to Beth Israel Hospital. There wasn't much on the market in the Boston-Brookline area that appeared suitable for goats.

When the ball game came on, we folded up the real estate pages, turned on the TV, and watched the Red Sox lose to the Tigers over at Fenway Park under a dark ominous sky.

After the game, we took Henry for a walk, and when we got back, we opened two bottles of Sam Adams, put together a refrigerator soup from the leftover chicken and various vegetables we found, and put it on low heat on the stove.

Then we undressed, showered together, dried each other off, and dozed in the bedroom while the soup simmered. Well, Evie dozed. I pretended while I lay there on my back staring up at the ceiling.

I kept seeing Ethan Duffy's face with duct tape over his eyes.

After an hour or so, Evie stirred and said she was hungry. We got up, made some coffee, and gave Henry supper. Evie and I ate the soup with oyster crackers, took coffee into the living room, smoked, sipped, and watched the night seep into the harbor.

And all that time, the cell phone never rang.

After a while, Evie said, "Well, I guess I better get going. Tomorrow's Monday."

"Why don't you stay the night?" I said.

She shook her head. "We don't live together, remember?"

"I know, but . . ."

"You're worried about that man."

I shrugged.

"I can take care of myself, Brady. I've done it all my life."

"This is different."

"I understand. I came here Friday night when you told me not to, and now I'm going home, even if you don't want me to."

"I'll follow you, then," I said. "Make sure you get there safely."

"What, so you can lead him to my house if he's following you?"

"Valid point." I didn't want to tell her that I suspected he already knew where she lived. "Okay," I said. "Keep your car doors locked and your pepper spray and cell phone handy."

"I will," she said. "And I'll call you when I get there. I'll lock all my doors. If I see or hear anything, I'll call the cops. Please don't worry about me. Okay?"

"You'll be careful?"

She smiled. "I'm always careful."

I brought along my .38 when Evie and Henry and I took the elevator down to the parking garage, and I kept it in my hand while she put her arms around my neck and kissed me hard on the mouth.

She bent down and gave Henry a pat, then turned, unlocked her car, and slid in. She started it up and rolled down her window. I bent and kissed her again. "You'll keep me posted on the job?"

"I'll consult you on the job," she said. "It involves you, too."

"I agree."

She smiled. "I'm glad you feel that way."

"Got your pepper spray handy?"

"I've got my pepper spray and my cell phone and my whistle," she said. "Relax."

"I'm not going to relax until you call and tell me you're home safely," I said.

"You're not going to relax anyway," she said.

Henry and I watched Evie drive out of the garage. Then we headed for the elevator. An elderly couple, neighbors I'd seen many times over the years but whose names I didn't know, were waiting for it to come down.

We nodded and said hello, and Henry and I waited beside them. The woman glanced down at my hand which, I realized, was still holding my revolver.

I hastily stuck it in my pocket.

She frowned and grabbed her husband's arm.

They got off on the second floor. As I remembered it, they lived on five.

TWENTY-FOUR

I sat beside the telephone until Evie called. "I'm here," she said. "Safe and sound."

"Took you long enough."

"Forty minutes, like always."

"It seemed longer than that. Doors locked?"

"Of course."

"You sure nobody followed you?"

She laughed softly. "I'm fine, Brady. I've got my pepper spray and my cell phone, and nobody can get in anyway."

"I wish we were living together," I said.

She was quiet for a moment. Then she said, "What did you just say?"

"I said, um, I wish you were here so we could be together."

She laughed. "That's not what you said."

"You know what I said."

"True," she said. "I just wanted to hear you say it again."

So I said it again.

I probably slept, but it seemed as if I lay awake all night waiting for the damn cell phone to ring.

It never did.

Monday morning Herm Alberts called me at the office to agonize over his prenuptial agreement. I reminded him that I'd laid out all the pros and cons of it for him, and that if he decided he wanted a prenup, all we needed to do was work out the details.

He said that he couldn't bear the thought of raising the subject with Lauren.

"It's an important decision," I said noncommittally.

"I wish you'd never brought up the subject."

"Hm," I said. "Sorry. It's my job, bringing up subjects." I cleared my throat. "Listen, Herm. A wise person once said, for most of life's decisions you should use your head. Gather as much information as you can, analyze it objectively, and let the facts tell you what to do. But for really important decisions, you should listen to your heart."

"Huh?" said Herm. "My heart?"

"I'm not telling you what to do," I said. "But I think this qualifies as a really important decision."

"What would *you* do? I mean, if you were me."

"I guess if I were you I'd be agonizing just the way you are."

"I mean, if you were getting married, would you insist on a prenup?"

"I'm not you, Herm. And I'm not getting married."

"When you were married, did you have one?"

"No. But that was a long time ago, and I didn't have any assets."

He was quiet for a minute. "You're not going to advise me on this, are you?"

"I'm not a marriage counselor. I'm just a lawyer. I want you to understand your options. It's your decision."

"A marriage counselor," he said. "We're not even married yet, and we should go to a marriage counselor?"

I didn't say anything.

"Screw it," he said after a minute. "I know exactly what my heart's saying to me." He hesitated. "Who is this wise person you mentioned?"

"Zee Jackson."

"Never heard of him."

"It's a her, actually," I said. "Let me know what you decide."

"I already know. I don't want any damn prenup."

"You've got time to change your mind," I said. "Think it over."

"No thinking required," he said. "I feel better already. In fact, I feel terrific. Thank you, Brady."

I hung up smiling.

The instant I hung up with Herm, my intercom buzzed. I pressed the button and picked up the phone. "What's up?"

"The police officers are here," said Julie. "Can you see them now?"

Julie knew perfectly well I could see them now. Promoting the illusion that I was always busy had become a knee-jerk reaction for her.

"I think I can squeeze them in," I told her.

A minute later, Julie opened the door and Saundra Mendoza and Matthew Keeler came in. Neither of them looked happy to see me. I wondered if Horowitz had decided to bring them into it, tell them about Ethan and my cell phone. "Julie offer you coffee?" I said.

"We're okay," said Keeler. "I know you're busy. We'll try to keep it short."

I nodded and gestured at the sofa in my sitting area.

The two cops sat beside each other, and I took the chair across from them.

Keeler glanced at Mendoza, then leaned forward. "I thought you agreed to let us know if you got any more phone calls."

I hesitated. The last time I'd seen these cops had been at One Central Plaza with the FBI agents. That was the day before my cell phone arrived. Before I knew about Ethan. It seemed as if it was months ago. "You mean calls that mention places where fires are going to happen?" I said.

"What other kind of calls are you getting?" said Keeler.

I shook my head. "I didn't get any calls about a fire. Why? Was there one?"

He nodded. "Last night in Southie. A warehouse. Wholesaler that imports electronic stuff from Japan."

"The spotted owl people again?"

He nodded. "Channel 7 got a tape this morning."

"Why that place?"

"Japan's a big polluter, I guess."

I shrugged. "Well, I didn't get any phone call about it."

Mendoza pointed her finger at me. "You're not holding anything back from us, are you?"

"Why would I do that?" *Did they know about Ethan?*

She glanced at Keeler, then narrowed her dark eyes at me. "You tell me."

I shook my head. "I didn't get any call about any fire. What makes the difference, anyhow?"

"We're trying to catch him, for Christ's sake," said Mendoza. "You're supposed to be helping us."

"If he didn't call you," said Keeler, "it means he's changing his pattern."

"And?"

"And if he keeps changing his pattern, he's going to be harder to catch."

I nodded. "I told you I'd cooperate."

Keeler and Mendoza exchanged glances. Then Mendoza leaned toward me and said, "There was a body."

"In the fire?"

She nodded.

I looked at her. I blew out a breath. *Ethan.* "Who was it?"

She shook her head. "It's gonna take a while to ID him." She hesitated. "You want to hear this?"

"Yes."

"You explain it," she said to Keeler. "You're the arson expert."

Keeler cleared his throat. "It's not that sophisticated. He uses gasoline for his accelerant. A couple sticks of dynamite, a primer, a battery, remote electronic detonation. He sets it all up, then moves away, gets his video camera going, and flicks his ignition switch. Last night, as near as we can figure, his victim was in the same room as the dynamite. Judging by the, um, the condition of the body, he had probably been doused with accelerant. No way to ID him visually. They're going to have to go to dental records, bone X-rays. We'll be lucky if they get anything definitive in a week."

"Jesus," I whispered. I looked up at him. "You said 'he.' This victim, it was a man?"

Keeler nodded.

"Old? Young? Short? Tall? Fat? Skinny?"

Mendoza narrowed her eyes at me. "Why? You got somebody in mind?"

Either they didn't know about Ethan, or they were waiting to see if I'd mention him. Maybe I should tell them. If he was the one who'd died in that fire . . .

No. The voice on the phone had been very clear. And Horowitz had agreed. I should tell nobody. I just had to hope that Ethan was not the corpse they'd found in the South Boston warehouse.

So I just shrugged. "After Walt Duffy and Ben Frye," I said, "I don't even want to imagine that it could be somebody else that I know. How did he die?" I patted the back of my head. "Like the others?"

"No," said Mendoza. "Worse."

"In the fire?"

She nodded.

I should've told them, I thought. I should've gone straight to Randall, given her the damn cell phone, told her about the phone calls and the apartment above the record store and the videotape. Dumped it on her lap.

Would that have saved Ethan? Maybe.

Maybe not.

And maybe this dead body wasn't Ethan. Maybe he was still alive.

I had to believe that. I had to play it out. At this point, I didn't see that I had any other choice.

"Mr. Coyne," said Keeler. "You okay?"

"No," I said. "Of course not. That's horrible."

"You can't help us with this?"

"I don't see how," I said. "I'm sorry."

"What're you holding back?" said Mendoza.

I shook my head. "Nothing."

She narrowed her eyes at me. "I don't believe you."

I shrugged.

"He's holding out on us," she said to Keeler. "I know damn well he is."

Keeler looked at me, then shrugged.

"We should take him to Randall," she said to him. "The sonofabitch knows something. She'll get it out of him."

"Don't play bad cop with me, Detective," I said.

"You ain't seen nothing," she growled.

"*Are* you telling us everything?" said Keeler.

I nodded. "Yes."

He peered at me for a minute. Then he turned to Mendoza. "I believe him," he said. "We know where to find him if we need him. You're not going to disappear on us, are you, Mr. Coyne?"

"Why would I do that?"

Keeler nodded. "Okay. Good." He stood up. "Come on," he said to Mendoza. "Let's get on with it, let Mr. Coyne get back to work."

Mendoza glared at me. "I know you're holding out on us," she said.

Keeler touched her shoulder. "Leave it, Sandy," he said softly.

Mendoza stood up, shook her head, and walked out of my office.

"It's her sister," said Keeler. "Poor kid. She's convinced she's going to die."

"Maybe they should make her take a leave of absence or something," I said. "She shouldn't be on the loose, harassing law-abiding citizens."

"Ah, she'd go crazy without the job." He held out his hand. "I apologize for her."

I shook his hand. "Forget about it."

"We'll be in touch."

I nodded.

I waited for five minutes, then called Horowitz on his cell phone. "Mendoza and Keeler were just here," I told him.

"That fire in Southie last night," he said. "I knew they were headed your way. What'd you tell them?"

"Nothing. They wanted to know if I got a call about the fire. I didn't. That's what I told them."

"Nothing about that videotape or the cell phone or Ethan Duffy?"

"I didn't say anything about any of that. Did you?"

"Me?" he said.

"I had the feeling they knew more than they were saying," I said.

"They didn't hear anything from me," said Horowitz.

"Roger," I said, "if that was Ethan's body they found in that fire . . ."

"If it ain't," he said, "and if you went ahead and told the cops everything and that fruitcake figured it out, he'd kill the Duffy kid, for sure."

I blew out a breath. "I'm trusting you on this."

"He's gonna call you," said Horowitz. "He's holding that boy because he wants something out of you. Hang in there."

"So you think Ethan's still alive?"

He laughed quickly. "Let's hope so."

"That's not very reassuring."

"Look at it this way," he said. "If you had told the damn FBI about that videotape and your cell phone and everything, Ethan would sure as hell be dead by now."

"How can you be so sure?"

"I got some ideas on this, Coyne."

"What—?"

"Not now. Gotta go. Keep doing what you're doing."

And he hung up.

Around noon Julie volunteered to take Henry for a walk. She said she'd pick up lunch for the three of us.

Ten minutes after she left, the cell phone rang.

"What?" I said.

"What did you tell them?"

"Who?"

"Those detectives."

"Nothing. I told them nothing. Let me speak to Ethan."

He laughed.

"If that was Ethan in that fire . . ."

"You're in no position to threaten me, Mr. Coyne."

"He better still be alive."

"He is," said the voice.

"Who was it, then? In the fire."

"Come on, Mr. Coyne."

"Let me talk to Ethan."

"Later," he said. Then he was gone.

I stared at the damned cell phone, with its evil green winking eye, for the length of time it took me to smoke a cigarette. Then I called Horowitz.

"He just called me," I said.

"The guy on the cell phone?"

"Yes. Him."

"What'd he say?"

"He said it wasn't Ethan in that fire."

"Good."

"Are we supposed to believe him?"

"If the kid was already dead, he wouldn't have called."
"What makes you think that?"
"Like I told you, Coyne. I'm trying to work on it. Unfortunately, I keep getting interrupted by phone calls."
"Gotcha," I said, and I hung up.

Twenty-five

Henry and I had just gotten back to my apartment after our last walk of the evening when the cell phone beeped.

I snatched it up, flipped open the lid, and said, "I want to speak to Ethan."

"Be patient, Mr. Coyne." He was still distorting his voice. Even so, I felt as if I should be able to identify it. There was something familiar in it. I was certain I'd heard that voice.

"I need to know that Ethan's all right," I said.

"You've been most cooperative so far, my friend. It would be tragic if you blew it now. Do as I say and you shall speak to young Mr. Duffy."

"Do I have your word?"

"Does my word really mean anything to you?"

"It's got to," I said.

He laughed.

I needed to find a way to get ahold of Horowitz. I took a deep breath, let it out slowly. "Okay," I said. "You're the boss. What do you want me to do?"

"Do not disconnect unless I tell you to. Understand?"

"I understand."

"Excellent. Now, first I want you to get your briefcase. Do it now. Keep the phone to your ear."

I went to the door where I always left my briefcase. "I've got it," I said.

"Empty it."

I took out all the documents and letters and piled them on the sofa in the living room. "It's empty."

"Now go to your car, Mr. Coyne. Bring that antique briefcase with you. As you go, tell me what you're doing. I want to hear your voice continually. Leave right now."

"All right. First I have to put on my shoes." I picked up my .38. "Okay. Now I'm getting my windbreaker out of the closet." I slipped the gun into one pocket. "Now I've got to fill my dog's water dish."

"Make it quick," he said. "Keep talking."

I told him I was heading for the kitchen, but I didn't tell him I was taking my wall phone with its extra-long cord off the hook and putting it face up on the counter. I turned on the faucet in the sink, held the cell phone close to the sound of running water, and pecked out Horowitz's number on the corded phone.

I heard Horowitz's voicemail answer. Damn.

I put the cell phone at my ear and bent close to the other phone. "Okay," I said. "My dog's got his water. Now I'm leaving my apartment. I'm heading down to my car." I left the other phone lying faceup on the counter. I didn't disconnect.

Henry followed me to the door. I held up my hand to him. He sat down and cocked his head. I gave him a quick pat, then went out and closed the door behind me. "I'm heading for the elevator," I said into the cell phone.

"Keep talking," he said.

Our connection got fuzzy in the elevator. If he spoke to me, I couldn't hear him. I kept talking anyway.

When I stepped out of the elevator into the parking garage, I paused with the cell phone against my ear, tucked the briefcase under my arm, slipped my empty hand into the pocket with the gun, and looked around the garage. This man had been here before. For all I knew, he was waiting for me behind a parked car.

"Are you still there?" I said into the phone.

"I didn't like that," he said.

"It was the elevator," I said. "Sorry."

"What are you doing now?" he said.

"Headed for my car."

"You've got to keep talking, Mr. Coyne."

The parking garage was eerily silent, the way it always was late at night. Somewhere the slow rhythmic plink of water dripping on wet concrete echoed softly. I saw nothing except dim orange light and dark shadows.

I went to my car, unlocked it, and slid in behind the wheel, narrating my progress all the way. I put the briefcase and the revolver on the seat beside me. "I'm in my car," I said. "Now I want to hear Ethan's voice."

"Why not?" he said. "Hold on."

I pressed the phone against my ear, and a moment later, a soft voice said, "Brady?"

"Ethan? Is that you."

"It's me." I recognized his voice.

"Are you all right?"

"I'm . . . yes, I'm okay."

"What's—?"

"That's enough, Mr. Coyne," said the voice. "Satisfied?"

"I'll be satisfied when you let him go."

"Just do as I tell you," he said. "Are you ready?"

"Of course I'm ready."

"Then let us begin. Do not doubt this, Mr. Coyne. If you do precisely as I tell you, you shall see the boy very soon. If you fail to obey me in any way, however small, you will hear him die. Do you understand?"

"Yes. Where are we going?"

He chuckled. "You'll see when you get there. Don't think, Mr. Coyne. Keep your head free of distracting scenarios. Just drive. Now. Start your car, pull out of your parking slot, exit the garage, and turn right on Commercial Street. Talk to me as you go. Give me a sightseeing tour. Boston after dark, eh?"

He directed me around the loop of Commercial Street that bordered Boston's Italian North End and merged onto Causeway Street near the North Station. Where Causeway butted onto Cambridge Street by Government Center, he told me to turn right. All along the way I named the restaurants and bars and nightclubs I passed, described the traffic lights I went through, and read the neon signs that were still lit at one o'clock on a Tuesday morning.

Once I put the cell phone down to fish out a cigarette and light it. When I picked up the phone and resumed my narration, he said, "What are you doing?"

"I just lit a cigarette."

"Keep talking, Mr. Coyne. I don't like to hear those silences. They make me nervous. You don't want me to feel nervous, I assure you."

So I kept talking. I did not tell him about the tantalizing

public phone booths I saw on the street corners or the two Boston PD cruisers I passed that were idling at the curb on Cambridge Street.

I had to keep trying to get in touch with Horowitz.

Precisely to prevent my doing that, I realized, was why he insisted on keeping me on the line.

At the rotary where Cambridge Street intersected with Charles he directed me onto Storrow Drive.

"Are we headed back to the record store?" I said.

He chuckled. "I told you, Mr. Coyne. Don't think. You lawyers think too much. That's your problem. Too much thinking, not enough feeling. Just drive."

"Can I ask you something?" I said.

"You can certainly ask," he said. "Don't expect an honest answer."

"Fair enough. My question is: Why me?"

"What do you mean?"

"Why'd you pick me to call about those fires? Why am I the one with this damn cell phone?"

"That's easy." He chuckled. "I've got something you want, you've got something I want."

"What—?"

"Besides," he said quickly, "I don't like you."

"Oh," I said. "We know each other, then?"

"Don't push your luck, Mr. Coyne."

"What do I have that you want?"

"All in due time. You are approaching the Harvard Bridge. Exit there, but do not cross the bridge. Swing around onto Mass. Ave. as if you were going to the Convention Center."

I did as he said. "Okay. I'm approaching Commonwealth. Stopping at the red light. Why don't you like me?"

"You're a bloodsucking lawyer, aren't you?" His voice had suddenly lost its cultured coolness. I heard a hint of profound hatred in it. Craziness, too.

It occurred to me that if I played it carefully, I might get him to drop his defenses and reveal something.

It also occurred to me that I could easily push him over whatever edge he teetered on. Then he would kill Ethan.

"What've you got against lawyers?" I said.

He hesitated, and for an instant I thought I'd gone too far. But then he laughed softly. "I thought I told you not to think, Mr. Coyne. We are not exchanging intimacies here. I am giving orders and you are obeying them. Do not forget that. Where are you now?"

"The library's coming up on my right."

"Go around the corner, find an empty meter, and park your car there."

I found a place to park on Huntington Avenue a little way past the library.

"Okay," I said. "I'm parked. Now what?"

"Look familiar, Mr. Coyne?"

"Oh, sure," I said. "The BPL, the Pru, the Hancock Building, the Plaza—"

"Don't fuck with me," he growled.

"I'm trying not to think," I said, "but I notice that my office building is right here."

"Bravo, Mr. Coyne. Go up to your office. Bring your briefcase with you."

And about then, finally, the lightbulb flashed in my head and I understood what he wanted. What he'd wanted all along.

But it didn't make much sense.

Why kill three men and kidnap a fourth for a few letters

about birds, no matter who'd written them and how old and important and valuable they might be?

My .38 was lying on the passenger seat beside me in plain sight. The last thing I needed was someone smashing my window and setting off my car alarm—or, for that matter, some foot patrolman stopping me.

I shoved the gun under the driver's seat. Then I picked up the briefcase, got out of my car, locked it, and crossed the street to my building. I punched the code into the keypad that let us tenants in after they locked up at ten every night, and I went up to my office.

"Okay, I'm here," I said into the cell phone. "Now what?"

"I'm sure you've figured it out by now, Mr. Coyne."

"You want those Meriwether Lewis letters, right?"

"Retrieve them from your safe, please."

"What are they worth?" I said to him. "Twenty-five, maybe fifty thousand dollars? There are plenty of easier ways for a master criminal such as yourself to make that kind of money."

"You should know," he said.

"What do you mean?"

"Lawyers." He laughed quickly. I heard no humor in it. "Fetch those letters and put them into your briefcase. Do it now. No more chitchat. It tests my patience."

I kept up a play-by-play in the cell phone as I twirled the dial, opened the safe, took out the envelope with the Meriwether Lewis-to-Alexander Wilson letters, put them into my briefcase, and closed the safe.

And as I did this, another part of my mind tried to piece together the information I had.

This man who was holding Ethan Duffy for the ransom of some old letters about birds seemed to have a profound dislike for lawyers.

Who did I know that didn't like lawyers?

I almost laughed out loud.

Who *did* like lawyers?

Everybody, sooner or later, ended up feeling he'd been screwed by a lawyer.

Even lawyers didn't like lawyers. Lawyers got screwed all the time by other lawyers.

Okay. This man was a member of the Spotted Owl Liberation Front. He liked birds. He thought of himself as a savior of bird habitat. He was on a righteous crusade against those he considered the enemies of birds.

I could almost understand trying to call attention to an issue you cared passionately about by burning down empty buildings.

But this guy killed people.

To glorify the spotted owl?

It was all out of proportion. It didn't make sense.

But, of course, there was no reason it should. The man was psychotic. Normal standards of proportion, logic, and rationality didn't apply, and I realized that no matter how carefully and thoroughly I tried to analyze it, to piece together clues, to understand the cause-effect nature of the man's motivation, the simple bottom line was: He was insane.

I'd been straining to identify his voice. I was sure I'd heard it before, but I couldn't place it, muffled and distorted as it was on the cellular phone.

"The letters are in my briefcase," I said. "Now what?"

"Now," he said, "if you continue to do exactly as you're told, you shall have your reunion with young Mr. Duffy."

"You get the damn letters and I get Ethan, right?"

"If all goes well, Mr. Coyne. It's up to you."

Twenty-six

Leave your office this instant," he said.

"Right," I said. "I'm going. I've got the letters. We're all set."

I was standing beside Julie's desk, and as I talked into the cell phone, I took her phone off its cradle so that it was lying faceup on her blotter. I hit the numbers 911. I didn't dare put Julie's phone to my ear. But when I heard the 911 operator's voice answer, I bent close to Julie's phone and said into the cell phone, "Ethan Duffy better still be alive when I get there."

"If you're not back in your car in two minutes," said the voice on the cell phone, "you can forget about the boy. Get moving."

"I believe you," I said. "I know you'll kill him. I'm moving."

I hastily printed the words. "Horowitz State Police" on a scrap of paper and left it on Julie's desk.

As I moved to the door, I heard the voice on Julie's phone asking for my name.

I didn't dare say anything else.

I left my office door ajar, exited the building, and headed to where my car was parked on Huntington. I hoped that what I'd said on Julie's phone would be recorded and the number would be traced. Then if that 911 operator was on the ball, she'd send a police cruiser to check out the office. He'd find the door open, see my note, and contact Horowitz.

As I chattered away on the cell phone, I looked up and down the street. A siren would be disastrous. So would police officers stopping me and asking me questions. My only hope would be to head them off by pointing to the cell phone at my ear, putting my finger to my lips, and hoping they'd get the picture.

A few cars and taxis were gliding along Huntington Avenue, but none of them slowed down to check me out. No police cruisers, no foot patrolmen, no SWAT teams, no helicopters.

I unlocked my car, climbed in, and put the briefcase on the seat beside me. "I'm back in my car," I said. "I've got the letters. Now what?"

"Now you drive," he said.

I reached under the seat, found my .38, and put it in my jacket pocket. Then I started up the car.

I reminded the voice that I was on Huntington Avenue, heading outbound, and he told me to keep going. Slowly and sedately, he said. And be sure to keep talking.

A minute later when I reported that I was approaching Symphony Hall, he told me to turn left on Mass. Ave. and then take a right onto Columbus Avenue. Then I found myself driving into the heart of Roxbury—not the most hospitable community for a middle-aged white man in a shiny new BMW to be passing through at two o'clock on a summer morning.

A little way past Madison Park High School, he told me to take a left, and then a right, and I figured he was trying to twist me around and disorient me. He was doing a good job of it. I didn't remember the last time I'd been in this part of the city. He kept directing me to make lefts and rights, and I found myself traveling on narrow residential streets lined with parked cars and trash barrels. I passed through neighborhoods of three-deckers and brick apartment complexes perched close to the sidewalks. Here and there clusters of young African-American men wearing baggy pants and backward baseball caps were gathered under streetlights, talking and smoking and listening to their earphones. Elderly men sat in twos and threes on their front steps, and when I drove by, they lifted their heads and watched me pass without expression.

I kept glancing into my rearview mirror. I hoped to see headlights a safe distance behind me, traveling at the same speed I was. Following me. Watching over me.

But every time I took a turn, whatever car might have been in my mirror kept going.

After fifteen or twenty minutes, I emerged onto Blue Hill Avenue, which cut through the heart of Dorchester—another Boston community that still bubbled with deep-rooted racial hostilities.

I'd been keeping up a running commentary on the cell phone as I drove. The voice said nothing except when he wanted me to make a turn.

"Franklin Park Zoo on my right," I told him. "Am I getting close?"

"Patience, Mr. Coyne. Left at the next traffic light."

And then I was gliding through more neighborhoods, taking lefts and rights that struck me as utterly random.

"That light ahead of you," he said into the cell phone, "is Washington Street. Go left."

"Okay," I said. Then, "I'm on it now."

"See Murray's Liquors on your right?"

"No. Wait. Yes, there it is."

"Just past it there's a gas station."

I saw it. There were orange barrels along the street, and piles of dirt were mounded around the island with the gas pumps.

"It appears to be under repair," I said.

"Renovation, to be precise," he said. "A major corporation, internationally notorious for oil spills and for the irresponsible disposal of toxic waste, and which spends millions of dollars annually to lobby for drilling rights in the Gulf of Mexico and in pristine Alaskan wilderness—headed, of course, by its team of fat-cat lawyers—has mobilized its customary arsenal of legal technicalities to squeeze out the local owners of this little neighborhood enterprise, and it is presently closed for renovations. You probably own stock in that corporation, Mr. Coyne."

"I hope not," I said.

He chuckled. "How irresponsible is that?"

"What?"

"Not knowing what vile enterprises you support with your investments. It's all about the money, isn't it?"

"I never thought of it that way," I said.

"No, of course you didn't. You're a lawyer. That's not how lawyers think. Okay. Just past the orange barrels there on the right you'll see a place where you can turn in. Drive around behind the building. You're just about there."

The front of the gas station was lit by a streetlight, but the area in the rear lay deep in shadows. As I pulled around to the back of the building, my headlights flashed on some heavy machinery parked against a ten-foot chain-link fence—a backhoe, a front loader, a bulldozer, a dump truck. There were two steel sheds the size of double-wide trailers flanking a big gas-powered generator, and in the corner stood a portable toilet.

"Park beside the Porta-Potty," he said.

I did.

"Good," he said. "Turn off the ignition and step out of the car. Leave your briefcase on the seat. Oh, and you better leave that revolver there, too. We don't want an accident now, do we?"

I looked around. He was watching me now, for sure, if he hadn't been all the time.

"You don't get the letters until I've got Ethan," I said into the phone.

"And you don't get the boy until I check the contents of your briefcase," he said.

"Sounds like a stalemate to me."

"Hardly," he said. "I will continue to live without those letters. But if I don't have them, Ethan Duffy will die. That is not my idea of a stalemate."

"What about me?"

"You, Mr. Coyne, are free to drive away right now. If that's your choice, I suggest you do it immediately."

"And if I do?"

"Leave the letters for me and Ethan Duffy's fate is in my

hands. Hm. I wonder what I'd do." He chuckled. "Drive off with the letters, and I'm sure your friends with the FBI will drop by to tell you all about it tomorrow."

I let out a breath. "Okay," I said. "The briefcase and the gun are on the seat. I'm getting out. Now what?"

"Try the shed on the left," he said. "Be gentle with the door."

I went over to the shed. It had a solid steel door and two rectangular windows.

I lifted the heavy latch, pulled the door open, and stepped inside. The sudden odor of gasoline slapped against my face. The fumes burned my nose and eyes. I staggered for a moment as a wave of dizziness hit me. I leaned back against the wall, fumbled for my handkerchief from my pocket, wiped away the tears, and then held it over my mouth and nose.

I looked around. The only light in the shed came from the half-open door and the two windows, and at first all I could see were the shadowy shapes of what looked like stacks of building materials.

Then I heard something . . . a human noise. A grunt or a sob or a groan.

"Ethan?" I said. "Is that you? Are you in here?"

I heard the noise again, a little louder this time. I blinked away the tears in my eyes, then squinted into the murky darkness, waiting for my night vision to kick in.

I heard the moaning sound again, and I followed it to the back corner of the shed. Then I saw him. He was sprawled on the floor leaning against a stack of wooden crates. His chin was slumped on his chest.

It was Ethan.

"Are you all right?" I said.

He lifted his head, groaned softly, then dropped his head. I saw that a strip of duct tape covered his eyes. His wrists and ankles were bound together in front of him, also with duct tape.

I put the cell phone on top of the crate, then knelt beside him and slapped his face gently. "Hey," I said. "It's me. It's Brady."

He took several deep breaths, then whispered, "Gasoline."

"I know," I said. "Are you okay?"

He groaned. "Awfully sick."

"I'm going to get that tape off you," I told him. "Brace yourself. Here goes." I grabbed a corner of the tape that covered his eyes, gave it a quick, hard pull, and ripped it off. Pieces of his eyebrows came off with the tape.

Ethan barely reacted. I wondered if he'd fainted.

"Sorry," I said. "You okay?"

He looked up at me, blinked at his tears, and nodded. "Thank you," he whispered.

Then I went to work with my pocketknife on the tape that bound his ankles and wrists. Duct tape is tough stuff, and it was a minute or two before I managed to free him.

When his hands were loose, I gave him my handkerchief, and he held it against his face. For a minute he just sat there, taking quick shallow breaths.

I held my hand over my nose and mouth. Even so, the fumes burned my lungs.

"He soaked me with gasoline," Ethan said. "He drenched everything. There's dynamite in here. Be careful. One spark will blow us up."

"Let's get the hell out of here," I said.

Ethan nodded. "I'm awfully scared."

The fumes were poisonous. I wondered how many minutes we had before they overtook us. I was feeling dangerously light-headed and nauseated.

"How long have you been in here?" I said to Ethan.

"Don't know," he mumbled. "I puked. Awfully dizzy. Must've passed out."

"Come on," I said. "You've got to stand up. Let's go."

"I'm wicked sick," he said.

I bent down, got my arm around his back, and started to haul him to his feet . . . and that's when the door slammed shut.

An instant later I heard the unmistakable click of a padlock snapping shut on the other side of the steel door.

"I'll be right back," I said to Ethan. "Keep breathing through the handkerchief."

I let go of him and went to the door. I couldn't open it. I slammed at it with my shoulder. It wouldn't budge.

The effort made me gag. The damp heat in the steel shed was overpowering. I was drenched with perspiration. Another wave of dizziness hit me, and I had to lean against the wall to keep myself from falling down. I pulled the neck of my sweat-soaked T-shirt up over my face, held it tight over my mouth and nose, and took a few shallow breaths. They tasted warm and humid. But the odor of my own body's sweat and adrenaline was stronger than the smell of gasoline, and after a minute my head cleared.

I went back to where Ethan was sprawled. "He locked us in," I said.

"We're gonna die," he said. "That's what he does. He kills people."

"Who?" I said. "Who is it?"

"I don't know," he said. "He never let me see him."

I groped around and found the cell phone where I'd left it on top of the crate. "You got the damn letters," I said into it. "Now let us out of here."

All I heard was static.

"Hey!" I yelled into the phone. "Answer me."

He didn't answer. Either he'd disconnected, or I'd lost his signal.

The hell with him. I dialed 911.

But there was only static.

Twenty-seven

I visualized the arsonist, the murderer, the lawyer-hater somewhere outside. Setting up his video camera, focusing on the shed where Ethan I were trapped, preparing to detonate the dynamite, to catch it all on tape.

"Is there a back door or a trap door or anything, do you know?" I said to Ethan.

"I don't know," he mumbled. "I can't . . ."

He turned his head and vomited.

Maybe it was the power of suggestion, but I felt bile rise in my own throat. I swallowed it back. My head was spinning and my lungs and throat and stomach burned. I was drenched with sweat, and my breaths were coming fast and shallow.

I pulled my wet T-shirt over my face and breathed through it. It didn't help much.

"We're gonna die," mumbled Ethan.

"Nobody's going to die." I knelt beside him. "You hear me?"

He didn't respond. His eyes were closed and his head was slumped on his chest.

I slapped his face. "You're pissing me off," I said. I slapped him again. "You are not going to fucking die on me. Got it?"

He blinked and looked up at me. "Okay, Brady. I'm sorry."

"And stop apologizing all the time."

He laughed softly. "It's how I was raised."

"We're going to get out of here," I said. "And you've got to help."

"I just feel shitty. I can't help it."

"Stay right there," I said.

"I'm not going anywhere."

I wasn't feeling so perky myself. I went to the front of the shed and looked up at the two rectangular windows. They were about a foot-and-a-half tall and three feet wide, and they were covered with some kind of screening material. They were a couple of feet higher than my head. Evidently their purpose was ventilation.

If I dragged over one of those wooden crates, we could climb up, push out the screen, and get the hell out of there.

Dumb, Coyne. There was a man with a detonator on the other side, and he was watching. If he saw a head pop out of that window, he'd press his button, and that would be that.

I forced my fuzzy brain to think about ventilation. Windows on just one wall wouldn't ventilate anything. There had to be openings on the opposite wall as well.

In the dim light inside that shed, I could see that the back wall was stacked to the roofline with wooden crates. I went back there, stood beside where Ethan was sitting, and looked up.

Along the top of the crates, directly opposite the windows on the front wall, I could see dim, diffuse light filtering in.

"Move away," I said to Ethan.

"What're you doing?"

"Just get out of the way."

He crawled toward the front of the shed.

The wooden crates were about four feet square, and heavy. I reached up, grabbed one of the top ones by the sides, and pulled. It took all of my rapidly-diminishing strength to edge it forward until it crashed to the floor.

Behind where it had been was a window matching those in the front wall.

I climbed up on the crates, sat on the top one, and kicked out the screen.

When I looked out, I saw that the bottom of the window was just even with the top of a chain-link fence that ran along about a foot from the back of the shed. Beyond the fence was a deep excavation. In the darkness, I couldn't see to the bottom.

"Ethan," I hissed. "Come here."

He didn't answer.

"Come on, man," I said. "Make it quick."

He just groaned.

So I clambered down off the boxes, went to where Ethan was sprawled, and hauled him to his feet. "You've got to help me," I said.

"Right," he mumbled.

I half-pushed, half-carried him to the pile of crates and boosted him up. "Go out the window and climb down the other side of that fence," I told him.

I was afraid he wasn't going to move. But he did, slowly. He crawled out head-first, and he was about halfway out when he just slipped away. A moment later I heard a thud and a grunt. Then nothing.

I pulled myself to the top of the crates and knelt there trying to catch my breath. I was drenched in sweat, suddenly drained of strength. Lights were flashing in my brain. I just wanted to curl up and go to sleep.

Gotta do it, Coyne. That man intends to blow you up. Any minute now.

I stuck my face out the window and took several deep breaths of cool, fresh air. Then I reached over to the top of the fence, and pulled myself out.

For a moment I teetered on top of the chain-link fence, gripping it awkwardly under my stomach, my front half hanging over the excavation, my back half still inside the shed. The sharp prongs on top dug into my hands and belly. My head was spinning, and when I tried to adjust my grip, I lost it, and I found myself falling.

I lost consciousness somewhere along the line, and I don't know how long I lay there in the mud before I came to. I tried to move and found that it hurt too much.

"Hey," I whispered. "Ethan. Where are you?"

Ethan didn't respond.

I lifted my head to look around. There was a shadowy shape off to my left. Maybe it was Ethan—or his body.

I began to hitch myself toward him when the earth seemed to bulge underneath me. Then came a tremendous thumping noise. It felt as if I were inside a bass drum and somebody had whacked it with a baseball bat.

Then the world lit up like a million suns, and the air went out of me, and everything abruptly went black.

There were men's deep urgent voices and bright moving lights and rough hands on me, lifting me.

Someone wiped my face with a wet rag. Then they strapped an oxygen mask over my nose and mouth, and I felt myself moving . . .

When I opened my eyes, there were red and blue flashing lights and bright flickering yellow lights. There were nervous voices and angry voices and laughing voices. Doors slammed and radios crackled and engines revved and roared, and in the distance a siren wailed.

The lights and the sounds sent darts of pain zipping through my eyes and ears into the center of my brain. I squeezed my eyes shut.

Then I felt a hand gripping my shoulder. I forced myself to crack open my eyes. A blurry face hovered over me. His mouth was moving, making sounds I couldn't understand.

I narrowed my eyes, tried to focus.

It was Horowitz. He was frowning, asking me something.

I shook my head.

He bent close to me. "How you doin', bud?" he said. His voice seemed to come from miles away.

I squeezed my eyes shut. I felt wretched.

"Don't try to talk," he said. "We'll do that later."

I was trying to think. Images ricocheted around in my brain, memory fragments that flashed and then disappeared before I could identify any of them. I knew I needed to share them with Horowitz.

"We got the Duffy boy," Horowitz was saying. "Thought you'd want to know."

I nodded. "Good. That's good."

Horowitz squeezed my shoulder. "Coyne," he said. "Open your eyes. I wanna show you something."

I forced myself to open my eyes. I blinked a couple of times, and they slowly focused.

Horowitz put his arm under my neck and helped me lift my head. "Over there," he said.

I looked to where he was pointing. Two uniformed police officers had a man by his arms. The man's wrists were cuffed behind his back, and they were half-dragging him to a cruiser that was parked near the steel shed.

The man had red hair.

I let my head fall back onto the gurney where I was lying. I looked up at Horowitz. "Keeler?" I said.

He nodded. "He blew up that shed. I thought you were inside."

I think I smiled. Then I closed my eyes.

Something was going "ping-ping" and something else was beeping softly and rhythmically. When I opened my eyes, the lights were dim and the ceiling was gray, and aside from the muted pinging and beeping, the silence was soft and furry and comforting.

My head felt swollen to the size of a beach ball. My body felt as if it had been trampled by all the bulls in Spain.

Something touched my arm. I slowly turned my head.

Evie.

"Hi, honey," I whispered.

She smiled. "Hi."

"I'm alive, huh?"

She bent over and kissed my forehead. "You're going to be fine."

"What hospital is this?"

"Beth Israel."

I closed my eyes and tried to think. Beth Israel . . .

"You work here, right?" I said. It was a great relief to make that connection. It meant my brain worked.

"Not yet," she said. "But it looks like I'm gonna."

"What time is it?"

"About ten."

I frowned. "Day? Night?"

"Night. It's Tuesday night, honey. You've been here since about three this morning."

"And you?"

She nodded. "I've been here since then, too. Detective Horowitz called me. He thought I should come right away. He said you might . . ."

I saw tears well up in Evie's eyes.

"I might what?" I said.

"You . . . your lungs and your heart. They didn't know how seriously they'd been affected by those poisonous fumes. And . . . and they were worried that you might have brain damage."

"You mean even more than before?" I said.

She smiled through her tears.

"I ache all over," I said.

"You fell on some rocks," she said. "Got a nasty concussion. But it was those fumes they were mainly worried about."

"So how does someone know when their brain has been damaged? My brain feels pretty fuzzy. But it usually does."

"Who loves you?" she said. "This is a brain test."

I groped around, and she grabbed my hand and held it tight.

"You do," I said. "That's an easy one."

She lifted my hand to her mouth and kissed my palm. "Then as far as I'm concerned," she said, "your brain is working perfectly."

"What about my heart and lungs?"

At that moment a nurse came into the room. "Awake, are we?" she said.

"He just woke up," said Evie.

The nurse bent over me. "How do we feel, Brady?"

"I don't know about you," I said, "but I feel great."

"Really?"

"Well, aside from my head and my body."

She smiled. "What else is there?" She looked about fifty. Short steely-gray hair, blue eyes, a spattering of freckles across the bridge of her nose, wide friendly smile.

"Okay," I said, "so I don't feel so hot."

The nurse pried up my eyelids and shone a little flashlight into my eyes, one at a time. Then she examined the various bags that were dripping stuff through the IV into the needle in my wrist.

"Well?" I said when she paused to write onto her clipboard.

"You are occupying a bed that some sick person needs," she said.

"So I can go home?"

The nurse smiled. "You are in Intensive Care. One step at

a time, huh?" She turned and said something to Evie.

Evie came to the side of the bed. "I've got to go now," she said.

"Aw . . ."

"Be a good boy," said the nurse. "She wasn't supposed to be here in the first place. But she made such a fuss, and that bossy policeman put his two cents in, and since it looks like she's going to be running this place . . ."

"I know how she is," I said. "You can't argue with her."

Evie kissed me on the lips. "I'll be back."

"Wait," I said. "I left Henry home. He's probably shitting on my rugs."

Evie smiled. "Julie picked up Henry this morning. He's fine."

After Evie left, the nurse adjusted my pillow and held a plastic glass for me so I could sip some water through a straw.

She said a doctor would be in to see me in the morning, then turned to leave.

"Wait," I said.

She stopped in the doorway.

"What about Ethan?" I said. "Your patient. Ethan Duffy. He was with me."

She shook her head. "I don't believe we have a patient named Ethan Duffy."

The following morning they moved me to a different bed in a private room and removed all the tubes from my body.

Horowitz came in around noontime. He pulled up a chair next to my bed. "You look like shit," he said.

"So do you."

"I've been working on this fuckin' case," he said. He needed a shave and his hair was rumpled and his eyes were bloodshot and his shirt was wrinkled. It looked like he hadn't slept for a couple of nights.

"What about Ethan?" I said.

He blew out a breath. "They've got him over to Mass General. Touch and go, last I heard."

"Is he gonna be okay?"

Horowitz shrugged.

"Find out for me, will you?"

Horowitz rolled his eyes. "I got nothing better to do."

"Please," I said.

He let out a big sigh, then got up and left my room.

He was back five minutes later. "Pick up your phone," he said.

The phone was on the rolling table beside my bed. I reached around, lifted the receiver, and said, "Yes? Hello?"

There was a hesitation. "Brady?" It was Ethan's voice.

"Ethan? How are you? Are you all right?"

"I'm okay."

"Are you really?"

"Well, I feel pretty crappy. But they say I'm going to be fine. How're you doing?"

"Me?" I laughed. "Oh, I'm fine."

"You saved my life," he said.

I glanced at Horowitz. He was sitting in the chair beside my bed with his arms folded, gazing up at the ceiling, trying to look bored.

"I'm the one who nearly got us killed," I said to Ethan.

"No," he said. "I owe you." He paused. "I got a nurse here wagging her finger at me. Gotta go."

"You take care," I said.

"You, too."

I hung up the phone and looked at Horowitz. "He's okay."

He nodded.

"So it was Keeler, huh?" I said.

"Yep."

"I thought his voice was familiar," I said. "He tried to disguise it, and I couldn't pin it down, but even so, I feel stupid that I didn't . . ."

"It's all over, bud," said Horowitz. "Don't worry about it. Somebody like me should've glommed onto Keeler, too."

"It was him who set all those fires, killed Walt Duffy and Ben Frye, trapped me and Ethan in that shed?"

"Yup. Killed Conrad Henshall, too."

"That was the third body?" I said. "The one they found in Southie?"

"Right."

"Why? Why was he killing people?"

"He's not ashamed of any of it, I can tell you that. He thinks he's the good guy." Horowitz cleared his throat. "Seems that Keeler had a daughter who died of leukemia a couple years ago. She was nine, only child. His wife had developed some plumbing problems, couldn't have more kids. The little girl was sick for years, in and out of hospitals, medical bills up the wazoo. There was other sickness in his neighborhood, too, besides Keeler's daughter and wife. Him and his neighbors figured it was this fertilizer plant, poisoning their wells. They wanted to get the goods on them, shut them down, recoup their medical expenses. Nail 'em to the wall, you know? So they tried to hire a lawyer. Guess what?"

I nodded. "No lawyer would take on the case."

"Exactly."

"It would be a contingency case," I said. "A few lawyers up against some mighty corporation. Years and years of litigation, millions of dollars to hire experts, take depositions, gather evidence, build the case—if there was a case—with poor odds of ever winning enough to break even. Lawyers aren't public servants."

Horowitz shrugged. "Keeler didn't care for lawyers to begin with, being a cop. So now he's grieving over his daughter, worried about his wife, furious at this fertilizer plant, and frustrated by every lawyer he bumps into. It drives him nuts. Pushes him over the edge."

"So he burns down buildings and finds a lawyer he can antagonize," I said. "Me."

"That's about it. He hooks up with this owl bunch and starts setting fire to buildings similar to that fertilizer place he figures killed his daughter. If he can't sue 'em, he can burn 'em down. Keeler's very good at that, being an arson expert. Then when you come on the scene, he's killing two birds with one stone. Getting back at the polluters and the lawyers at the same time."

"But what about Walt Duffy and Ben Frye? Why'd he have to kill them?"

"Duffy was the main man of SOLF," he said. "The organizer. The ringleader. Just like Agent Randall explained to you. The FBI was all set to subpoena him. They'd been conferring with arson people and the local cops, so Keeler was in on it. He got to Duffy first. Killed him to shut him up, took his computer and cell phone. Duffy must've said something about those letters before Keeler whacked him on the head."

"What about the letters?"

"It wasn't really the letters that Keeler was after," Horowitz said. "Duffy had slipped a couple pages of computer printouts in with them. The printouts listed the e-mail addresses of what looks to us like every member of the Spotted Owl Liberation Front in the northeast. Including Keeler's. Duffy had you deliver it to Benjamin Frye, who was sort of his second-in-command, so he could carry on after they nailed Duffy."

"So Walt must've told Keeler what he'd done."

"According to Keeler, he threatened to go after Duffy's son, so Duffy spilled the beans to him. Keeler didn't want that list with his e-mail address on it floating around."

"So then," I said, "Keeler went after Ben, but by the time he got to him, he'd given the letters, along with the printouts, back to me. Ben never even knew the printouts were there. That's when Keeler started haunting me. Calling me on the phone, mugging me in my parking garage, hoping I still had the letters in my briefcase."

"And when he realized you didn't," said Horowitz, "he snatched Ethan Duffy, hooked you up with that cell phone, and sent you on your scavenger hunt. He figured you'd do anything to get Ethan back."

"He figured right," I said. I thought for a minute. "So why'd he kill Conrad Henshall?"

Horowitz shrugged. "Ethan was hiding out in that little apartment over Henshall's shop. Keeler had to get him out of the way."

I thought about all that, and it made sense. "So how *did* you find us at that shed? Did you get my message? I called you from home, got your damn voicemail. Or was it that 911 call I made from Julie's phone? The note I left with your name on it?"

He shook his head and smiled. "That voicemail you left

me, all I could hear was the sound of running water. I didn't hear about that 911 call you made from your office until this afternoon. That didn't matter anyway. It was that cell phone of yours."

"What do you mean? Keeler had me tied up on that phone the whole time."

"I set it up when we were at the ball game," he said. "Slipped one of those little bugs the size of a dime under the leather case. After that, I heard everything that was said within twenty feet of that phone. Followed that entire conversation he had with you last night. Knew where you were every minute."

"You knew Ethan and I almost died in that shed?"

He shrugged. "We did the best we could, Coyne. It was tricky."

"I wasn't complaining."

"Keeler had an electronic detonator with him, see," he said. "There was dynamite in that shed, and it was soaked with gasoline. If we'd spooked him before you got out . . ."

"He blew it up anyway," I said.

"Yeah," said Horowitz. "You had me kinda worried there for a minute."

TWENTY-EIGHT

They made me stay in the hospital until Saturday. Evie came into my room around ten in the morning. She had clean clothes for me.

"Thank God," I said when I saw her. "My angel of mercy. Get me out of here."

She came over to where I was sitting on the edge of the bed in my humiliating hospital johnny. "I'm gonna pamper you all weekend," she said, sliding a soft hand under my hem.

"I don't want you to pamper me too gently," I said. "Sometimes I like it rough."

"We'll see how you're feeling, big guy."

They insisted on pushing me out in a wheelchair. Liability, you know.

When Evie and I were settled in her car, I said, "Let's go see Ethan."

"Right now?"

"Please."

While I was laid up in Beth Israel I kept in touch with

Ethan's progress at Mass General. They'd moved him out of Intensive Care on Thursday.

Ellen Bramhall, Ethan's mother, was sitting with him when Evie and I walked into his room. When she saw me, she stood up and gave me a hug. "Thank you," she whispered. "You saved my boy's life."

I didn't understand why people kept insisting I'd saved Ethan's life. The way I figured it, if it hadn't been for me, he wouldn't have been kidnapped in the first place.

I shook hands with Ethan, then introduced Evie to him and to Ellen. Ethan's head hadn't been shaved in a while. It was covered with brownish fur. I noticed that they'd removed the stud from his nose, too. He looked pale and fragile and very young, lying there on his white pillow.

We chatted for a few minutes, and then Ethan said, "Mom, I need to talk to Brady for a minute."

Ellen frowned for an instant, then smiled quickly and said, "Oh, you mean privately."

He nodded. "If you don't mind."

Evie stood up. "Come on," she said to Ellen. "Let's find the cafeteria. I need some coffee."

After the women left, I pulled a chair close to Ethan's bed. "What's up, partner?"

"You said you were my lawyer, remember?"

I nodded. "You think you need one?"

He rolled his eyes. "The cops've been asking me a lot of questions. About me, about my dad. There's some things you should know."

"I know your father was involved with SOLF. The Spotted Owl Liberation Front."

"Right," said Ethan. "So was I."

I nodded. I realized I wasn't surprised.

"I didn't think my father knew about me," he said. "I was going to tell him after I—after I actually did something. Did something to make him proud." He shrugged. "I knew about him, though. I guess I thought it would be a way I could, I don't know, earn his respect. Have something in common with him. You know what I mean?"

I nodded. I knew how it could be with fathers and sons.

"That FBI lady told me about the list of e-mail addresses they found," Ethan said. "Mine was on that list."

"Is she telling you that they're going to prosecute you because your e-mail address turned up on a list?"

"That Agent Randall," said Ethan, "she's like threatening me. Wants me to tell her everything I know. I keep telling her I don't know anything. The only people I know of who were in SOLF were my dad and Connie." He swallowed. "And they're both dead."

"Conrad Henshall?"

"Yes. What happened to him is my fault. I got him into it."

"You never torched a building, did you?" I said.

Ethan shook his head. "With SOLF, you were pretty much on your own. You just e-mailed back and forth with them. With my dad, actually. They didn't organize you or tell you what to do. They didn't even know who you were. You could pick a building or something and you and your team could just . . . just go burn it down and make sure SOLF got credit." He smiled. "Connie and I, we were a team. Our own little two-man cell. We'd drive all over the place, scouting for a good target. We found dozens of them, but Connie, he always decided they weren't quite right."

"Henshall was protecting you," I said. "Keeping you out of trouble."

"Yeah, I gradually began to realize that. We spent a lot of time together, pretending to be eco-terrorists. It was kinda fun." Ethan smiled. "He was being a father to me. And I guess I was a son to him. He didn't have kids, and me, I felt like I didn't have a father. I could talk with Connie about anything."

"What about that apartment over the record shop?"

"Connie owned the whole building," said Ethan. "He kept saying he was going to rent out the apartment, but he never did. He used to spend the night there sometimes when he had a fight with his wife. Or if me or one of the other people who worked for him needed a place to crash, he let us use it. Connie was a good guy." He looked up at me. "So am I in trouble?"

"You didn't do anything criminal," I said. "You can't be punished for guilt by association."

He shrugged. "I guess I need a lawyer to convince Agent Randall of that."

"Sure," I said. "You got one."

"Thank you."

"No problem," I said. "We've got other lawyer-type things to talk about, too, you know."

"I know," he said. "I already thought about them. My mother and I have been talking. My father's will, right?"

I nodded.

"I know I'm his only heir," said Ethan. "I know the only thing he left me is his house. I guess I'm supposed to make sure his collection of bird stuff goes to museums and libraries, right?"

"That's my job," I said. "It's all my job. You don't have to do anything. The issue is, until you're twenty-one, your mother is your trustee."

"Meaning what?"

"Meaning she's the one who makes the decisions about your, um, your inheritance."

"We've already talked about it," he said. "That's not a problem."

"Good."

"We know what we want to do."

"Well," I said, "as your lawyer, I should know, too."

"As soon as we can take care of my father's collections," he said, "we want to sell his townhouse. The money will pay for my college. I'm going to go stay with Mom and Jonathan and live in a dorm or an apartment or something when school starts. Like a normal college student."

"Whatever 'normal' means," I said.

Ethan smiled. "Does that sound okay?"

"It sounds very sensible. You'll have a lot of money left over, if I'm any judge of Beacon Hill real estate. Your father owned that place free and clear. We'll set up a trust fund for you. In a couple years when you're twenty-one, it'll be yours."

"Cool," he said. "I can use it to make my first movie."

I smiled. "Your lawyer will undoubtedly try to hook you up with a good financial adviser."

Ethan rolled his eyes.

"That's the sort of boring, sensible thing lawyers do for their clients," I said. "Still want me?"

"After what you did for me?"

"Listen to me," I said. "The most generous way to look at what I did was this: I got you into trouble, then I did what

I could to get you out of trouble. You don't owe me anything."

"I still want you to be my lawyer."

We shook hands on it.

"I don't know what to do about Henry," he said after a minute.

"My secretary's taking good care of him. Don't worry about Henry."

"But once I move out of Dad's house, I'm going to have to sell him or something."

I started to say, "You can't do that." But I didn't. Instead, I said, "Your mother won't take him?"

"It's not her. It's Jonathan. He won't allow animals in his house. Mom's upset about it, but she won't stand up to him. I don't want to make a problem for her. Jonathan's an asshole, but I guess she's stuck with him. He's probably pissed about me living there as it is. I feel bad about Henry."

"We'll find a good home for Henry," I said.

"I hope so." He hesitated. "I've been having this thought. About my father."

I nodded.

"I think he knew I was involved with SOLF," he said. "I think he recognized my e-mail address on that list. I think he got rid of that list when he knew they were going to subpoena him. To protect me."

"If you're thinking—"

"That he got killed because of me?" Ethan nodded. "That's what I'm trying to figure out. The day it happened?" He blew out a long breath. "He picked a terrible fight with me. Told me he couldn't stand having me around. He hated how I looked, how I acted, hated my friends, my lifestyle. Everything about me. I told him if that's how he felt, I was leaving.

He said good, go, he didn't want me around."

"He knew something was going to happen," I said. "He didn't want you involved."

He nodded. "That's what I think now. But at the time . . ."

"You were upset."

"Yes. I went to Connie, asked him to let me stay in his place over the shop. Told him I didn't want anybody to know where I was. That night you came looking for me and saw Phil?"

I nodded.

"I was there. Upstairs. I figured Dad had sent you looking for me."

"You didn't know what happened to your father?"

"Not until I went back to the house. I had some things there I needed. That's when I saw the crime-scene tape on the doors."

"The police were looking for you, you know."

He nodded. "Sure. I figured I was a suspect. I should've turned myself in before Keeler kidnapped me and killed Connie. But I was scared and upset. I didn't want to talk to anybody. I called you to tell you I was okay so you'd stop looking for me. I blew it. The whole thing. If it wasn't for me . . ."

"Nobody blames you for anything," I said.

"My dad was protecting me. He picked that fight with me to get me out of harm's way."

"Yes," I said. "I'm sure you're right."

"And he passed on that list to Mr. Frye to keep my name out of it. That's what got him killed. Both of them. Connie, too. Trying to protect me."

"That's not how it was," I said. "Your father passed that list on to Ben Frye because he wanted to keep SOLF going.

That's all. That had nothing to do with you. Don't blame yourself for what happened to your father."

"You think?"

"I'm certain," I said, although I wasn't.

Ethan smiled—a bit sadly, I thought. "I don't know whether I should be relieved or disappointed."

"Your father loved you more than anything," I said. "Never doubt that. He just wasn't very good at expressing it."

"I'm gonna be better at it with my kids," he said. "It's a hard way to grow up, feeling that your father doesn't notice you."

A few minutes later Evie and Ellen returned, and for another half hour or so we all sat there in Ethan's room making small talk.

Then Evie glanced at her watch and stood up. "This man," she said, jerking her head at me, "is just out of the hospital. I need to get him home so he can rest and get his strength back. I have big plans for him."

Ellen giggled and Ethan grinned. I think I blushed.

On a blustery Wednesday morning toward the end of July, Evie and I drove Ethan and Henry to Plum Island. Ethan and Henry rode in the backseat. Henry kept his nose pressed against the window. Ethan held Walt Duffy's urn on his lap.

As we drove, Ethan explained to Evie that Plum Island, at the mouth of the Merrimack River on the Massachusetts north shore, was one of the prime bird-watching spots in all of North America. Sea birds and shore birds used it as a resting place on their migrations, and many parts of it were preserved as a sanctuary for nesting piping plovers and other endangered and threatened species. Rare birds, tropical and Arctic and even European, were sometimes blown off-course to Plum Island by storms, and when that happened, word circulated fast in the bird-watching community.

Before his accident, Walt had haunted the place with his camera. "My dad loved birds more than anything," Ethan told Evie. "And he loved Plum Island. It seems like an appropriate place to leave him."

We crossed the bridge from the mainland, turned right, followed the sandy road that cut between the sand dunes and the salt marsh, paid at the gate, and stopped in the parking lot by the public beach. The lot was surprisingly full for a cloudy, cool mid-week morning, even in prime sun-bathing season. The cars sported plates from as far away as Pennsylvania and Ohio and New Brunswick.

Ethan carried Walt's urn. I held Henry's leash in one hand and Evie's hand in the other. We followed the path through the dunes, and when we topped the rise at the beach, we saw that a crowd of about a hundred people were gathered there. It was a strange sight on a beach. They were all barefoot, but the women were wearing dresses and most of the men wore jackets and neckties. Many had binoculars strapped around their necks. They watched us as we approached.

Then somebody clapped.

The slow applause grew as we walked toward them, and when we stopped, the crowd of people formed a silent circle around us. Then one gray-haired woman stepped forward. I recognized her, and after a moment I remembered her name. It was Gladys Whyte. I'd met her walking her dogs on Mt. Vernon Street.

She went up to Ethan, touched his arm, and said, "All of us—" she waved her hand, indicating the other people

"—are birders. Fans of your father. Walter Duffy was an icon in the birding community. We came here today to say goodbye to him. I hope you don't mind."

Ethan blinked a couple of times, then shook his head. "I know my father would be honored. Thank you."

And then, while gulls and terns, sandpipers and oystercatchers, cormorants and eiders, and, no doubt, myriad other more exotic species that I couldn't identify wheeled over the water and paddled in it and tiptoed on the wet sand and squawked and tweeted and cooed back in the marsh grass, Ethan waded out to his knees.

I let Henry off his leash, and he paddled out to Ethan. The rest of us remained at the water's edge and watched as Ethan took the top off Walt's urn, held it high, and tipped it over.

As we drove back to Boston, Ethan, from the backseat, said, "I hope you guys will let me make lunch for you."

Evie started to demur, but I squeezed her wrist. "That would be great," I said. "We'd love to." To Evie I said, "Ethan's a great cook."

She looked at me sideways. I just smiled.

"I didn't know you'd invited people to your little ceremony today," I said to Ethan.

"I didn't invite anybody except you guys. I guess I might have mentioned it to Mrs. Whyte the other night when I was walking Henry. I didn't even know she was a birder."

"There are millions of birders," I said. I was wondering if any of those folks who'd met us on Plum Island loved birds so much that they burned down buildings.

For some reason I didn't think so.

Ethan opened a bottle of cabernet from Walt's wine cellar and made crabmeat-and-avocado-and-lettuce sandwiches on pita bread and a tomato-cucumber-onion-and-basil salad, and we ate at the table in the walled-in patio behind Walt's—now Ethan's—Mt. Vernon Street townhouse.

Henry lay under the table, alert for falling crumbs.

Titmice and nuthatches flitted in the feeders, and song sparrows splashed in the bath. Ethan was continuing to tend the bird garden as Walt had done.

"This is such a beautiful spot," said Evie after several minutes of silence.

"I've got to sell it," said Ethan. "It's no place for a college kid."

"That's a shame," she said.

Ethan glanced at me, then said, "It makes me sad to think of some non-bird person living here."

"Do you really like it?" I said to Evie.

"Oh, yes," she said. "I love it. It's spectacular."

"Want it?"

She turned and frowned at me. "What did you say?"

"Would you like to, um, live here?"

She dropped her chin down onto her chest and peered up at me out of the tops of her eyes. "What exactly are you saying, Brady Coyne?"

I glanced at Ethan. He was smiling. "I mentioned to Ethan that I might have a buyer for his place," I said to Evie. "I know a lawyer whose office is in Copley Square who likes to walk to work, and this lawyer has a . . . a dear friend, a bird lover, in fact, who's recently taken a job at a hospital here in the city. The only question is whether the lady is ready to, um . . . to cohabit . . . I mean, to live with . . . that is, to share her life with the lawyer."

Evie reached for my hand. "Say it straight, please."

"Okay." I took a deep breath. "Will you, Evie Banyon, come live with me, Brady Coyne, in this house?"

"This is a commitment, you know," she said.

"I've thought deeply about it," I said. "I am not being frivolous."

"A *giant* commitment."

"Yes. I agree."

"Scary."

"Yes, indeed."

She put her hand on my shoulder and leaned toward me. I kissed her on the mouth.

"Okay," she said.

"Is that like 'I do'?"

She smiled. "Almost exactly."

"We'll have to keep the feeders filled and the bushes and flowers tended," I said. "This will have to be a bird garden forever and ever."

"I love birds," she said. "And I love gardens. You know that."

"You shouldn't be too precipitous," I said. I gave her my most serious expression. "There's, um, something you should know."

"Oh-oh," she said. "What?"

"Somebody else will be living with us."

"Oh?" She frowned. "And who might that be?"

I glanced at Ethan. He nodded. I patted my knee, and Henry scrambled to his feet, plopped his chin on my thigh, and looked up at me with big adoring eyes. I scratched his ears and arched my eyebrows at Evie.

She smiled. “Henry?”

I nodded.

“Awesome,” she said.